THE STOLEN KINGDOM

BOOK ONE IN THE
STOLEN KINGDOM SERIES

THE STOLEN KINGDOM

Copyright © 2019 by Bethany Atazadeh

Contact Info: www.bethanyatazadeh.com

Front Cover Design by : Guilherme Ambrósio

Model Photography by : Oswaldo Ibáñez

Hard Cover Wrap Design by : Stone Ridge Books

Editor: Claerie Kavanaugh

ISBN: 978-0-9995368-2-7 (paperback)

Second Edition: April 2020

9 8 7 6 5 4 3 2 1

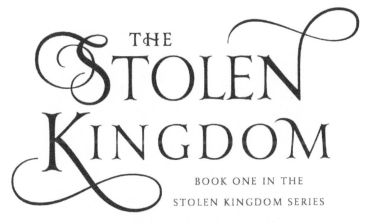

THE STOLEN KINGDOM

BOOK ONE IN THE
STOLEN KINGDOM SERIES

BETHANY ATAZADEH

GRACE HOUSE PRESS

ALSO BY

BETHANY ATAZADEH

THE STOLEN KINGDOM SERIES :

THE STOLEN KINGDOM

THE JINNI KEY

THE CURSED HUNTER

THE NUMBER SERIES :

EVALENE'S NUMBER

PEARL'S NUMBER

MARKETING FOR AUTHORS SERIES :

HOW YOUR BOOK SELLS ITSELF

GROW YOUR AUTHOR PLATFORM

BOOK SALES THAT MULTIPLY

OTHER :

THE CONFIDENT CORGI

PENNY'S PUPPY PACK FOR WRITERS

SIGN UP FOR MY AUTHOR NEWSLETTER

Be the first to learn about Bethany Atazadeh's new releases and receive exclusive content for both readers and writers!

WWW.BETHANYATAZADEH.COM

AHDAMON

J I N N

SAGH

HODAFEZ

H U M A N
KINGDOMS

W   E

S

RUSALKA

DRAGON
CLIFFS

KESHDI

AZIZ

PIRUZ

BARADAAN

Chapter One

Arie

MY HANDS SAT CLENCHED in my lap. I didn't play with the gold and pearl fabric of my dress, or tap my fingers on my throne, or even twitch an eyebrow. But underneath my skirts, my toes tapped a steady rhythm, counting down the seconds until dinner.

Normally, I adored holding court with my father. Learning to rule meant everything to me.

But not today.

Not for the last few months, actually.

We'd listened to the nobles list their complaints for nearly four hours now. My head buzzed with voices, like a swarm of locusts. The more people in the room, the louder they pulsed until the pressure was unbearable.

At least if I kept still and avoided drawing attention to myself, it was more manageable. I sat as quiet as the serving girl concealed in the corner. But she wasn't wearing the gold circlet of a princess woven through delicately braided hair. She didn't have long, black curls falling on expensive gold-lace sleeves. Or a white pearl dress, designed to remind eligible men of a wedding gown. Lucky girl.

A white-haired Shah, lord of a small province in our kingdom, stood in the open space before my father and I.

"King Mahdi," Shirvan-Shah railed, in the middle of an outburst. "I didn't want to bring this to your attention if I didn't have to, but this dispute is over far more than my son and Marzban-Shah's daughter." Spittle flew from his mouth as he paced the marble floor between us and his rapt audience, who waited their turn. "It pains me to speak of such things, but I'm afraid I must…" He dropped to his knees before my father's throne and bowed his head.

I wanted to roll my eyes.

"As I'm sure you're aware, the Marzban family has Jinni-blood running through their veins…"

I leaned forward.

Too late, I caught myself and sat back.

No one noticed. All eyes were glued to Shirvan-Shah, who let the silence draw out, until it lay thick and expectant over the room. He cleared his throat and stage whispered, "I believe she may have a Jinni's Gift."

Horrified gasps and murmurs replaced the silence. The corners of his mouth twitched upward as he stood. I found myself hating him.

"That's a strong accusation to make without proof," my voice rang out. I couldn't help myself. "What if she's innocent?" I clutched the arms of my throne, leaning forward. "Are you willing to risk ruining a young girl's life simply because she didn't find your son a good match?"

Every onlooker shifted their gaze from Shirvan-Shah to me. The hum in the room grew louder. I regretted my words immediately.

"Arie," my father scolded. It wasn't my place to judge in these hearings. Not yet. My role was to learn and observe.

"Sorry, Baba." I bowed my head, hating the disappointment in his tone.

Whispers grew louder as I became the center of attention. My head throbbed.

"Continue, Shah." My father tipped his gold scepter toward Shirvan-Shah.

As the focus shifted back to the older man, I sighed softly, resisting the urge to sag back against my throne. Imitating the serving girl once more, I sat stiff and upright, barely breathing.

The Shah eyed me before easing back into his speech. "The princess makes a fair point." He dipped his head toward me, tenting his bony fingers. "However, I fear Marzban-Shah's daughter's Gift is evident. There's rumor of her sheets turning to iron, as well as her bathtub, and other common household items."

This time I guarded against any reaction. When those around me gasped, I chastised myself, *Don't be too still either.*

"What kind of Gifting is this?" my father muttered.

"I'd never heard of its likeness, Your Highness," Shirvan-Shah stepped closer, though he didn't lower his voice in the slightest. "There are too many different Jinni's Gifts to keep track of. I thought perhaps it was like Aaran-Shah's Gift, where he knows what to plant and helps the seedlings grow. Or Yazdan-Shah's son who can turn commonplace items into gold. But it seems that, as usual, this woman's Gift is dangerous."

Why do they see danger in women while men are trusted? I pushed down the urge to question him, but it was difficult. *Her Gift seems harmless.* Especially when compared to other Jinni's Gifts I'd heard of growing up—the ability to travel across kingdoms in a heartbeat, shape-shifting, swimming in the depths with the Mere-folk, soul-stealing... That last one may have been more of a child's bedtime story than truth, but I'd never been entirely certain. *How can we know anything about the Jinn when even the entrance to their land is a secret?*

"Thank you for bringing it to my attention," my father said with a sigh. The laws regarding Gifted women had been passed before I was born. While the stories differed on how the decision came to be, the verdict was clear: Gifted women were dangerous. They must go to trial and be closely examined. If they failed the trial, their Gift was to be severed.

I'd been too young to witness the last Severance, but my blood ran cold as my father added, "She will be dealt with immediately."

Dealt with.

I clenched my teeth to keep a flood of words from escaping.

A neighboring prince's Gift had surfaced just two months ago. Of course, his Gift had been deemed safe. But it'd been years since anyone had discovered a Gifted woman.

My father turned to the cleric. "Schedule a hearing. And arrange a search party to see if anyone can find a Jinni. We'll likely need a Severance." The cleric scratched notes on his parchment.

The blood drained from my face. The hum in the room grew louder. Another Shah stood to go next, but I stopped listening. My heart pounded as I waited for the worst of it to manifest. Bracing myself, I still felt completely unprepared when it happened.

The princess looks like she's about to faint.

It was someone else's thought forming in my mind—the tone of it high and shrill. Though I'd doubted the sensation when the episodes had first begun, certain I was losing my mind, it was undoubtedly a thought. Now, I could usually distinguish which thoughts belonged to me versus those around me.

I tried to ignore the stranger in my head. But as one of my ladies-in-waiting, Havah, stepped forward to offer me a cup of cool water, her thoughts intruded as well.

She looks horrible.

It took everything in me not to wince as I accepted the cup. As I thought about the ruling, it was hard to swallow.

I didn't know the full details of a Severance. But the Gifted woman's fate was certain: death.

Whether a day, a week, or even a month or two after the fact, she wouldn't live long. They always said it was an accident. The women hung themselves, or slipped in the bath, or fell from their horse... But I knew better. Someone killed them. What a horrible punishment for an innocent girl who couldn't help herself. I hated that I had to keep silent. But if I didn't...

If my kingdom—if my own father ever learned of my Jinni's Gift, would he do that to me?

* * *

When the bell tolled in the keep across the castle, my father dismissed everyone to get ready for dinner. "We'll resume with Yik-Shah in two day's time."

I stood a split second after he did, rushing toward the back door to avoid the crowds as I all but fled the throne room, trailed by my ladies-in-waiting. I led the way up the curving staircase, down a long hallway, and entered my rooms.

My sitting room at the entrance held a dozen comfortable chairs and a table, meant for entertaining guests without allowing them the intimacy of my bedroom, though there was a small bed hidden along the wall where my ladies-in-waiting took turns staying the night in case I required anything.

"I'll call if I have need." I dismissed them, entering my personal rooms. Locking the door, I crossed to my bathing room and stared into the floor length mirror.

Havah was right. My warm, golden skin was pale; a sharp contrast to the soft black hair that flowed loosely over my shoulders. I touched my lips, still a vivid red, and the paint came away. Dipping a clean towel in fresh water, I scrubbed until my face was clean. Water dripped on my elegant dress, but I didn't care. As I set down the towel, my hand shook.

A knock sounded.

With a sigh, I moved to open the door. "Time to get you ready for dinner, Arie-zada," Havah called me by my childhood nickname, a shortened version of my formal title, *Shazada*. She stepped through the door, to stand beside it. *You go through so many dresses.*

I turned to hide my reaction as I waved her in, moving to the balcony for some fresh air.

"Sirjan-Shah paid you so many compliments during the last courtship tour, I could hardly keep up," Havah said.

I stared at the sea, eyes searching for a glimpse of one of the Mere out of years of habit, though I'd yet to see one. Waves crashed against the cliffs below, and I struggled to tune out Havah's thoughts as I replied, "His compliments were shallow." I knew, because his flattery was interlaced with thoughts of my treasure and how he could best get his hands on it.

Or maybe you're shallow, Havah's thoughts washed over me like a bitter rain.

I winced.

She ignores them all. I couldn't tune her out, no matter how hard I tried. *I'd give anything for attention like that.*

When I glanced back to where she sifted through my closet for a suitable evening style, she only smiled. If not for the way my Gift had manifested over the last six months, I'd never have guessed her thoughts.

What did she have to be jealous of? Her bronze skin was smoother than mine, her lips fuller. Her brown eyes more slanted and her hand more talented at lining them with coal. Her hair shone just as dark and long as my own. We could be sisters, but for my tiara and the quality of my clothes.

"What about Tahran-Shah?" she asked, pulling out a red, sleeveless dress that would cling to me. She helped me remove the white pearl gown. "He's very handsome and his—"

"Is there anyone who interests you, Havah?" I interrupted, stepping into the red dress.

"No one, Arie-zada." She used the term of endearment almost like a weapon. Making me like her. Want her by my side. Except now that I knew the truth, I couldn't hear it the same way.

I allowed her to lace the dress tight, so it wouldn't slip, though I secretly drew deep breaths until she finished. No sense in being miserable during dinner.

Havah held out the top piece to finish off my dress. I slipped my arms into the gold lace sleeves. It settled delicately over my collarbone and shoulders, making the ensemble appear modest, though it didn't even reach the dress. Havah buttoned it in the back.

How could any man want a mere servant when they're in your presence?

I swallowed a sigh. The constant invasion of thoughts was exhausting. Even if people weren't thinking of me, there was always an ominous, low hum in my mind. The hum would swell into a buzz and threaten to form. It made me so tired, I could hardly think.

I swayed on my feet.

She wants to be crowned heir apparent on her 18th birthday, yet she can't make it through a full day of court.

"Just stop."

Havah froze.

Hands outstretched, with a hair pin still in her mouth, she met my gaze, confusion written across her face.

Not again. I cursed myself inwardly for yet another slip. I couldn't seem to control my tongue.

"Stop… worrying over the men in my life, my friend." I smiled to take the edge off my words. "I know you want the best for me."

"Ah…yes, Arie-zada. Of course. As you wish…" Only a tiny crease between Havah's brows gave her feelings away as she pinned my thick curls up, to better offset the enormous gold earrings dangling from my ears. As I turned to stand before the mirror, they tickled my shoulders.

Just as I'd begun to relax, Havah returned to her previous train of thought, *How can she rule Hodafez, if she can't even stomach a Severance?*

I ground my teeth. *For the love of Jinn, can't you think about anything else for two seconds?* I wanted to scream the words, but I managed to stay silent for once, until she was done.

So beautiful, she thought, stepping back, and this time the tone was a bit kinder. More admiration, less contempt.

"Thank you," I murmured into the silence.

She paused once more.

My eyes widened. I forced myself to breathe. Lifting my chin, I stared at myself in the mirror, patting my hair. "Ah… it looks lovely."

It was enough.

"You always look lovely," Havah replied, moving to store the leftover hair pins.

I slowly let out my breath.

Each time I slipped up, I feared the worst.

I reached out to grasp Havah's hands, searching her smooth face for a friend, wanting—needing—to know I wasn't alone. "I'm sorry I snapped earlier. It's just… it's impossible to know if a suitor is truly interested in me…"

I stopped, unable to put into words the real problem: I knew exactly what they were interested in. My wealth. My throne. Even my people, occasionally. But never me.

Havah's face softened. Her hands squeezed mine back. "How could anyone not love you? You only need to let your guard down long enough for a nice young man to get to know you. Now come, it's time for dinner."

I let her lead me through the front room where my other ladies stood waiting, out into the carpeted hallway that softened our footsteps, and downstairs toward the dining hall. The hall that held an entire room filled with people eager to prove Havah false and bring my worst nightmares to life.

She was wrong. No one could know me, or the truth. *If they knew the truth, they wouldn't love me. They'd want to kill me.*

Chapter Two

Arie

AFTER DINNER, I ENDURED a few more hours in the Great Hall, pretending to listen to the storyteller and musicians, before claiming a headache and retiring early.

I paced across my bedroom, stopping at my balcony to gaze out at the black depths of the sea and the way the moonlight lit a path across the waves. It made me want to jump out onto the water, follow the path wherever it led, and never return.

When it felt as if hours had passed, I picked up my candle and cracked open the door between my bedchamber and the outer room. Tonight, it was Farideh who slept there, ready to come to my aid. Fortunately, she was a heavy sleeper.

I tiptoed through the room into the dark, silent hallway on slippered feet. My candle flickered as I crept down the stairs and slipped inside the castle library.

Passing dozens of bookshelves that stretched twice my height, I pushed through velvet curtains that led to a little room at the back. It was pitch-black without the moonlight coming through the windows. The smell of books and dust grew stronger, tickling my nose. But the room was empty besides the books and work tables, which was all that mattered. My reading material over the last few weeks had to be kept secret at all costs.

Glass boxes guarded the ancient books. One thick volume rested against the back wall, old and worn, that no one was allowed to read, but was too full of information to burn.

I set my candle on the table. It lit up the small pocket of space surrounding myself and the book. The enormous volume was turned to the title page:

The Land of Jinn

Lifting the heavy glass lid, I set it aside before leafing through the pages, one at a time. I'd found the book only a few nights prior, after searching the library for a book from Jinn for months, with no success. Each night I could get away, I came here to read a bit more—always making sure to turn it back to the title page and replace the glass before slipping out.

The pages in the first section, *Laws and Lists,* were dense: this land had been merged with that land, and this law passed underneath a similar law, and so forth. I'd gleaned very little from it beyond the first sentence, which declared, "Each individual Jinni must honor the code of Jinn or risk banishment." I held back a sneeze as I flipped past that section.

Next was *Spells and Secrets,* written in a language I didn't recognize. The last few nights I'd studied them anyway. The pictures on each page shimmered as if they might come to life at my signal, but what that signal might be, I couldn't guess.

On one page, a clock, on the next, a sundial. A tea kettle. A candle. Seemingly random objects. But tonight, I noticed a pattern in the spells that I hadn't seen before: each object told time. Whether obvious, like the pocketwatch, or through items that didn't seem designed to mark time at all: a tea kettle which would boil after a certain number of minutes passed. A candle that might last for hours, but would eventually burn out.

Interesting, but meaningless, as far as I could tell. I didn't know how I could use the spells if I couldn't even read them; I made note of it and moved on.

After the last page of spells, I discovered a third section: *History and Households.*

I snatched my candle, bringing it closer and leaning in to read. My eyes caught on the page where my fingers fell. There was handwriting in the margins.

I bit my lip. It looked like—could it be my mother's? I recognized her handwriting. The style was utterly unique; the way her letters curved and her script flowed—if indeed it was hers—reminded me of a never-ending ribbon.

I squinted at the words. *The humans believe the race of Jinn to be nearly extinct.* I followed the swirled script to the next line and stopped. *They fear us.*

Us?

It couldn't be. I stepped back, glancing over my shoulder as if someone else might see the offensive words. I'd assumed after my Gift formed that somewhere in my family's lineage there was Jinni blood, but not...

Was my mother... did she mean that she'd been Gifted like me? Or what if—no. *It's not possible*, I repeated to myself, but it didn't feel very convincing. Had my mother been a full-blooded Jinni?

I flipped through the book, barely remembering to be gentle with the worn parchment, searching for another note in the margins.

The pages upon pages of history ended and genealogies began. *Households.* They listed family trees in tiny print, starting with two names and expanding into hundreds, crammed onto the page like ants swarming a crumb.

I almost missed it.

There, at the very bottom of one of the family trees, directly under two full-blooded Jinni's names, another descendant's name was scribbled in...

My mother's.

Chapter Three

Arie

WHEN I STRODE INTO the grand hall the next morning, I was in no mood to greet anyone. I had my ladies-in-waiting surround me instead of hanging back, creating a natural buffer and giving me a reprieve from inane conversation.

After last night's revelation, I'd flung the book back to the title page, dropped the heavy glass overtop, and raced back to my quarters in a panic. My mother was from Jinn. A full-blooded Jinni. Which made me only half-human and half—I couldn't even finish the thought. What were the implications of this? My father *had* to have known. Or did he? He would've told me, would've wanted to prepare me, if he'd known himself. Right? And what about the court? If they knew—if even one person knew—they'd almost certainly be watching me in secret. Waiting for me to reveal a latent Gift. If I hadn't accidentally already done so. I'd lain awake the entire night trying *not* to think about it. And now I felt like walking death.

I didn't notice the servant approaching until he spoke. "Your father requests your presence in the throne room," he said, bowing. I nodded, moving past him toward the high table for breakfast. "He said it's urgent," the young man added before I could sit.

I paused, letting go of my skirts. "What could possibly be so important that it can't wait until I've had a hot meal?" I ignored his thoughts about my deep blue dress and the strip of skin it revealed at the smallest part of my waist. Lifting my hands, I let the dozens of silver bracelets clink together noisily to catch his attention.

He cleared his throat, clasping his hands together as he bowed again. "I believe it's because we have a guest. King Amir of Sagh."

I dismissed him, and the servant hurried away. Heading toward the throne room and leaving my ladies-in-waiting behind, I barely noticed the people I passed. Why was the neighboring king here?

Though King Amir was as old as my father and his dark hair beginning to gray, his face was more youthful with thick black brows, few wrinkles, and a long nose that made him look regal. He was wealthy enough to bribe anyone he pleased, which he often did. The king of Sagh should be likeable. Yet, no matter how nice he seemed, I often left his presence feeling oddly uncomfortable.

Because Amir had a Jinni's Gift.

Leaving behind the grand tables where courtiers feasted and a storyteller entertained them, I followed the long hall to the throne room, but paused outside. I took a deep fortifying breath before pushing through the heavy door.

The throne room felt larger without the crowds. Quiet. As the door closed, the wave of thoughts died down like the tide going out until there was only the softest whisper. They grew stronger as I approached the small room at the back, where I spied two people through the open door.

My father stood by the enormous work table in the back. Papers were strewn across the stained wood, lit by sunbeams. Usually I'd find him muttering to himself as he sorted through them, forehead wrinkled. Today, he stood by, letting King Amir review Hodafez's materials and goods for himself. I frowned at the audacity. Standing in the shadows of the pillars, I couldn't seem to will my feet forward. Maybe I could hide in my rooms and claim to be ill.

"Your kingdom is so small," Amir tutted as he leafed through the papers. "And the castle too. If my fortress were this size, it'd be indefensible." My father didn't say a word. Odd. "You're fortunate, you know," Amir continued, rounding the table. "The way Hodafez rests on a cliff, surrounded by mountains or sea on all sides; it's impregnable. Otherwise, I'd have taken it by force years ago. You'll forget I said that, of course."

"Of course," my father finally spoke.

And that—his immediate agreement and the fact that he truly meant it—that was the reason I hesitated to enter. Amir's Gift was powerful.

The memory of his voice the first day I'd met him still gave me shivers. "Give me the bracelet, Arie," he'd murmured in that deadly monotone.

As a six-year-old, the thought of losing my jeweled bracelet had made my eyes well up with tears. But as I'd begun to wail, he'd whispered, "Hush."

And I had.

Even as a child, I'd fought the compulsion to obey, but in the end, he'd left the castle with my jewels and the command not to tell anyone. It'd taken me years to break free of that order.

What he'd done was forbidden. It broke the Jinni code. But I had no proof; it was a woman's word against a king's.

His Gift might be weak compared to a full-blooded Jinni, but I stared at him now the way I would eye a cobra. He was deadly. Unpredictable.

Though my father and Amir were around the same age, my father's hair had turned white instead of gray, and he had permanent laugh lines around the corners of his eyes. I expected them to notice and greet me, but if my father saw me, he didn't say a word, and Amir ignored me as well.

"You called for me, Baba?" I forced myself to walk up to them. My footsteps echoed in the quiet room.

"Arie." My father held his arms out to me, but tucked them absently back into his belt before I reached him.

"Hello, princess. We've been waiting for you. Your father has news. You'll be very excited." Amir's deep syrupy voice flowed over me, and I found myself feeling oddly eager. My father just smiled.

"Oh that's right, it was our little secret," Amir clapped a hand on my father's shoulder, smirking. "You may speak of it now. I'm sure your daughter would like to hear the news from you."

"Yes, yes," my father said, coming to life. "I have good news for you, Arie."

"That's what Amir tells me," I replied, wary. Amir scowled at the way I left off his title. He always was a stickler for formalities, despite the fact that we were both royals.

"Mmm, yes." My father smiled at my forehead instead of my eyes. "We have finally found you a husband!"

I blinked. First at 'finally,' and then at 'husband,' but he wasn't done. "You are to be married within the week. A wedding! If your mother was still alive, she'd be so happy." And indeed, he had actual tears of joy in his eyes as he finished.

Amir and my father studied my face for a reaction, but I felt nothing. This was ridiculous. "Married to *whom?*"

"To myself, of course," King Amir said, stepping forward to take my hand. His fingers felt cold. "When I knelt down on one knee, you were in shock, but you've come to admire me and look forward to our marriage. I can see you're very pleased."

Though not one word was true, I responded to his influence, smiling back at him.

"I remember." A small voice in the back of my mind yelled that it'd never happened, even though I saw the mental image of Amir on one knee, holding a ring. I glanced down at my bare finger, feeling confused and thrilled with my engagement all at once. My father hugged me and repeated his excitement. Amir simply smiled and nodded.

"I'm sure we will make each other truly happy," he said, as he bent over my hand and kissed it. Only his thoughts jarred me back to reality. *Your kingdom will finally be mine.*

I froze. Amir had turned back to the papers on the table and missed my reaction.

He couldn't know I'd heard him. I might wonder what my father's reaction would be to my Gift, but if Amir ever found out, I knew exactly what he would do.

"Another Gifted woman? Shameful," Amir said as he slapped a paper onto the table. My muscles tensed, certain he'd heard my thoughts, even though that was my Gift, not his. He shook his head, gesturing toward the paper. "I've half a mind to just hang her." My heart stopped. But he meant the girl from yesterday—the one who could turn things to metal.

The way Amir's face twisted in disgust before he moved on reminded me of a day, years ago, in the Court of Kings. When the idea of a Severance had shifted from a rarity so uncommon that a famine was more likely, to a frequent custom that was widely accepted.

Amir's hair had been dark then, his form more muscled, but he'd been just as convincing. He'd stood in the middle court, among reigning kings seated around him, and a wider audience of royal families and nobility in the surrounding balconies. "A Gifted woman is dangerous. You've all seen the results."

Back then my mind hadn't enough strength to fight his influence, and I'd nodded along with everyone else. We'd just witnessed the aftermath of another Gifted woman—a kingdom burned to a crisp. Or so I'd believed. Now, I wondered if it'd been set up to convince the kingdoms to remove women with Gifts once and for all.

A few of the kings had resisted Amir's sway. "She deserves a fair trial, just like a Gifted man," one had said.

But others aligned with Amir. "Women can't handle this kind of power. They're too emotional. I vote we sever all their Gifts."

"Agreed," said another. "The toll on them is too much, it would be better if they were allowed to live a normal life."

Arguments rose and fell, but in the end, Amir had shrugged. "We will give women a sound and reasonable trial. But we all know how it will end."

The woman had hung herself.

I shivered at the memory, strategizing the best way to resist Amir without revealing my Gift. But my silence stretched too long. Amir glanced over his shoulder. "You *are* happy, are you not?"

Forcing myself to give in to the waves of influence washing over me, I beamed up at him. "I'm delighted to marry you. When will our wedding take place?" Clenching my fists within the folds of my skirts, I tried not to fidget.

My father hadn't said a word. He stood, gazing at nothing, as Amir set down the paper and held out his hands. "Come." I swallowed and obeyed, keeping my smile pasted on. When he gripped my fingers, I focused all my energy on not pulling them away. "We'll be married in a fortnight on Summer's Eve," Amir said. "The feast and entertainment will make the perfect wedding celebration, don't you think? Best of all, the entire kingdom has already been invited and everyone nearby will be encouraged to attend. Your father has already given it his blessing."

I blinked at that. The Summer's Eve feast was less than two weeks away. Amir mistook my silence for the same blank reaction as my father. He cupped my cheek with his hand. "You will be a beautiful bride." I let my face light up the way he expected it to, and he turned away. "You're dismissed."

How dare he dismiss me in my own home? My blood boiled as I glared at his back. I almost forgot to obey, but forced my feet to move toward the door, touching my father's arm as I passed. "Baba," my voice came out too bright. "Could we have a private moment to celebrate? Maybe we could have some champagne?"

"I'm not sure we should celebrate just yet, Arie-zada." My father patted my arm. His face was slack and his words came out slow, as if he had to mull over each one individually. "It's still a secret."

"Oh, it's not a secret anymore," Amir replied, not even glancing up as he picked up another paper. "That sounds delicious. Go pour three glasses. I'll join you in a moment."

At the command underneath Amir's voice, my father turned to obey, and I followed, hurrying to shut the large oak doors behind us. My father pulled out the champagne and began to pour the drinks.

"Baba." I took his hands and squeezed, searching for some sign that he was present, that the distance from Amir gave him his mind back. "You know I can't marry him." My whisper was urgent, desperate. "Please tell me you'll stop this!" I was only 17. That might be old enough to get married. But it was far too young to marry someone as old as Amir. My father had always agreed with me before.

"Mmmhmm, King Amir thought you might be uncertain, but he knows you'll come around." Baba patted my hand before he pulled free and turned back to pouring.

This wasn't him. I stepped back with tears in my eyes. *It's not his fault,* I told myself as I hurried toward the side door. I needed to escape before Amir arrived.

Walking down the hall, I kicked through a door when no one was looking, letting it crash into the wall behind me as I strode on, blinking back tears of frustration. I didn't know what to do. No one else saw past Amir's manipulation. I was alone.

Chapter Four

Arie

WHEN I REACHED MY room, I dismissed Havah the moment she finished drawing my bath. I sank into the soothing heat with a sigh. But the peace was short lived.

Havah returned before I'd had a minute to myself. "Your father expects you to sit beside King Amir at dinner tonight," she told me, laying out my towel. "He said you'll be announcing your engagement—a thousand blessings on your wedding, I didn't know! Which dress should I set out for the evening?"

"I didn't know either," I told the ceiling, not wanting to see the misplaced jealousy on her face any more than I wanted to hear it. "Pick whatever looks good. I'd like a few moments alone, please."

She left in a huff, but as soon as she closed the door I felt relief from her thoughts. The walls muted them as they would a voice, and for that at least, I could be grateful. I needed to think of a plan.

Our little kingdom was small, but it wasn't defenseless. If Amir decided to threaten us, maybe we could fight. We had the sea on one side and the benefit of height on the other. There was only one winding road up to our little fortress and it was well-protected.

Staring into the bubbles, I smacked the water. It didn't sound like Amir planned to go home or even leave our castle between now and the wedding.

I pictured the stables, where my favorite horse had his own stall, no doubt being groomed and fed right now. How hard would it be to sneak away? Steal down to the stables in the dead of night, saddle up, and ride off? I could seek refuge in a neighboring kingdom... No, Amir's men would stop me before I left the castle gates.

I gave up on relaxing, splashing my way out of the tub. Drying off, I heaved the towel at the wall, wishing it would smash and break instead of land without any impact at all. I felt equally useless.

Straightening my shoulders, I called for Havah to return and help me dress. I didn't *want* to leave. I loved my father. I wanted to rule. And I couldn't imagine life away from him and my home. As Havah did my hair, I clenched my jaw at the two young women in the mirror. There had to be a way out of this.

* * *

By dinner, my hair was dry and I'd calmed down. This would all be handled by the end of the meal. I hadn't endured years of training in court etiquette just to let one difficulty ruin my entire life. This was *my* kingdom.

The royal court milled about in the Great Hall, conversing, waiting for my father and I to be seated before finding their tables. A wave of their thoughts, mostly unclear, surged over me.

"To the high Shazada, much beauty," a girl said. She was just a year or two younger than myself, displaying a crown of dark braids and a shocking ability to bow so low in such a tight dress.

I hid a smile as I dipped my chin and accepted her wishes, returning my own. "To the daughter of Marzban-Shah, many admirers," I replied, remembering how she'd turned down a sour proposal. If only I could take her aside for some tips on how to do the same.

Maybe she could help me, the girl thought even as she stood. Her smile trembled and her eyes blinked too much, something I may not have noticed without the thought. Why did she want help? When I stared too long, she blushed and apologized, melting away into the crowd. Only when she turned her back did I remember: she was the Gifted girl. Maybe a part of me had wanted to forget. A very large, guilty part. I swore to myself I would try to help her the moment I resolved my unwanted engagement.

One difficulty at a time.

I moved through the room, greeting everyone who approached.

"To the high princess, a happy marriage."

"To the Madani family..." I struggled to find a response, "much wealth."

"To the high Shazada, a blessed marriage."

I wanted to groan. "To the Berange-Shah... a good day." It was a disgraceful response, but I couldn't find it in myself to care. I picked up my pace, making my way toward the raised dais at the front of the room where I would sit with my father and King Amir, and hopefully avoid any further conversation.

When my father and King Amir joined me, I managed a smile, though it was mostly teeth. The king didn't seem to notice, only nodding as he pulled out his chair. I expected to hear my father's thoughts about my attitude, even if he didn't voice them, but there was only silence. Strange.

Across the room, everyone sat at the long tables, and a hush fell. The pressure of their thoughts increased.

Such a pretty dress, an unfamiliar woman's voice.

This engagement ruins everything, another woman. *She was meant to marry my son!*

I'd grown accustomed to not reacting during meals, but still I flinched. This wedding would *not* happen!

With a flourish, the musicians played a rolling trill of excitement to signal the start of the feast, and the silence broke. I breathed a soft sigh as the noise level returned to normal, the music plucking along light and airy. Everyone's focus returned to their food. Amir patted the hound who lay at his feet.

The first course was served. Stewed venison from my father's hunt last week, prepared with flavoured sauces, herbs, and spices. The servants held out bowls of water for us to wash our hands before we ate, but Amir waved them away. "I've already washed," he told them.

I blinked when they didn't react, glancing at my father when Amir dipped his dirty fingers directly into the bread trencher before us, ripping off a piece. The stale bread from the kitchen that served as a thick long plate was meant for holding food, not for eating, but Amir ignored dinner etiquette altogether.

Baba frowned. "Even a king should respect his peers and wash for dinner."

"Oh, but I have, can you not see?" Amir spread his hands. A hair from his hound that clung to his sleeve drifted down onto the table. He spoke loud enough for the whole room to hear, and those who were listening nodded, returning to heaping their plates with food. Of course he'd washed. How could Baba question him?

"My mistake," Baba hurried to agree, lifting his spoon. "I do apologize." The room waited respectfully for him to take the first bite, before they began their meal.

I could've choked as another dog hair drifted through the air toward my bowl.

Why is she unconvinced? At Amir's thought, I stopped watching the hair and smoothed my frown into a peaceful smile, as if all I ever wanted was to sit there and eat. I pretended to bump my bowl, moving it to the left—the hair just missed it—and took a bite. Amir would call for a Severance if he sensed even a whiff of my Gift.

Strange.

The word came through crystal clear, which meant he was still thinking directly about me.

I swallowed my bite, not daring to look up, and scooped another.

She has a strong mind. He had no idea how strong. *I'll have to keep an eye out for her...*

The thoughts faded. I focused on breathing. In. Out. Don't draw attention. Bite after mindless bite. *At least if he ever plans to murder me, I'll have forewarning,* I tried to console myself. But it didn't help. To even think of going through with it... I shook my head, gripping my bowl with both hands to keep them from trembling.

Soon, the notoriety of our guest diminished and the noise tripled as conversations and drinks flowed.

I stayed silent. My father wasn't one to chat during meals, and Amir was focused on the food as well. The meat tasted like dust in my mouth. The servants served fruit and nuts to cleanse our palates before the next meal. I picked at the grapes.

The next course was more exotic. Roast peacock. Our cook always took every opportunity to impress guests, and there was a generous helping of leeks, onions, and peas incorporated into the sauce that soaked into the bread platter.

I nibbled at the bread, dipping it in the sauce to give it some taste. If Amir had paid me any attention at all, he would've noticed my anxiety, but instead he devoured his meal, draining another cup of our finest wine.

Only when he'd picked over the last course full of baked apples, candied pears, and a cheese platter, did Amir settle back into his chair with a belch, and turn to address me, "What are you doing tomorrow, my bride-to-be?"

The term of endearment made my skin crawl. I swallowed, pushing a smile onto my face, though it didn't reach my eyes. "I thought I'd go for a ride in the morning." I'd always loved to ride, even more so as my Gift took over. Anything to get out of the castle.

"Oh no, I don't think so," Amir said, dipping his dirty fingers in the water bowl finally, though it was too late to be helpful, then wiping them on the bread bowl so that no one else could eat it. "Can't have the future Queen of Sagh out riding around the country like a vagrant, can we?"

I couldn't tell if he was using his Gift, or if it was just my fear of disagreeing with him, but I fought to find the right words. "No, I suppose not…"

Amir grabbed the trencher, pulling yet another chunk of bread from the side and dipping it into the last bit of leftover sauce. "Glad that's settled," he said through a mouthful. "Don't you worry now. You're going to be a very happy bride."

This time, his Gift swept over me and I had to fight it. He pushed back his chair and stood, making his way out. There was no need for me to pretend my acceptance. He'd grown so used to the effects of his Gift, he'd just assumed. I should be grateful for that. Because if he'd turned back even once, I knew he would've seen the fury written all over my face.

I crushed the bread in my hand until it was a solid lump. It was either that or cry in front of the entire court.

I glanced at my father who still sat beside me, stiff and silent. What had Amir done to him? Same wavy white hair and beard, same gold crown perched on his head. Same warm, brown eyes, except the warmth had vanished, leaving a blank expression I'd never seen before.

"Baba," I whispered so no one would overhear. He started to turn to me. "How can you let this happen?" Hurt slipped into my tone and I had to stop before my voice broke. At my words, his eyes stopped at a point on the table, transfixed. He continued chewing, as if he hadn't heard me. What had Amir said to make him come to an abrupt halt at even the slightest reference to the wedding?

Staring down at my trencher, I tried to eat a few more bites so I wouldn't be hungry later.

"Can you pass the cheese?" my father said out of nowhere.

Speechless, I lifted the platter and handed it to him. "Do you want the grapes too?"

"No, no," he replied right away. It felt almost normal. "I have my wine."

"Of course, Baba," I whispered, watching him finish his meal and stand to leave.

"Goodnight Arie-zada," he said, patting my arm. He moved toward the closest door.

"Baba, wait," I stood on impulse, and followed him out into the hall, before wrapping my arms around him and burying my face in his tunic, feeling his scratchy beard on my forehead.

He tilted his head to peer at my face. "What's this? What's come over you?" His voice was gruff, but his thoughts were concerned, *Something's wrong...* As he pulled back and unwrapped my arms, his eyes were alert and normal. Had Amir's spell worn off?

"It's King Amir," I babbled. "He's trying to force me to marry him and he's convinced you to—"

My father pulled out of my embrace and turned to go.

"Baba, wait!" He didn't. And worse, I couldn't hear a single thought from him, as if he couldn't absorb any conversation about the wedding. What had Amir commanded him?

"Why don't you hear me?" I cried after him as he rounded the corner. He didn't respond. He couldn't. I swallowed back tears, holding onto that thought. It wasn't his choice. He didn't mean to leave me alone. It wasn't his fault.

I ran to my rooms before anyone could see me cry. He couldn't help me. He couldn't even help himself.

I went to bed that night wide awake, ignoring the teardrops trailing down my cheeks and hitting my pillow as I wracked my mind for a solution. A way out. I'd do anything— absolutely anything—besides marry the king of lies.

Chapter Five

Arie

WHEN I HEARD HAVAH'S slippered feet come in the next morning, I was ready. I didn't even roll over. "I'm not getting dressed today Havah, you can go."

She curtsied. "Yes, Princess Arie." Ever the obedient one. Unlike me. "I'll get you some breakfast."

"Two helpings please," I called after her before she left the room. "Extra bread and fruit. And cheese!"

Her thoughts were judgmental, but she didn't say a word, only nodded and left, letting the door swing shut.

It wasn't long before she came back with a full tray and another servant helping her carry the second. "King Amir requests you join him and your father in the library."

"Tell him I'm not feeling up to going out." If he wasn't in my presence, then I could feasibly disobey without him suspecting my Gift, couldn't I? "It's my time of the month. I'll be staying in my room today."

I ate as much as I could stand and wrapped up the leftovers, carefully hiding them in the back of my wardrobe. At first, I expected Havah to return or Amir himself to show up, disregarding etiquette that forbid him from entering a lady's bedchamber, but he must have accepted my excuse because no one came, except Havah to bring the noon meal, and much later dinner. Each time, I asked for extra servings of everything. Though they thought I was acting strangely, they obeyed.

As the day dragged by, I went over my options one last time, making certain this was the best choice.

My father, King Mahdi of Hodafez, was vacant and disconnected from his own kingdom, his own daughter. He couldn't save me. Our armies weren't strong enough to fight Amir's, even if he hadn't had the advantage of his Gift. They couldn't save me. My father was well-loved, so others might fight with us. But how could they even begin negotiations with Amir in their midst? He'd seen our weakness and exploited it. No one could save me.

There was only one thing he hadn't accounted for.

I was not a weak woman. I could save myself.

* * *

As darkness fell, I had Havah bring me food one last time; who knew how long I'd need my supplies to last. Once finished, I dismissed her. "I'd like to be by myself tonight, you may go. I won't need you until morning."

Though extremely offended—it was her turn to stay the night in my outer rooms in case I needed her—she went. That was all that mattered right now.

As soon as she shut the door, I flew to my dressing room. Now that I was finally alone, I needed to hurry.

My travel bag was stuffed to the brim with food and hidden on the back shelf. It was lightweight, but too conspicuous with the intricate designs, beading, and jewels. Ripping them off earlier in the day had felt almost physically painful.

Next, I removed my nightgown and slipped into a shift, followed by a simple gray dress I'd picked out hours ago. It was meant to be embellished with another lace top piece that decorated my arms and shoulders but little else, with a suggestive cut-out over the cleavage. Instead, I pulled on a more modest—and warmer—top piece made of a soft white wool that covered my arms completely and most of my torso. It was difficult to button it in the back without Havah's help, but I managed, and then added a warm spring cloak to my ensemble as well, just to be safe. Summer was on the horizon, but the nights could be cold. Underneath my skirts I'd pulled on warm leggings and riding boots.

I stepped up to my floor length-mirror, pausing for a moment to study myself. The simple brown cloak over a gray and white dress still looked far too rich for a commoner. I tugged the cape closer together and tied it. My posture screamed nobility. Curving in my shoulders, I lowered my chin, imitating our servants, pulling the hood of the cloak over my head.

It would have to do.

"Why does everything have jewels or lace or trains?" I muttered as I turned and tripped on the excess fabric of the gray dress. Did village women even have trains?

I sighed. Of course they didn't. Why would they? There was no need for frivolous clothing as a working woman. I swallowed. It wasn't the thought of working that terrified me, it was the number of unknowns; my mind spun at the uncertainties.

I shook my head. This was for the best—not only for me, but for my father as well. Amir couldn't very well force my father to marry him. As long as I stayed away, our kingdom would be safe from his clutches.

Turning sideways to see the back of my dress in the mirror, I took the knife I'd used on the bag earlier and carefully cut the train off. Much better. The cloak would cover any jagged edges.

I pulled my long hair back in a braid, winding a strip of leather around the tail.

Focus. No time for fear.

I left the useless gray fabric on the floor of my dressing room. The goal was speed, not secrecy. Once they figured out I was gone, they wouldn't need to see the evidence of my plan to guess what it was: blend in. Disappear.

Picking up my travel bag, I untied the strings, packing another cloth full of cheese, sliced bread, fruits, and nuts leftover from my last meal.

My eyes caught on the tiara on the dressing table behind me. Back-tracking, I placed my crown deep in the bottom of the bag. A backup in case things didn't go as planned; another kingdom might be willing to harbor a princess, at least briefly. Returning to the dressing room where I'd discarded the jewels from my travel bag, I stuffed those inside the bag as well, before pulling the drawstring tight. They would fetch a good price, if I couldn't immediately find work.

The bleakness of my future spread over me like a heavy cloud, weighing me down. I fought the urge to crawl back into bed and go to sleep. *This is for Baba,* I reminded myself. For my kingdom. And for me. It was better for everyone if I was out of Amir's reach. With time, Amir would leave, and I could return.

Swallowing hard, I stepped up to the enormous mirror on my wall: the final stage of my plan. The silver spun edges of the mirror twisted with designs, hiding the entrance to the secret tunnels behind it—which were never to be used except in dire circumstances, such as a revolt or a fire. My situation definitely qualified as a crisis.

Behind this mirror, the tunnel led past my father's room—which wouldn't help—and also past my mother's old rooms—which had been sealed off since her death—exiting out of the castle through the stables on one side, and out onto the cliff walls on the other.

Feeling along the edges of the mirror, I searched for the hidden pressure point. It'd been years since I'd even thought of the tunnels, much less used them. My fingers slipped over along the edge, finally landing on the piece of metal that was discretely detached from the rest of the ornamentation. There was a satisfying click.

Picking up a candle, I swung the mirror open. The hinges squeaked in protest and I winced. If I ever returned—no, *when* I returned—I would make a point to oil each of the doors—

"Where are you going?" Havah's voice stopped me, one foot over the threshold, and the other out. My grip on my bag tightened. I didn't know if I could hurt her. But if she was going to sound the alarm...

With a candle in one hand and my bag in the other, I lifted my chin, holding myself tall, and answered simply, "Please don't tell anyone."

Havah's cheeks were pale. "Is this... because of your wedding? I don't understand, why wouldn't you talk to your father? He's always been reasonable before. I'm sure if he knew you were about to—"

"He can't know!" I interrupted, setting the candle holder down on a nearby table with a bang. "His mind is not his own. And I'm not entirely sure yours is either." I advanced toward her, a step at a time.

She faltered backward, holding her hands up in protest. "Of course I'm—are you suggesting—he wouldn't! It's against the law!"

"What good is a law if there's no one to make him keep it?" I snapped. But I stopped moving. As far as I could tell from her thoughts, there was no deception in her. "Havah, do you trust me?"

Her lower lip trembled, but she nodded. "I do." Her thoughts echoed her words. She was telling the truth. For the first time since my Gift had developed, I found myself grateful for it.

"Answer me this: have you spoken with Amir one-on-one—even for a moment—since he came to visit?"

She shook her head and whispered, "No."

Could she keep it hidden from me if she didn't think about it? "That's not very convincing," I pushed.

"I swear to you," Havah dropped to her knees, surprising me. "I won't tell a soul you're leaving. I'll pretend to fall violently ill for the next few days to avoid running into him."

When I didn't immediately answer, she glanced up with a fervent light in her eyes. "If you think that leaving Hodafez is necessary, I swear on all of Jinn that I will help you." I let a beat pass, listening. Her eyes squinted in confusion but she waited with me. Only when I felt certain she was telling the truth did I answer.

"It *is* necessary," I repeated what I'd told myself earlier. Stepping forward, I reached down and pulled her to her feet, until we were eye to eye, and made my own vow: "I won't let him have our kingdom."

"We can't let him have *you* either," Havah added. "It occurred to me that he's at least twice your age!"

A smile touched my lips. "That too." I grasped her arms and squeezed. "Thank you."

She squeezed back and bowed her head. I shouldn't have been so harsh on her. Everyone had jealous thoughts. But in this moment, she was loyal and true.

I turned back to the mirror, but Havah caught my arm. "You can't go that way," she said. "King Amir's men are everywhere."

"How do you know where the tunnels lead?" I asked, pulling out of her grip. "Only the royal family is supposed to— you shouldn't know about them at all."

Havah groveled under my scowl. "I... my mother told me... and her mother before her..."

Brows raised, I heard her regretting this revelation, worrying that I might remove her from her position as a lady's maid or have her punished. I placed a hand on her arm. "Let's at least see for ourselves," I said in a kinder tone. After all, I couldn't leave her behind. She could still change her mind about keeping my secret.

Gesturing to my bedroom door, I added, "Bar the door before we go." Something I kicked myself for not doing earlier.

When she returned, we each took a candle and stepped inside the tunnel, pulling the mirror closed behind us.

There were torches along the walls at steady intervals, but I ignored them. The candle was enough. There wasn't time to waste.

Winding around rooms, we descended first one staircase to the ground floor, then another to street level. We closed in on the stable's secret entrance. There was no peep hole, no way to see the other side without cracking open the stone door.

Nerves strung tight, I pressed the latch and caught the door before it swung wide. Loud, drunken voices sang out from one of the nearby stalls. They were either playing a game, drinking, or playing a drinking game.

I pushed on the stone until the latch clicked shut, hoping no one heard. "You were right," I whispered to Havah. "Let's try the seaside exit."

I'd wanted my horse, for the fastest departure, but on foot would still work, if we hurried. The night was waning.

We retraced our steps to the ground floor of the castle, then the second, entering a third, smaller tunnel that narrowed until my shoulders nearly touched both walls. It exited at the uppermost part of the cliffs, only a stone's throw from the watch towers above.

Remembering the guards stationed there, I gave Havah my candle and motioned for her to back up. I felt my way up to the stone door. The latch took forever to find in the dark. Before I opened it, I pressed a finger to my lips to remind Havah of the guards. She nodded, staying put in the narrow passageway. It was unlikely they'd hear us with the waves crashing against the cliffs. Far more likely they'd spot our silhouettes scurrying down the mountainside.

Pulling the door inward, I leaned out, searching for the watch tower. When one of the guards turned to look down at the cliffs, I ducked back inside. Why did the moon have to shine so bright tonight?

I couldn't risk this exit either.

Hissing in frustration, I pushed the heavy stone door shut once more, returning to Havah. She didn't say a word until we'd traversed the long tunnels back to my bedchamber.

My candle was nearly burnt out. As we'd walked, I'd struggled to think of another escape route. But we'd been in the tunnels too long. There was only one option left.

I set my candle on a nearby table, before facing Havah. "You must never tell anyone of the tunnels," I began. "And even more importantly, don't tell my father what I'm about to do."

She followed me over to my bed, where I proceeded to remove the sheets and blankets.

"Tie these together," I said. "Two knots. Make sure nothing will pull them apart."

Nodding, she obeyed. Minutes creeped by as we created a rope. I rubbed my eyes, which burned. Morning couldn't be far off now. I fought the urge to give up.

At some point, Havah must've pieced together my plan, but she didn't say a word, only helped me finish the rope.

"Do you think you could stay here until morning? Keep them out as long as possible?"

I knew I was asking too much, but Havah only nodded, remaking my bed with my heaviest winter bedding and stuffing pillows under it to form a princess-shaped outline. "I'll tell them not to disturb you—and pretend I've just come to check on you if they do come in."

I hugged her on impulse. "Thank you, Havah." My throat was tight. I couldn't waste any more time. I tied an extra knot at the top of my travel bag. Pulling it over my shoulders, I tied it again over my chest as a precaution.

At the edge of my enormous balcony, I threw the rope of bedsheets over the ledge, wrapping it around the rail and tying it tight.

Each summer, men dove from the cliffs into the water below. The warrior's leap, they called it. As long as you leapt far enough out, there were no rocks and the water was deep. It was the height that was terrifying. I'd never braved the jump—my father would never have let me—and I'd never had a desire to.

My balcony was two stories higher.

But it was designed for privacy. Which meant it was the only part of the entire castle that was left unguarded.

Leaning over the thick stone ledge, I tested the rope, before swinging a leg over to follow. The bedsheets dangled in mid-air, the same way my heart dangled in my chest, dropping into my stomach. Would they reach low enough?

I couldn't find the will to move. Straddling the stone railing, I stared down. The water below was pitch-black and clouds passed over the full moon, darkening the skies and hiding the stars completely.

Havah stood in the doorway, hands clutched in front of her mouth to keep her thoughts to herself, though I heard each one of her fears just fine.

I had to jump. No one would ever expect it.

For the millionth time, I tried to conceive another way out. But the guards were loyal to my father, which made them loyal to Amir. I'd never make it. This was the only way.

Chapter Six

Arie

THE DARK WATER RIPPLED in the moonlight. Tightening my grip on the bedsheets, I awkwardly climbed over the stone railing until I was hanging from the edge along the outside. My muscles seized up. It took enormous effort to slide down the sheet at the pace I intended, without slipping.

My arms burned with the effort of holding my weight plus the bag full of food, which threw me off balance whenever the wind blew. When I reached the first knot, I sucked in a breath. What if I hadn't tied it tight enough? I braced myself for a fall, but the knot held.

Hand over hand, gripping so tightly my fingers grew numb, I reached the end of my makeshift rope with much too far left to fall. The cliff diving took place much lower than this, and even then, only the most skilled swimmers attempted it. What if I sunk so deep I couldn't find my way to the surface?

And what about the Mere? Would they interpret a princess entering their kingdom as a threat?

Stark terror gripped me. But there was no going back now. My trembling muscles would never carry me back up. Cramps took over my arms, making it hard to keep my grip. I swayed there, suspended at the end of my rope, gathering the nerve to jump.

Before I had a chance, I felt a knot begin to slip, dropping me lower, and lower, and then I was falling. I held in a scream, air stealing my breath, before I hit the water. The frozen sea hit my body like a punch to the gut and I sank so deep that the moonlight didn't reach me.

Flailing wildly in the dark, I kicked toward what I hoped was the surface. There was nothing to guide me. My lungs burned. Had I swum toward the ocean floor instead of the surface? Just as I began to lose hope, my hand broke free of the water and reached open air.

I gulped deep mouthfuls, panting as I tread water. It was freezing.

My skirts tangled around my legs and my bag on my back weighed me down. Remembering all the food inside, I hurried to untie it and hold it up, but it was a losing battle. I started swimming, struggling to hold it up with aching arms and kick through the lurching waves at the same time.

The cliffs were close, but I couldn't waste time resting there. I needed to swim across the bay. If I could reach the shore of the neighboring kingdom of Keshdi, that would put some distance between myself and Hodafez. But could I make it that far? The frozen depths and the murky black water made me shiver as I kicked.

Flipping onto my back, I floated to catch my breath, dragging in deep lungfuls of air. This could work. Holding my bag over my stomach to preserve at least some of the food, I kicked. The thought of sharks or angry Mere below made me push harder.

The silhouette of the castle grew smaller and smaller. It made me expect to see Keshdi over my shoulder each time I looked, but even though I swam on and on, until the burning in my chest grew even hotter than the muscles in my arms and legs, it didn't appear.

Eventually, I stopped looking back and focused on kicking. If I let myself stop too long, I'd sink.

My strength was giving out when I saw the twinkle of lights on the water and glanced over my shoulder to see the coastal city of Keshdi rising above me. The white sand of the shore glinted in the moonlight.

The last stretch was the hardest. Something brushed against my leg and gave my muscles new life. Heart pumping so fast it burned, I finally felt the sand beneath my feet and waded out of the water.

My legs shook. My bag was soaked through. My shoes and leggings chafed, squelching loudly with every step. I was too tired to peer inside at the damage the water had done to my supplies.

I took two more steps and sprawled out on the shore to rest. But the first hints of the rising sun touched my skin, and panic made me drag myself to my feet and set off through the trees. I could see the town through the branches on my right, but I stayed hidden, pushing through foliage and searching for the nearest path as I dusted off sand. A small dirt road curved up ahead.

It was past dawn now; the sun warmed my skin but I shivered at the thought that in just a few short minutes, my ladies-in-waiting might check on me and find Havah instead. Once they discovered I wasn't in my room, they'd alert my father. Who would then tell Amir. In the daylight, the cliffs of Hodafez rose close behind me across the bay. Too close.

There was almost no one on the road, besides a woman and her two children heading toward Hodafez. I slipped through the underbrush, heading in the opposite direction and staying out of sight, just in case.

By the time my clothes were nearly dry, the steady plodding of horse hooves sounded on the dirt road. I stopped and hid behind a tree. My legs felt like soggy bread—I couldn't walk much further. A farmer passed by with a wagon full of wheat held down by a blanket. *I have to take the risk.*

Slipping out of the woods, I crept up to the back of the wagon, lifted the edge of the blanket, and jumped inside. I nestled into the hay, pulling the blanket over me, and held my breath. The cart didn't stop.

With a sigh of relief, I let myself relax, just for a moment. It was cramped, but soft. The wheat tickled my arms and neck, but I ignored it. I'd stay here just until we reached the town of Piruz. I knew enough of the high-born families there to feel safe and it would bring me far enough from Amir's clutches. The sun beat down on the blanket over me, lulling me to sleep. My whole body ached. A nap sounded divine.

It felt like only a minute had passed since I dozed off when the wagon jerked to a stop. Blinking, I frowned at the blanket above me. The air had grown overly warm and the prickly wheat made my sweaty skin itch. How long had I been asleep? I hadn't meant to still be in the wagon when it stopped.

"Only one more mile to town," the farmer said. Was there someone with him? Or was he talking to himself? I tried not to rustle as I shifted. The sound of him patting his horse reached me, softened by the blanket. The horse stomped its hoof. "Calm down," I heard him mumble, "We'll be there soon."

Muffled footsteps approached the wagon bed. I held my breath. His hand grasped the edge of the blanket. But he only tucked it into the sides more firmly where I must've loosened it, before his footsteps shuffled off. A moment later, I heard him relieving himself.

I held as still as possible when the farmer's footsteps returned, but he only climbed up and slapped the reins. The wagon lurched back into motion.

How far had he said the next town was? A mile? I should walk the last stretch. I didn't want to be anywhere nearby when he came to unload the wheat.

Crawling toward the back of the wagon, I peered out from underneath the blanket to find the sun at its peak in the sky. My eyes watered as they adjusted. I'd slept much longer and gone much farther than I'd planned.

With care, I took my bag and slid out onto the ground, landing as softly as I could, crouching in case he heard my fall. After making sure he hadn't noticed me, I ducked into the trees. A few stray pieces of wheat had spilled out onto the road and others still clung to me. I brushed them off.

Once within the trees, I opened my bag to view the damage the saltwater had done to my food. My nose wrinkled at the smell. Tossing the bread and cheese without looking too closely at the colors they'd taken on, I nibbled at the fruit and nuts that were left, wishing I'd packed more.

The jewels were still in the bottom, along with my crown if I grew desperate. I tried to smile. It shouldn't take too long to walk the last mile to town. I would get a hot meal there.

This is for the best, I reminded myself again. This was the only way my father could be free of Amir. I just needed to find a place to stay for a while; wait him out.

Though I climbed over fallen logs and circled the underbrush, the horse and wagon were so slow they barely gained any distance from me at all, coming back into sight after every bend.

As I considered stepping out into the road and passing them, now that I was far enough from home, I heard galloping hoofbeats fast approaching.

Two men rode past wearing the colors of Amir's guard.

I pulled back into the trees, breathing hard.

They overtook the farmer and ripped the blanket from the back of his wagon before he could even stop his horse. With a few words exchanged that I couldn't make out, they took off down the road toward town.

After that, I walked even slower, unsure what to do now. If they were searching for me ahead, I didn't want to deliver myself right to them. The trees began to thin and the city walls came into view.

The city was enormous. It started abruptly, with houses made of pale limestone and roofs that shone burnt-orange in the sun, stretching out before me as far as I could see. I'd come quite a bit further than I'd intended; at least half a dozen cities past Piruz. I'd never seen Aziz from on foot before, but I recognized it immediately from the way the city stretched out into the water like a claw. My stomach growled and my feet ached. Still, I didn't enter.

Approaching the outskirts, I stopped at the solid wall that surrounded the city. There were only three entrances. Even now, in the heat of the day, there was a line to pass through the largest gate before me—too many people. Better to avoid being seen. To the left, the road led to a tall building with stables; the streets of Aziz weren't wide enough for horses. Were the guards there, or had they entered the city on foot? I could only assume they were still looking for me, since they'd never returned down the road.

On a gamble, I circled the city until I came to the gate by the sea. Only then did I allow myself to enter Aziz.

This entrance was smaller, probably meant for the city's inhabitants rather than trade. I followed the cobblestone streets inward, trying to ignore the trapped feeling from the narrow streets and the sensation of being pressed between the pale buildings which grew darker and more sinister in the shade.

On the far side, the castle of Aziz rose above the rooftops, well-protected by the intricate roads, the thick wall, and the sea. I'd stayed there before. On the outside, it was modest.

Designed to hide the wealth of this city, though anyone who looked closely could see that the people were clearly taken care of.

Details I'd never noticed from my previous visits struck me now that I was on foot. Lanterns hung from doorways, open windows held clothing strung out to dry. Here and there, a person would pop into sight, before turning down another street. As I descended deeper into the city's valley, the bustle of the marketplace came into sight. I walked faster.

The smells of fine food and spices made an easy trail to follow. At the edge of the market, the narrow streets opened into an enormous bazaar, filled with people and stalls selling all kinds of wares.

Carpets were laid out to claim spaces, lined with baskets full of different food and cloth. Even more carpets hung on display, along with jewelry, scarves, and a million other items for sale. Awnings were put up at random to provide shade from the heat of the sun, which was making its way back down toward the horizon.

I fished out the smallest jewel, though it was likely still too much, approaching a vendor selling sausages with a butter-cheese on flatbread that made my mouth water.

Setting my bag on the ground, I waited my turn to bargain. I'd never done this before. As I stood there, a blind woman sat begging only a few feet away, holding out her bowl to a passing stranger, but he only scoffed and continued on.

Moved, I stepped out of line without thinking. Placing my hand gently over hers, I set the tiny jewel in her bowl. She frowned at the sound, picking it up and testing the feel of it. As her eyes grew round and awed at the edges of the jewel, I slipped back into the crowd, smiling at the way her face lit up. Her hopeful thoughts of the 'nice stranger' reached me as she made her way out of the square.

Turning back to the vendor, I moved to pick up my bag.

It was gone.

For a moment, I could only stare at where it had been, trembling. "Where is my bag?" I demanded of the people in line. "Who took it?"

They only scowled at me.

"You!" I pointed to the man who stood where I had been, "Did you take it?" He shook his head, trying to ignore me, but I stepped closer to him, grabbing his arm, "Did you see who took it? Which direction did they go?"

He shook me off, angry now. "How dare you? Where is your husband or father to stop this inappropriate behavior!"

I backed away, glaring at him. Only his thoughts of calling the city guards halted my retort.

Instead, I scanned the area, searching for someone leaving, possibly in a hurry, carrying my bag. There! I pushed through the crowds, running after the brown bag in the distance, but as I got closer, I knew it wasn't mine. Swiveling, my eyes skimmed over the nearby people, but there were just too many. It was a lost cause.

How could I have lost everything in one moment?

I stood there at the edge of the bazaar, breathing hard, searching for the thief without success. The little food I had left, my spare clothes, my jewels, and my crown. All gone.

I sprinted back to where the blind woman had sat, shoving past people in my haste... but she was gone as well.

"Excuse me," I called to a passerby. He ignored me, striding on. Blinking, it took me a moment to remember: to them I wasn't a princess. "Excuse me, please," I spoke more firmly to a passing older woman. She slowed, but just barely. "Have you seen anyone with a brown bag?" I hurried to keep up with her as she strode down the street, but she didn't answer. "Please," I gritted my teeth and begged, "Someone stole my bag—it has all my belongings in it—have you seen any sign of someone running, maybe, or—"

"No. Go bother someone else."

The ill treatment was jarring. When I stopped, she moved on without a backward glance.

Standing in the dust of the marketplace, I stepped aside to let a group of people pass, then further back as the crowds jostled me, until I stood against a wall in the shade.

My stomach growled as the smell of the sausages wafted toward me, emphasizing the enormity of what I'd lost. How could I have been so stupid?

Stepping into the shadows of an alleyway, I tried to organize my thoughts, to plan, to think of something.

I listened for thoughts from those around me, but for once, all I heard was a soft buzz.

No one gave me a second glance. No one cared.

It felt strange.

Hugging my arms to myself, I pulled the cloak tighter around me, and despite the heat of the day, I shivered. For the first time, I was truly alone.

That girl's been lurking for an hour now, a foreign man's thought startled me. *She looks like she's going to steal something. I think I'll wave down the next guard to pick her up...*

I didn't waste any time melting into the crowds, making my way to the opposite side of the bazaar. I eyed another vendor selling fresh, warm flatbread, beef, and yogurt. My stomach gurgled. I pressed a hand against it and tried to form a plan.

Clearing my throat, I stepped up to the woman ladling yogurt and beef into the flatbread. "Tomatoes?" she asked her customer, "Cucumber?" They paid for their meal and left, and her dark brown eyes landed on me. "One?" she asked, already preparing to make another.

"I'd like to," I began and she picked up a second flatbread, opening the mouth of it to fill it up. "No, no," I hurried to add, "I mean I'd like to, but I don't have any coin,

and was wondering if I could work for you in exchange for—
"

"You can't pay?" she interrupted.

I shook my head, lifting my chin higher. "I can work for it," I repeated.

"I don't need any help." She waved me away.

My pride wouldn't let me grovel. I passed her stall to one just a few carpets further, and tried again.

The man there was even less interested in speaking with me. "Paying customers only," he snapped. "Move along."

I forced myself to try once more at a fruit stand; anything that would fill my stomach.

"Please, do you have any work?" I tried a different approach. "All I ask for payment is a meal."

All the wrinkles on her forehead deepened as she mulled it over. "What can you do?"

"I can… ah…" My mind raced to find an appropriate answer. Run a kingdom? No. Address courtiers? Definitely not. Plan a banquet? "I'm a fast learner—"

"I'm afraid I can't help you, young lady." She was kind enough to pat my hand. "Maybe come back tomorrow. If sales are good…" she trailed off with a shrug.

I nodded and moved on, wandering aimlessly. The sun was setting. Shopkeepers were beginning to tear down. There was no point in asking anyone else; their day was over. They were going home to a warm meal and soft bed. I, on the other hand, untrained, unqualified, and useless, would not be experiencing any of those things tonight.

Chapter Seven

Arie

I QUENCHED MY THIRST at the town well, telling myself I was full and ignoring the way my stomach rioted. I would try again tomorrow. The sunset turned orange, pink, and gold as it touched the edges of the rooftops.

I needed to find a place to sleep before it grew dark. The thought of sleeping out in the open was hard to fathom. Pulling my hood up to avoid unwanted attention, I tried not to dwell on it for too long. *I've made it this far…*

Dusk fell quickly. In the graying light, I nearly ran through the last few streets out of the city. No one gave me a second look. I entered the forest outside the city, eyes on the growing shadows around me, peering over my shoulder every few steps. I listened more carefully than I ever had in my entire life, making sure no one followed. The hum of nearby thoughts faded as I delved into the underbrush. I didn't know where I was going or how far, but hoped it would come to me soon, because I could barely see.

A nagging worry followed me. *What if I can't find my way back?* Glancing around in the dim light, I noticed a small clearing with soft, tall grass that grew up to my waist. A promising hiding place.

Wading through the grass at a snail's pace for fear of snakes or other creatures hiding within, I stopped in the center, feeling the ground to make sure it was dry before bending the long grass into a makeshift bed. It offered a slight cushion. I wrapped myself in my cloak for warmth in the cold night air and lay down, using my arm as a pillow.

The moon was still nearly full. Here, away from the light of the city, the stars glittered above me as the sky turned a deep black.

The silence felt like a physical weight—like I'd lost my hearing. The irrational fear that this might actually be the case had me checking my surroundings every few minutes. But the soft buzz of cicadas slowly rose in the air and I finally realized what was missing. This far away from town, away from people, there wasn't a single thought. A complete absence of my Gift. It was heavenly.

A possibility crept into my mind that I'd considered before, but had never known how to act on.

My Gift could be removed.

Before, in the castle, pursuing a Severance had never been an option. Admitting my Gift and submitting to trial meant revealing the truth to whoever was killing Gifted women. Even if I'd found a way to keep my abilities hidden as I looked into a Severance, I knew one thing for sure: only a Jinni could perform the rite. And a princess searching for a Jinni couldn't be kept secret for long. Back home, it hadn't mattered if I'd wanted a Severance or not; it wasn't safe.

But now… If I could find a Jinni, removing my Gift might finally be possible. I stared up at the night sky as the stars winked on, one at a time, soaking up the peaceful silence. This supposed 'Gift' had always been more of a curse. If it were truly possible to be free of it… it could save my life.

* * *

Instead of waking rested, the emptiness gnawed at my insides like a tiny creature clawing at my ribs, pulling me out of sleep before it was even fully light out. Every part of my body ached. In the night, the dark silhouette of the trees shifting in the wind had made me jump more than once, and the noise of the cicadas, though comforting at first, had made it nearly impossible to sleep. I stood stiffly, glancing around the empty clearing as I stretched and yawned.

Pulling my cloak back on, I set out the way I'd come. My feet were covered in blisters from all the walking yesterday. Before I even reached the outskirts of town, the smells of baked bread and stews cooking wafted to me on the wind. My stomach pinched me. Hard.

One step in front of the other, eyes on the stone wall in front of me, I pushed on, entering the town. The soft buzz of nearby thoughts settled over me again as if they'd never left.

I paused in the quiet alleyway, before going further. Closing my eyes, I tried to remember the maps in my father's throne room. If I went to the castle, would they recognize me without my crown? Or worse, what if King Amir's guards were still here searching and they dragged me back home?

In the growing heat, feeling thirsty, hungry, and discouraged, I struggled with indecision. Should I take risk going to the castle just for a meal or keep trying to find work?

"You just gonna stand there with your eyes closed?" a male voice asked. I jerked, eyes flying open to find a tall, well-dressed young man around my age leaning against a green door on the stairs above. He was chewing on soft, fresh flatbread, and his dark hair fell across his face as he smirked at me. My mouth watered, but my heart pounded. I hadn't meant to draw any attention.

Drawing myself up to my full height, I hid my discomfort that he was a half-head taller and only a few feet away, looking him up and down. Taking time before speaking was a common intimidation tactic in the courts. I'd learned it the same year I'd learned my letters.

But to be honest, I was at a loss for words.

How had he managed to startle me? If he was looking right at me, clearly thinking about me, shouldn't I have heard his thoughts?

You take your sweet time. There, finally. His first thought.

"You take your sweet time," he said on the heels of the thought, matching it, down to the exact words. They blended together.

Speechless, I frowned at him, concentrating. My Gift had never done this before. Thoughts never lined up this smoothly.

Pretty, but strange, he thought. And then shocked me by saying, "You're pretty, but strange."

My lips parted. Who said *exactly* what they were thinking? I studied him. He shrugged, mistaking my silence for a dismissal and turned to go.

"Wait!" I found my voice and called out. He turned back, golden-brown eyes studying me as he took another bite of bread. I had no clue what to say. There were no leering thoughts underneath his words, no twists of phrase, no secret dismissals or disrespect… well, nothing that he kept hidden anyway.

"I'm, I just—" I stumbled over my words. Frustrated to be caught looking like a fool, I lifted my chin, straightened my hood, and cleared my throat. "I was just wondering where you bought the bread." I swallowed the drool that formed when I said the word.

He paused, holding the last bite in front of his open mouth, pulling it back slowly. *She's hungry.*

"I'm *not* looking for handouts," I said, before he could verbalize that last one. My pride wouldn't let me take some stranger's leftovers. I'd figure something out. "I just need directions. I'm... new in town."

"You sure are," his thoughts and words overlapped, and that smirk returned. Pointing over his shoulder, he shrugged. "The market's that way. Can't miss it."

Though I already knew where the market was, I thanked him and moved down the street, trying to keep a steady, non-desperate pace for appearance's sake.

I like her.

I paused mid-step at his thought. Turning to face him, I stared up into those eyes and spoke without considering my words. "What was that?" His brows rose at the blunt question. He hadn't actually said anything.

"I just—I thought I heard something..." I faltered. The seamless blend of his words and thoughts had thrown me off kilter; the last straw in my tired, confused mind. I just needed to hear him lie once so I could move on.

Squinting at me, he didn't answer right away. After he finished chewing, he shrugged. "I was thinking... you're a little odd." Ha! First lie. I nodded to myself, turning away, when he added, "And I like it."

Again, I paused. Looking over my shoulder at him, I croaked out, "You... like it?"

"Sure," he shrugged again. "It. You. Stop making such a big deal out of it," he said as my brows rose in shock. "Go get your bread." And he walked off without a goodbye or another word.

I blinked at his back.

Turning toward the market, I tried to forget him, but I'd never met someone so honest. It took away the advantage I'd grown so used to.

As I entered the market, I wiped the frown from my face, shaking off the irritation. No need to worry about it anymore. I'd never see him again. *Focus on getting something to eat.* The smell of freshly baked bread, spices, and roasting meat flooded my senses, making me clench my fists until little crescent nail marks were indented in my skin.

I made my way through a new section of the bazaar, feeling too intimidated to try asking for work just yet, staring at the different spreads. Little tent awnings stretched out from the buildings on one side of the street, shading the tables underneath, full of all different wares, including food, food, and more food.

My stomach ached with a hollowness I'd never experienced before. I felt briefly murderous. All my high morals flew out the window when I saw a table left unattended.

I could spend the day asking for work again, only to be very likely turned away with yet another round of laughs. Or…

No. I shook my head, walking past the open booth and on down the street. Stealing was the very reason I didn't have coin to buy food in the first place.

In the doorway of the shop ahead, a young woman stood sweeping dirt and debris out onto the street. "Pardon me," I called, walking around a cart in the street to approach her, "Do you have any work for the day?" I began.

"No," she snapped.

"Please," I continued, humbling myself to beg. I had no other choice. "I could sweep for you, or–"

Without a word in reply, the woman turned to go inside and slammed the door in my face. *Trying to steal my job,* she thought as she did. *And she was filthy too.* I flinched. Had sleeping in the field left me looking that poorly after one night? I ran my hand through my hair, trying to straighten it. A piece of the sweet-smelling yellow grass fell to the ground.

The shopkeeper at the booth next to me saw me turn toward him, and before I could even open my mouth to ask, he shook his head in silent rejection.

A man with a thin mustache and hair slicked over in an effort to hide his balding head, stepped up next to me, sliding his hand down my arm. I jumped. He whispered in a deep voice, "I know where someone as beautiful as you could have work in minutes." His face was just inches from mine.

I stepped back even as he spoke, yanking my arm away. The sudden urge to call for help hit me, but who would come? I called on all my courtly training, standing tall and strong, and glared at him. "How *dare* you," I demanded in a loud tone. "Leave me at once!"

But my anger hardly affected him at all.

He had the audacity to step closer, still whispering, "Down the street, two blocks, ask for Elam if you change your mind." He snaked a hand out toward me as if to stroke my arm yet again. I lurched out of reach with a shudder of disgust.

As he skulked off, I felt more frustrated than ever. His offer was quite clear. Between that and stealing a loaf of bread, I knew which I would choose in a heartbeat.

Before I could think too hard on it, my feet turned back toward the unmanned booth. Not knowing how much time I had before the owner returned, I picked up my pace. Hurrying toward it in a mix between a casual walk and a desperate jog, I pulled my hood up, trying to blend in.

The table was still unguarded.

It wasn't ideal. The sun was shining. The streets were filled with booths and shopkeepers and crowds, all of whom might see my next move. But I was no longer thinking straight or strategizing much further beyond: get bread, eat bread.

I glided past the table, reaching out a hand.

One warm loaf in my grasp, I curled it in toward me. *That was smooth,* someone's thought rose above the wordless hum, and I froze. Someone was thinking about me. Someone had seen.

Chapter Eight

Arie

THE VOICE WAS FAMILIAR. I glanced behind me in the direction it had come from, but in that split second of indecision, another man stepped out in front of me. I hadn't seen him underneath the awning. His eyes landed on me. Dropped to my hand. I slipped the soft bread beneath my cloak, but it was too late.

"Thief!" the shopkeeper screeched, pointing his stubby finger at me. "Stop her!"

I ran, dodging hands that reached out to grab me, but I didn't get far. Someone seized my cloak, yanking me to a stop. Others latched on until they held me firmly in place. I gripped the bread so tightly that the middle caved in and it threatened to break in half.

Why did she stop? She could've made it. There was that familiar male voice again. I swung my head around, trying to glimpse the owner of the thought. Over my shoulder, as the shopkeeper shoved through the crowd yelling orders, I spotted him. Golden eyes. He leaned against a building, watching the scene unfold.

A hand clamped down on my wrist, yanking the bread in my hand above my head for everyone to see. "This woman stole from me," the man screamed over the crowds, drawing attention. "I call for the maximum punishment for the crime! Do I have three to bear witness?"

My mouth was dry. The maximum punishment in most kingdoms was either slavery or death, depending on the leniency of the crown. "Let me go!" I struggled to yank my arm from his grip without success. The bread dropped to the ground. "It's just bread! It's not even worth anything!"

"Not *worth* anything!" The man's face reddened.

"I'll witness," a woman snapped, crossing her arms as she glared at me. "That's the only way they truly learn their lesson." No mercy there.

"So will I," a man intoned, shuffling supplies from one hand to the other. This was ridiculous. What kind of people reacted so harshly over a piece of bread?

The shopkeeper twitched as he waited for a third. "Who else? Come, I don't have all day!"

A pause. *Maybe not everyone in this city is insane.* But, no. Even as I thought this, two more voices sealed my fate. I tried to pull away again, startling him, but he was stronger and faster, and so were two strangers standing nearby.

The crowd closed in. There was nowhere to go even if I could break free. I stilled, feeling bruises form under their fingers. The shopkeeper untied the rope securing his tunic, wrapping it around my wrists. The sharp rope bit into my soft skin. I flinched as he tightened it. "She belongs to me now!" He raised his voice so all the onlookers could hear, adding,

"She'll fetch a high price at the auction tomorrow, if anyone is interested!"

He yanked on the rope, leading me back to his shop. How had this happened? Was this how people truly lived? As the crowd dispersed, a grin spread over his face and he added to himself, "I won't have to work for weeks."

I stumbled along behind him, unable to escape, listening to him ponder the price I might fetch tomorrow. I clenched my fists. We'd see about that.

"Sit." He pointed to a narrow spot against the wall between the heavy baskets of bread and wares.

I considered running, but he was already determining that he would beat me if I tried. I lowered myself to the ground with as much dignity as I could muster and sat.

Tying the end of my rope to a large basket full of heavy cloth, he didn't say a word. *Try to escape through the market with that. See how far you get.*

"Maybe I will," I muttered.

His eyes narrowed in on my face and his hands stilled on the rope. "Say again?"

My heartbeat roared in my ears and I couldn't breathe. He could *not* find out about my Gift. "Maybe I will... sit."

He shoved the basket back against the wall at my impudence, which dragged me with it, knocking me sideways. By the time I caught myself, he'd already turned back to the front of his booth.

I stared at the knotted rope around my wrists and the dirty carpet underneath me. My empty stomach squeezed even tighter than the rope. When the shopkeeper's back turned, I immediately set to work on the knot, but I paused and fell back as soft leather shoes stepped onto the carpet in front of me.

"Good morning, Haman," a smooth male voice said. I lifted my gaze to find the boy with those golden eyes standing in front of us.

He gave my captor a charming smile. "How fortunate. I'm looking for a slave and now I overheard you say she's going to auction tomorrow. Why don't I save you time and buy her from you now?"

"I think not," the shopkeeper huffed. "No doubt she'll cause a bidding war. I'd be a fool to sell her to you now."

No. The initial shock was wearing off as the full scope of my situation sank in. "I'm *no one's* slave!" I snapped at both of them, standing halfway, before the heavy basket stopped me.

The shopkeeper's hand swung at my face before I had time to react, cracking across my cheek and knocking me sideways. I fell into the limestone wall behind me. Sharp pain spread across my face and side. Blinking back tears, I stayed standing, glaring at him.

"Ah," golden eyes said, shaking his head. "I'm not sure I'm interested in damaged merchandise." The shopkeeper's hand stopped mid-air, where it was raised to slap me again. I couldn't tell if he was saving me or the 'merchandise,' but I appreciated it.

Don't stop, golden eyes thought when I stilled, and it sounded like a groan. He wanted me to struggle? I hesitantly tugged at the ropes that held me there. The basket hardly budged an inch, but irritation spread across the shopkeeper's face. I dragged the basket a bit further, testing its weight.

That's it, golden eyes thought, even as he raised his hand, thoughtfully stroking the dark stubble along his jaw. "Come to think of it, obedience is key. I'm not sure she'll be worth buying after all."

As golden eyes nodded farewell, turning to go, the shopkeeper's greedy gaze shifted to me. *She's going to cost me more than she's worth. I should sell her while I can...* I risked another tug on the ropes to compound those feelings, even as I wondered why I was trusting golden eyes at all. I couldn't tell what the shopkeeper thought of him, but his white tunic and overcoat were embroidered with gold thread in delicate ornamental designs, and his pants were dyed a rich, expensive red, which all spoke of wealth.

No doubt the shopkeeper could see a missed opportunity as easily as I could. He hurried to untie me, dragging me to the edge of the carpet. "I suppose I could sell her to you now," he called after the well-dressed stranger, a desperate tone in his voice.

Even knowing golden eye's strategy, I couldn't help but be impressed at his indifference as he paused and turned around. "How much?"

"Four hundred."

"Tohmans?"

"No, rice kernels. Of course, tohmans!"

Golden eyes whistled. "You're trying to steal from me, even as you sell me a thief?" He laughed and turned to go once more.

This time the shopkeeper dragged me out into the crowds as he lowered his price even further, and I knew we'd met a master bargainer when golden eyes graciously accepted, paying the man and taking my ropes so smoothly the shopkeeper didn't have time to wonder if he'd been tricked until we were already walking away.

Glancing over my shoulder, I noted the shopkeeper counting his coin as he returned to his carpet. I felt multiple eyes on me; no doubt the same ones who'd just witnessed against me before. I would wait to struggle until the crowds thinned. I listened intently for golden eye's plan for me, so I could anticipate if I should run or fight, but he didn't think about me at all; the hum of his thoughts focused on something else.

He kept the rope loose between us, never pulling me along, slowing his pace to match mine instead.

I picked a place up ahead, at the end of the market where the streets narrowed again—I could use the walls to my advantage, knock him into one, a well-placed kick—but we veered off course unexpectedly.

He stopped beside the stall with the elderly woman from the day before. She greeted him warmly, eyeing me as she accepted the coin he set down in exchange for some fresh fruit. Handing it to me, he only said, "Take it slow."

Stomach growling, I barely heard him, following mindlessly as I bit into the soft fruit and ate until all that was left was the core. Nibbling at that, my stomach reacted and I understood belatedly why he'd warned me.

I hadn't even noticed we turned down a new street, so focused had I been on the fruit, until he took my hands in his and gently slipped the rope off, tossing it to the side.

"Do you still want some bread?" he asked before I could form any words. Was that a trick question? I nodded, even as I frowned in confusion. He waved for me to follow and we strode down the new street until he found a stall with flatbread. "Is this okay?" he asked, and again I nodded, shocked into silence by the strange treatment. No one asked a slave what they wanted.

I took a step back at that thought. I was not and never would be his slave. Now that my hands were free, I should run. But I stood fixed in place by his offer of food.

She's scared, he thought as he purchased the bread, staring at me. Accepting two loaves, he stepped back up to me. "You're scared," he commented, just as I was debating if I should run now or wait until his back was turned.

"No, I'm not," I retorted. I was terrified.

Yes, you are. "Yes, you are." It set me off balance.

He held one of the loaves of bread out to me silently.

"You don't have to do that." I didn't take it. Accepting bread from him felt like accepting that he owned me, which I would never do. My father always said my pride would be my downfall. It just irked me that this boy was so cocky. Who was he anyway? Was he one of the princes? He couldn't be. I would've met him in previous courtship tours if he was.

"A simple thank you will do." He smiled as he took my hand, flipping it over so he could place the bread in my palm. My fingers curled over it as if they had a will of their own. He stepped back, crossing his arms and tapping a finger as if to emphasize that he'd wait.

"Thank you," I ground out. It came with difficulty. I hated being told what to do.

"You're very welcome," he said. If I hadn't been so annoyed at him, I would've laughed. Instead, I scowled and crossed my arms. As I did, the bread got in the way and I stopped mid-movement, giving up all thoughts of making a stand, to bring it to my mouth instead. Taking an enormous bite, I closed my eyes and groaned in happiness.

"That's not very civilized," he taunted. I responded by stuffing an even bigger bite in my mouth before I'd finished the first. "So," he said when I didn't reply. "What's your name?"

My mouth was full to the brim. My court advisor would be ashamed of my poor manners. I garbled around the mouthful of bread, "I'm not going to tell you my name. It's none of your concern."

"Well at least give me a nickname or something. Otherwise I'll have to give you one. I'm thinking I'll probably go with 'Bread Girl.' Or maybe 'Starving Sister.' Or–"

"Arie!" I interrupted, swallowing the enormous bite. He cocked his head, unable to understand what I'd said. "Just call me Arie," I repeated once I'd swallowed.

I took a more modest bite. He was ruining my meal. But I was too busy chewing to worry about where to go next. And I had to admit, if only to myself, that I felt a little safer with him nearby. Just the thought irritated me. I needed to learn how to protect myself. Maybe I could learn to carry a walking staff.

I was still mulling that over when he disrupted my thoughts. "I'm Kadin. But you can call me Your Highness."

I jolted. Had I been wrong? Was I speaking to another royal all this time? His clothes did seem rather rich. But one glance at his face revealed he was joking. I raised a brow and took another bite.

"Kadin," I began, trying to think of a diplomatic way to tell him I wasn't going anywhere with him.

"You mean Your Royal Highness Majesty Kadin," he corrected me.

"I definitely don't," I replied. "That's not even right." I stopped myself from adding anything further. Why would a village girl know or care about exact titles? He raised a thick, dark brow, thinking the same thing, but stayed silent.

"Listen, that was a good grab," he turned to continue walking, and I found my feet moving to follow. Maybe I could let him buy me a bit more to eat before I took off. "If you hadn't paused, you'd have been free and clear." He glanced over at me. "So why'd you hesitate?"

I opened my mouth to tell him it was *his* fault. After all, he'd distracted me. But I couldn't answer without giving away my Gift, so I only shrugged.

"With a little training, you could be pretty good. You could work for me, if you're interested. A few small jobs now and then."

I didn't miss that he was purposely vague. "Are you going to force me?"

"No."

No? I stopped walking and when he noticed, he stopped too, turning to face me, waiting. His thoughts didn't tell me anything, which meant he wasn't strategizing a way to drag me into it, wasn't thinking about me at all. Just waiting.

I studied him. Ornate patterns on his long overcoat. Only the rich could afford all that detail. Dark hair that fell in front of his eyes with that five o'clock shadow that made him look just a bit disheveled and one-hundred-percent mysterious. "What is the opening for?" I asked slowly.

"The pay is good, but the job is risky. I can't tell you unless you agree."

Risky? What did that even mean? "Well… if you can't tell me, then I'll have to say no."

Tensing, I prepared to run, waiting for the slightest thought of grabbing me. I raised my chin and kept my face clear of my plans.

He only nodded. "Okay. That's a shame, I had a good feeling about you. If you change your mind, we're on East Rice Street." And he turned on those fancy leather shoes to leave. My lips parted in surprise.

I stood in the middle of the busy street, still holding the last bit of my bread, staring at his back as he strode away. Why did I feel like I'd made a mistake?

As he reached the corner, his final thought grabbed my attention, *I can't let a pretty girl keep me from finding a Jinni.*

Chapter Nine

Arie

"WAIT!" I CALLED BEFORE I could stop myself, running after him. He was looking for a Jinni? My thoughts from the night before, of finding a Jinni willing to sever my Gift, came rushing back.

I rounded the corner to find Kadin standing there, waiting, brows raised. Slowing, I stopped in front of him, mouth open. I closed it. He hadn't actually said that last thought out loud. I wracked my brain for another way to bring it up. I'd have to take a risk. "I'll do it."

The way he studied me made my toes curl. I swallowed, but held his gaze, unwavering.

"Why'd you change your mind?" Again, so straightforward, saying exactly what he was thinking. It was growing on me.

Of course, I couldn't do the same. I shrugged. "I need a job."

"This isn't just any job," he cautioned me and I felt déjà vu from his conversation with the shopkeeper just a few short minutes ago. He'd hooked me, and now he had *me* chasing *him*.

"You really are a master manipulator, aren't you?" I said on a whim, trying this new angle of being unusually direct myself. It felt good. No beating around the bush. He chuckled. It was all the encouragement I needed to keep going. "You said if I agreed, you'd tell me what the job is. So, what is it?" I crossed my arms, aiming for a posture of confidence, but it felt defensive.

He studied me. *Should I tell her?*

It was the first time I'd seen him uncertain. So careful. If it was such a big secret it must be something unlawful or forbidden... and he'd wanted to hire me after seeing me steal. As he searched for a way to partially reveal the truth, his thoughts confirmed my suspicions and my words slipped out, "You're a thief."

His brows rose at my accusation. My breath hitched. Why couldn't I keep my mouth shut? But he didn't deny it.

"You want *me* to come steal things for you?"

"I haven't decided, honestly."

Even though I knew he was turning the tables again, making me pursue him, it still worked. "I suppose I have some experience. What's the job?" As if I stole often. As if that wasn't my first time. Would he buy it? "I'll consider working for you, if you tell me everything."

He only laughed. "I'd be a fool to tell you everything. You'll have to earn our trust first." Instead of pushing him toward sharing his secrets, I'd helped him decide not to.

I could kick myself.

On impulse, I stepped closer, speaking softly, "I've heard rumors around town... that you're looking for a Jinni?" I hesitated at the last second, turning it into a question, worried he hadn't told anyone and I'd just given myself away.

He frowned. Lifting his chin, he crossed his arms. "You've only been in town a day. Who told you? And how come you didn't say something until now?" He wasn't quite buying it, but he hadn't denied it either. I could work with that.

"This is what I do," I told him. "It's my job to find Jinn for people who're looking. I just… wanted to make sure you were worth working for first."

I was reaching now. Men hunted the Jinn occasionally, but a woman? Nonetheless, I'd already started down this track. Too late to turn back now. I stretched myself to my full height even though I only came up to his chin.

"Who told you I was looking?" Kadin repeated. He wasn't gullible. His thoughts were suspicious, and he didn't hide them from me, speaking almost as soon as he thought them, "Are *you* a Jinni?"

I took an involuntary step back. "Of course not." I caught myself. I couldn't afford to appear defensive. Lowering my arms to my sides, I shook my head at him and smiled, as if it were obvious. "Don't you know anything about the race you seek? You can recognize a Jinni by their pale skin, paler than any human." I quoted my mother's book as I held up my arm, gesturing at the warm tone, far darker than any Jinni, although much lighter than my father. "But more importantly," I added, as another detail from my mother's book returned to me, "They *always* have blue eyes. As you can see—" I gestured to my face. "—my eyes are brown."

"It could be a trick," he replied.

He had me there. Could they disguise that feature? I didn't know. My knowledge was so limited; I'd only just begun to read the book when I'd left home… But I needed him to believe he needed me, so I lied. "No," I shook my head. "Not possible."

"How do I know you're telling the truth?" he asked then. So candid.

"You don't," I said, choosing to be equally direct in return. "But you can test me, if you'd like. I can find a Jinni."

The truth was, I only knew limited bits and pieces of the methods; the book had been extremely vague. I needed him to help me with the rest. Including survival. "Hire me, and I'll help you track and find a Jinni in under a week's time." A bold statement. I had no idea if it was true, but I needed work, I needed coin, and I needed time to plan.

"There's something odd about you," he replied. "Tell you what. Come to dinner." Though he didn't mean for me to hear it, I caught the thought that followed. *At least we can give her something to eat before we make any decisions.* "If you can convince my crew, then you're hired."

"Your crew?" My stomach wanted to ask more about dinner, but I made myself focus.

"There's six of us total." Those warm golden eyes watched me closely. He still didn't quite buy my lie. "Thought you would've heard that when you were making inquiries."

Best not to reply to that.

"Do you promise I'll be safe?" I asked. I didn't mean for my voice to get so high and shrill at the end.

"I give you my word," he replied. But I listened for his thoughts. No sign of deceit. No ulterior motives. He meant it.

I let myself relax, just a little. My feet ached, my stomach still pinched me as if to say one meal was not nearly enough. Once I let my guard down, weariness overcame me. I could've slept right there in the street. "Okay," I said. "Dinner it is."

Chapter Ten

Arie

KADIN BROUGHT US TO a small abode on the edge of town. Made of the same pale limestone as the other buildings, I recognized the green door with peeling paint. It was where I'd first met him. An oddly small place for someone dressed like him.

In the early afternoon heat, the streets and roofs were empty. No one lounged outside to witness me enter.

My steps slowed.

Kadin strode ahead, confident, head held high. But I'd gotten enough of his thoughts in piecemeal to know he was as unsure as I was.

He glanced back as he pulled out a key. "Changing your mind?"

"No," I said after a long pause, uncertain.

Remember the Severance, I reminded myself. *For me, and maybe... maybe for Amir?*

That was an idea I hadn't considered before. It would certainly solve a lot of problems.

This is about more than just a job and a meal. I limped toward the green door on blistered feet with as much dignity as I could muster.

Unlocking it, his fingers curled around the handle and he pushed it open, ushering me in ahead of him. Stepping inside, I blinked, waiting for my eyes to adjust, appreciating the cooler air after the sun had beaten down on me without ceasing the past few days.

A low sofa stretched the span of three walls in the small front room, all three sides covered in brightly colored pillows. The decorative window covering let light in through a hundred different designs making patterns across the walls and floor. It was a beautiful home, but there was nothing personal, no paintings or tapestries. An older man lounged at the table, which held the noon meal.

My mouth watered.

The man didn't look up, busy working with a knife and a piece of wood. He was nearly my father's age and his skin was even darker than Baba's. His head was shaved smooth, but he'd allowed a carefully trimmed beard to grow.

Kadin cleared his throat. "We have company," he told the man, who glanced up at me. "This is Arie. Arie, this is Illium."

The older man nodded, once, and returned to his work. The complete lack of thoughts about me proved his disinterest was real.

A younger man came through the kitchen door holding a tray with steaming cups of tea. Kadin repeated the introductions, adding, "This is Naveed."

The younger man was closer to my age, and I assumed Kadin's as well. He had light brown skin, closely cropped black hair, and warm brown eyes.

He set the tea down and stepped forward. Not saying a word, he just smiled and squeezed my hand.

Hello, he thought and let go, still not speaking.

It should've made me feel ill at ease, but it didn't. I smiled back. "Wonderful to meet you both."

Illium grunted, focused on his whittling.

Naveed nodded in reply. *You as well.*

I began to feel nervous, but held myself still and composed, trying to hide it. *Did he somehow sense my Gift? Is this a test?*

"Each member of my crew has a job," Kadin said, pulling my thoughts away from the strangely quiet man. "Illium is in charge of potions and poisons. Naveed is my eyes and ears." Again, a grunt from one and a nod from the other.

Naveed's hands moved lightning fast, almost like a dance, and I heard his thoughts as he spoke to Kadin. *Tell her what happened.*

"Naveed is unable to speak," Kadin added. "He lost his tongue many years ago when one of the princes decided they didn't like something he said."

I swallowed, suddenly very aware of my own tongue. Kadin said the words casually, but a muscle tightened in his jaw and there was fire in his eyes.

His thoughts were only a soft hum since he wasn't thinking of me.

Had he been involved somehow?

He sat on the sofa, gesturing for me to join them.

I chose the empty side across from Illium, and a few feet from Kadin, perching on the edge. I eyed the food, but tried to focus on Kadin's words.

"You'd think Illium over there is mute as well." Kadin joked, which eased the tension in Naveed's shoulders as he settled onto the sofa by Illium. "But his silence is by choice."

The older man's hands never stopped moving, but he flung one up in a crude gesture before returning to his work, and Kadin laughed.

I picked at the dirt under my nails, feeling completely out of my element, but forced myself to stop. Turning to Naveed,

I cleared my throat. "I'm sorry that happened to you." I knew it hadn't happened in our kingdom or I'd have heard of it, yet I still felt responsible. Rulers should be just and fair.

He smiled. *She's kind.*

I watched his hands as Naveed signed and Kadin translated. "He says don't worry about it."

I pressed my lips together and nodded, but knew I wouldn't forget his story anytime soon.

"Arie's here for a meal," Kadin told them both, running a hand through his thick, dark hair. "I'll explain more when the others get here."

Naveed waved toward the food on the table, offering me a bowl.

"Yes, please. Thank you," I said in a rush, leaning forward.

He filled the bowl with rice and vegetables. It was simpler than what we ate back home, yet tasted better than any meal I'd ever had.

I'd only taken a few bites when the door burst open, startling me. Three men entered mid-conversation, shutting the door and stepping into the room before they noticed me and fell silent.

"This is Arie," Kadin began all over again, and introduced them to me one by one. "This is Ryo, Daichi, and Bosh." Each of them waved.

Nice.

How'd she get here?

She's pretty!

The onslaught of thoughts made my head ache, but I tried not to wince as I greeted them.

Ryo gave me a wide smile that he assumed worked on all the ladies as he sat down first. "Make room, make room," he said, grinning at me. I scooted over to the bench where Kadin sat as they crowded in, but I didn't have far to go. I felt oddly aware of Kadin's presence, even though we weren't touching.

Daichi moved slowly, more cautious, and if his thoughts were any indication, a bit shy. He and Ryo were both handsome, with black hair and almost equally dark eyes, the only difference was while Ryo was clean shaven with closely shorn hair, Daichi's most defining features were his beard and topknot. Both had tattoos that swirled out from underneath their shirts, which spoke of them hailing from Bafrin in the East.

"You're taking all the food," Daichi grumbled as Ryo scooped more and more until he'd made a tiny mountain in his bowl.

"Oh, shut it, I worked harder than you." Ryo took his time scooping yet another helping, which only made Daichi grumble more.

"Those two are cousins," Kadin murmured as they bickered. "But you'd think they were brothers the way they argue."

Normally they would've had my full attention, and the quiet boy seated in the corner would've gone unnoticed, but his thoughts were louder than all of the conversation combined. *She's so pretty. I wonder if she's older than me? I wonder if she likes Kadin? She probably likes Kadin...*

I ducked my head, focusing on my bowl instead of the boy. He looked younger than the others, tall and gaunt with gangly arms and legs, like he'd missed a lot of meals growing up or had just recently grown a foot. The dark fuzz on his upper lip grew in patches.

As they settled in to eat, they talked less, and I inhaled my food. I found myself grateful that men could only think about one thing at a time. Focused on the food—or in Illium's case, the strange little object he was carving—the quiet allowed me to finish my own meal in peace.

With the warm food in my belly, I started feeling sleepy.

"More?" Kadin asked, taking the bowl from my hands. I nodded, embarrassed but still hungry.

He scooped another helping, handing it to me before he sat back down.

The light from the window reflected the gold flecks in his brown eyes and distracted me until he spoke to the others, "Arie here tells me she's an expert in the Jinn."

Their thoughts assaulted me all at once and I couldn't even separate them in the jumble.

Ryo winked at me. "That true, gorgeous?"

"It is," I managed a weak smile. "I'm trained in hunting the Jinn."

"Says she'd be a good addition to our team," Kadin added, and then took a bite. It seemed that was as much introduction as I would be given.

"The question is, why are you all looking for a Jinni?" I asked. Did they want some extra help to steal something? Or did they want to steal something *from* a Jinni?

Illium blew the wood shavings from his lap in the silence.

The others watched him, none of them replying. Bits and pieces of their thoughts flooded my mind. *Why does she want to know…how does… can we trust… she telling the truth?*

It was overwhelming. I pressed a hand to my forehead, rubbing my temples. I didn't know if I'd ever learn to pick a thought out of a group when they all coincided like this.

Hopefully, if this went according to plan, I'd never have to.

I cleared my throat and added, "You know what, it's none of my business. All I need to know is if you want my help."

"We definitely need your help," Bosh said, licking his finger as he spoke. "We haven't had *any* luck—" he cut off as Kadin lifted a few subtle fingers. "Um… today that is…" he faltered, trying to recover.

Kadin sighed and shook his head.

I bit the inside of my lip to keep from smiling.

Naveed set down his bowl to sign something. Kadin didn't translate, but I overheard, *How did she know?*

"That's what I want to know too." Kadin replied, still not bothering to interpret for me. He signed something further. *She has secrets. Don't know what they are yet.*

You have such a soft spot for the unfortunate souls, Naveed signed back, shaking his head at Kadin with a small smile. At first I thought my Gift was growing and expanding to all thoughts, until I realized Naveed meant me.

I schooled my face not to react, scooping up the last kernels of rice until my bowl was clean. Kadin wasn't as convinced as I'd hoped.

He finally spoke, "I figure we can hear her out. See what she knows. What do you all think?"

Illium shrugged, turning over the wood to scrape away at a new place, speaking for the first time. "Whatever it takes." His deep baritone voice surprised me. It was soothing and melodic, with the cadence of a natural speaker.

Kadin nodded. "That's a yes from Illium," he said to me as Naveed signed something. "And from Naveed as well."

Ryo spoke with his mouthful. "I vote yes."

Daichi lifted his spoon in agreement.

"Definitely," Bosh's voice came out a bit higher than he might've intended, "We need a lady in the crew."

"A lady, huh?" Ryo teased him. "Trying to flirt, are we?"

Bosh blushed and stuttered, "I just meant, for all the, you know, for when we need to get into certain places that—"

"We knew what you meant, Bosh," Kadin cut him off.

Why did I get the feeling Bosh was about to say something Kadin didn't want me to hear? Were they looking for a Jinni or were they thieves? Or both? Kadin set down his bowl to give me his undivided attention. "So, Arie. How do you go about hunting a Jinni?"

Their gazes turned to me. "Before I start," I said, clearing my throat to buy myself time. "I should ask what you already know?"

Kadin frowned. *Is it a ploy? Maybe she's using us and doesn't know anything.*

I kept my face clear and open, not letting a single twitch reveal I was doing exactly that.

"I suppose it wouldn't hurt to exchange information," Kadin said slowly. I could tell the men trusted him; they waited for him to continue. "We know the Jinn are drawn to certain objects. Ancient relics and antiques. But we're not entirely certain which ones. Daichi—" he waved to the bearded man, "—show her the artifact."

I eyed the tattoos curling around Daichi's thick arms as he pulled a small, circular item out of his pocket.

At first, I thought it was a metal ball. He held it out to me and I accepted, feeling the cold weight of the object in my palm. "It's a doorknob…"

"Close," Bosh spoke up, "It's a door *knocker*." He grinned at my surprise.

When I glanced back up at Daichi, a blush had risen above his beard.

He held out his hand to take it back and I returned the odd metal door knocker.

"Why…" I trailed off, not knowing where to start.

"The Jinn are known to appear at auctions looking for particularly old items," Kadin explained.

Naveed took my bowl and I pressed my hands together, unsure what to do with them.

Everyone was finished, but we stayed seated, listening to Kadin. His men clearly respected him. It made me wonder what he'd done to earn such loyalty.

"It's believed that certain antiques may be enchanted for different Jinni, to enhance their Gifts. Different objects for different abilities." Kadin clasped his hands together, speaking quietly. His words reminded me of the book full of Jinni spells back home. "At first we searched for individual items." He gestured to the door knocker. "But if you don't know what you're looking for it's nearly impossible to know if you're chasing the right item. We were never able to find a Jinni that way. A while back we decided to try auctions with some success."

"Success?" Ryo scoffed. "We've been to dozens of auctions. In almost as many towns. We've seen *one* Jinni."

Illium looked up sharply at Ryo.

Without this reaction, I'd have missed it. They hadn't been here long. That explained why there was nothing personal in the décor, nothing to speak of a home.

Kadin only shrugged. "We made the mistake of waiting for the last Jinni to win the bid before trying to meet him. He disappeared before we could approach."

"We even tried coming back the next day," Bosh added helpfully, "You know, when the bidders pay for their winnings and pick them up? But he'd already came and went."

Kadin waved a hand. "The important thing is, we know an auction is the best place to find a Jinni. And now we know, the best way to gain an introduction, will be to possess the item they're bidding for. Then, they'll have to come to us."

The puzzle pieces fell into place. I hadn't known that, but I finally remembered what I'd noticed in the Jinni book back home. It was a tidbit that would immediately place me as an expert now. Except... the door knocker didn't make sense. "Was a Jinni actually bidding for the door knocker?"

"I told you it was stupid," Ryo muttered.

"Shut it," Daichi snapped, shoving the piece back into his pocket, growing redder.

"We were experimenting," Kadin pacified the men, speaking to me and ignoring the muttered jabs at Daichi over his 'precious door knocker.' "We've spent a few months traveling from one auction to the next. Usually we bid low and let someone else outbid us, once we feel confident the other person isn't a Jinni. But in a few rare cases, our bid ended up being the highest."

"Yeah," Bosh joked, trying to impress me, "like when this dingbat thought a Jinni would want something as stupid as an old piece of a door."

"I said, *shut it,*" Daichi stood so fast he knocked the table in front of him, spilling a half empty cup of tea.

Naveed jumped up to catch it, mopping up the spill before it reached the floor.

"Daichi, why don't you go get some air," Kadin said lightly.

Glaring around the circle, Daichi stomped out the door and it slammed shut behind him.

Instead of being ashamed, Bosh chuckled, and Ryo and Illium joined him.

Kadin's lips quirked, but he resumed his explanation as if nothing had happened, leaning back against the bench. "That's all we know. Your turn." His sharp gaze met mine, deceptively casual but I knew from his thoughts that he was convinced I was about to reveal how little I knew.

I shouldn't have been offended. He was wise to be skeptical, right even. But if he hadn't thought I had true information then this whole meal had been charity. It made me bristle. "It's not just any artifacts they want," I told Kadin with a tone of authority, shaking my head at him. "They need to be *timepieces.*"

I paused, waiting for a reaction.

Kadin only frowned, studying me.

"You know, items that mark time in some form or fashion," I prompted, keeping my features still, trying not to be nervous. I didn't have any other information to share. If he'd already discovered this, I was in trouble.

"Like a sand glass?" Bosh's voice was hopeful.

"Or a pocket watch," Ryo added. "Or a sundial…"

I hid my relief with a laugh. "Exactly like that."

"Timepieces," Kadin mused. He was watching me too closely. His expression hadn't changed. "That narrows it down, but there will no doubt be a variety of options. How would we know when a Jinni might bid?"

"I'll know," I declared. In truth, I had no idea, but I needed them to take me with, or all of this would be for nothing. "Up until now, you've been guessing. But if you take me with you, I guarantee I'll find you a Jinni."

I met each of their gazes, letting confidence ooze out of me, and heard each of them begin to believe it.

I only hoped I was right.

Kadin studied me. His men watched both of us. "Alright," he said, even as he thought it. "You're in."

I grinned. I couldn't help it.

For a long second, Kadin didn't look away. *You're going to break my heart, aren't you?* He stood to pour himself another cup of tea, not showing even a hint of the thought on his face, making me feel like I'd imagined it.

Worried my face was turning red, I glanced around the room and said the first thing that came to mind, "Let's find a Jinni!"

They cheered, raising glasses in agreement.

Kadin sat back down as they settled. I half-expected him to address the thought he'd had, since he'd been so direct up til now, but he turned the conversation to planning so fast it felt like being twirled one too many times. "The next auction is tomorrow," he began. "Which means we'll need to finalize the details tonight."

He described what they knew of the next day's auction.

Naveed caught me staring at the teapot and poured me another cup.

I smiled my thanks, only half-listening to Kadin until he said, "We'll use Arie as bait."

I almost choked.

"Because she's so pretty?" Bosh asked. Normally men kept those thoughts private. But he was utterly serious.

"Because she's a so-called Jinni-hunter," Kadin smirked as he gave me the title.

I guess, in a way, that's exactly what I was.

"The real bait is the artifact, though, right?" I spoke up.

"I suppose you're right." Kadin smiled. Only when his thoughts proved in line with his words did I smile back.

Their excitement was contagious.

They plotted all through the afternoon and into the evening, with a few card games mixed in.

When the heat of the day cooled, we moved up to the roof. Sitting in the night breeze, full of good food, I lounged in a chair and watched the sun set over the ocean, almost happy.

Except when I thought of my father.

The men had stopped worrying about me unless I asked questions, so I'd grown quiet, content to listen. Mostly, they forgot to think of me altogether, except for Bosh.

I think I'm in love, the thought floated to me out of nowhere.

I avoided his gaze, though I didn't think he knew he was staring.

I've found the girl I want to marry. I wonder if she'd dance with me at Summer's Eve…

"Bosh, focus," Kadin chastised him when he caught the young man gawking.

Bosh turned away, probably thinking about his embarrassment now.

I sighed softly, and Kadin frowned. He didn't miss a thing. I'd need to be careful of that.

I leaned my head against the chair, letting my eyes slide shut. But they flew open seconds later as Kadin thought, *She's tired.*

"Come with me." He stood, leading me back inside and downstairs. "I'll show you to your room."

I followed him down the hall, trailing a finger along the brightly colored walls, watching paint peel off under my touch. Their clothes spoke of wealth, but this dwelling was falling apart, and the furniture was sparse. "How long did you say you've been here?" I asked Kadin as we stepped into the bedroom at the far end.

"I didn't," was all he said in response.

Not long then. I was bursting with questions, but I decided to wait. I could pick up more by being invisible than by asking him anything.

Kadin busied himself picking up someone's pack, stuffing clothes and miscellaneous items lying around the room inside. "This'll be your room while you're working for us."

"Working with you," I corrected him.

No reaction.

He finished filling the pack as I moved toward the rickety bed, eyeing the blankets. *This isn't the time to be picky.* After two days of barely eating or sleeping, the warm food in my belly had me swaying on my feet. "Wait... Is this your room?"

"No," Kadin said. "It's your room." Which I took to mean yes, it had been. He carried his pack toward the door. "Rest. There'll be time to plan more tomorrow."

I nodded and he closed the door.

Why did I trust him? His thoughts were comforting, but some men were just better at hiding their feelings and plans...

I shrugged as I dropped onto the shaky bed. I'd be more careful when I woke up. Now I needed to listen to my body, which was begging for rest. Curling up, I barely even noticed the rough blankets and lumps in the mattress as I drifted off to sleep.

Chapter Eleven

Arie

A HANDHELD MIRROR. A set of silver spoons. A lavish settee.

I stood in the middle of the town square in a crowd of people watching the auction.

Each item the auctioneer's lackeys held up passed slower than a seven-course dinner. Or at least that's what it felt like.

He yelled over the crowd, speaking so fast I struggled to follow, pointing here and there at bids only he seemed to see.

I sighed, fanning myself with a large leaf I'd found. It felt like I was being gradually cooked by the sun.

A dozen men stood guarding the prizes of the day, and the crowd pressed in closer, making us a mess of sweaty bodies pressed together.

Not a single timepiece so far.

At least none that I was aware of. I'd accidentally bid on the first piece of the morning when I'd brushed my hair from my face, so now I kept my hands carefully below my neck to avoid the same mistake. The tension building in my muscles mixed with the anxiety and overwhelming number of thoughts in such a confined space, was forming what promised to be a spectacularly awful headache.

I glanced around the square yet again. Standing in the midst of a crowd of people, I searched for any sign of a Jinni, but of course, I wasn't entirely sure what I was looking for. Neither were any of the men in the crew, though they were spread out across the square nonetheless, eyes peeled for a sighting. Pale skin and blue eyes. Such small things would be so easy to miss in this mass of sweaty people.

I watched the men circulate through the crowd. Kadin kept a close eye on me. He was trusting me to bid for their little group today, so he needed to calm down and give me some space. Between him, his men, and the hum of so many in the crowd, I could hardly think straight, much less make out his thoughts. But from his expression, he clearly wasn't convinced I would come through today. I made a face at him.

He only raised his brows at me and hid a smile in response.

The heat of the sun made me so tired, I almost missed the next item when the auctioneer held it up. It was small, no more than the size of my palm, and rose slightly taller than it was wide. Beautiful gold metal designs framed the thin base and stem, billowing out into a round bulb the size of both my fists put together. Thick green glass with a perfectly shaped opening at the top. It would glow a mellow, warm-green light when lit.

An oil lamp.

My instincts responded to the lamp. Oil lamps only stayed lit if they had oil. If you filled them to different markers, you would get different amounts of time before it burnt out.

Which meant that, in a way, it *marked time.*

I bid on it impulsively, raising my palm leaf high.

Kadin frowned at me, looking like he might break his cover and come over to rebuke me in person.

But I simply raised a brow at him, as if to say, *Think about it.*

His frown softened, turning puzzled.

I continued to bid, even as the amount rose higher and higher. I may have been sheltered in our castle, but even I knew when the price grew steep.

It made sense, considering the lamp's base was made of gold and the delicately blown glass looked detailed and ornate, making it very valuable indeed.

Even though I couldn't see most of the group while I focused on our lamp, their combined thoughts hoping I was making the right decision felt oppressive.

The auctioneer's words flew by, as people kept bidding. "This beautiful item is going fast, if you don't bid now you'll lose it, bid now, do I have a bid? You there, sir? Ma'am?"

I bit my lip, confused, had I lost it? I raised my leaf high again.

"Young lady, you already have the highest bid."

I blushed as he continued to rally the crowd.

"Do I have anyone who dares to risk the young lady's ire and take it off her hands? Bid now, or forever go without."

Listening closer, I paid more attention to the other bidders. I began to worry the cost was too extreme. Kadin hadn't given me permission to bid this high.

His frown deepened, but he didn't try to stop me.

Then, just as I was about to back out, I felt it.

A sense I'd only ever felt around a few others. One in particular: King Amir. I'd assumed it was just because the king made me uncomfortable. It was always so small and insignificant, less noticeable than goosebumps, almost like a breeze. This time it was magnified one-hundred-fold, yet the breeze didn't touch the leaf in my hand or the clothing around me.

I lifted my hand to stay in the running and raised up onto my tiptoes to see who might bid next.

The internal breeze didn't have any sense of direction and I worried it was my imagination, until I saw a pale hand rise in the crowd, adding his bid to the rest.

I glanced over at Kadin.

Worry lines creased his brow, but he nodded for me to continue.

So, I did.

It rose even higher.

Between the crew's lavish clothing and their humble living space, I couldn't honestly predict what they had to spend, but one by one, the other bidders backed out, until between the auctioneer's calls, the only hands that rose were mine and a Jinni's.

I waved my makeshift fan in the air once more, bidding slightly higher, wondering if even my crown cost this much. Could they afford such a ridiculous sum?

When the auctioneer urged the crowd to beat my latest bid, there was only stillness.

Was the Jinni still there? Had he given up?

The auctioneer proclaimed the final price, naming me the winner.

The lamp was mine.

As the auctioneer moved to the next item, I wove through the crowd and stepped to the side where the employee wrote down my information. I signed a promise of purchase note. We had until the end of the week to pick it up and pay for it.

Now what?

I heard his thought as if it were a shout amongst whispers: *Why does she want my lamp?* It was so crystal clear, as if he'd spoken to me from mere inches away.

I whirled around, looking over both my shoulders, expecting to find him right there behind me.

But I was alone.

It was definitely a Jinni.

Goosebumps broke out along my skin as I scanned the crowd, searching for him. I'd never heard a Jinni's thoughts before, but now I knew without a sliver of doubt. We'd found him.

Hello, Daughter of the Jinn, he spoke directly to my thoughts again, and this time he added a direction to it, making it come from my left, in a way no one had ever done before.

How does he know I have Jinni-blood? Can he sense me the way I sensed him?

Panic flooded my senses, and despite the sweltering heat, I felt ice-cold. *Does that mean he knows of* my *Gift too?*

I waited for those surrounding us to turn and stare at me in horror, until a more rational part of me reminded myself that he hadn't spoken aloud. No one else had heard it. When I turned toward the 'sound,' I found him immediately. Staring at me.

Tall and thin, he stood still amongst the sea of people, hands in his jacket pockets. He had a hook nose, clear, sky-blue eyes beneath dark black brows. His pale, almost-translucent skin was so clear his veins showed beneath, giving his pale skin the slightest hint of blue. His tall forehead spoke of intelligence and his long black hair, almost to his shoulders, was swept back. His stance was casual. Un-hurried. He allowed me to take it all in, with eyes wide and my mouth open, before he continued his internal conversation with me, *I wish to buy your lamp.*

I didn't know whether to think my response back to him or speak it out loud.

In my indecision, I simply stood there, planted in place.

Kadin approached me from the side, while we still stood staring. "Well?" he asked. "Did it–"

"Kadin!" I interrupted him. "Did you get what you wanted? I got what I wanted, so I'm happy." It sounded like I was a rambling fool.

As smart as he was, Kadin somehow didn't catch on. "Are you okay? Did you spend all that coin just because you thought it was pretty?"

Without warning, the Jinni stood next to us, joining our conversation. "I don't mean to intrude."

Kadin jumped as if he hadn't seen him until he spoke.

I smirked ever so slightly. *Now* he caught on. There was no mistaking a Jinni now that I'd seen one.

"I would like to speak with the lady regarding her latest purchase."

"Of course," I agreed.

When he turned to Kadin, patiently waiting for him to depart, my smirk turned into a full-on grin. I wiggled my fingers at him as he turned to go.

"Very good," the Jinni said, facing me. He held a cane. He seemed too young for a cane, only a half-dozen or so years older than myself. Was he older than he appeared? Some legends said the Jinn lived forever. His eyes did seem ancient. Then again, he held the cane more like a weapon than something he needed for support. "How much for the lamp? I can pay you double what you've purchased it for."

"If you can pay double, why didn't you keep bidding?" Kadin called from a few feet away, eyes narrowed.

"I prefer not to draw unwanted attention to myself," he replied, turning to Kadin with one raised brow, waiting.

Kadin's scowl deepened, but he took the hint and moved back until he was out of hearing distance.

"I don't believe I caught your name," I said, curtseying and giving him my most charming smile that usually gave me a thought or two. "I'm Arie."

The silence from his mind felt almost intentional. I had no way of knowing for sure, but my instincts had me wondering if he was capable of hiding his thoughts? Who knew what the Jinn were capable of? Maybe he could hear all my thoughts right now.

He sighed. "Gideon."

It fit him. "Nice to meet you, Gideon."

He nodded at my effort to start with pleasantries, but only said, "I'm waiting expectantly for your answer."

I knew for sure Kadin wanted a chance to speak to him, which was the next step in his plan. The next step in mine had been different. I'd wanted to ask him to describe this so-called "Severance." I'd wanted to know if he would sever my Gift. And I'd wanted to ask if he would also sever King Amir's. Then the king would never have the upper-hand in Hodafez again.

But on the spot like this, the enormity of my request hit me and I couldn't bring myself to ask.

I needed more time to think it through and form the right words. To get to know this Jinni a bit better first. After all, a Severance was a lot to trust a stranger with. Especially a Jinni. "Maybe we could meet somewhere quieter and discuss it?"

Gideon sighed again, long and drawn out. Would he agree?

The Jinni culture was full of rules that they strictly adhered to. A code of honor. A true Jinni would never steal, no matter how easy it might be for him.

At least, that's what we'd been taught in stories growing up.

Now was the moment of truth.

"So be it," Gideon finally replied. Rubbing the bridge of his nose, he asked, "Where would you like to meet?"

Chapter Twelve

Kadin

THIS IS FOR YOU, *little brother,* I thought, watching Arie speak with the Jinni.

My plan had worked. Finally. After months of searching for a Jinni, this strange girl had shown up and we'd found one at the very next auction. I'd never admit it, but I hadn't been sure it was possible. A small part of me had wondered if the Jinni were just a myth like everyone thought back home. But now, this tall, soft-spoken, formidable member of their race stood in front of me, in the flesh.

And he'd just shoo-ed me away.

I ground my teeth, waiting from an appropriate distance, until Arie beckoned me to rejoin them.

I hurried to do so.

My men all watched anxiously from their concealed positions within the crowd.

"The lady wishes to speak somewhere private." The Jinni skipped small talk in a strange mixture of bluntness combined with impeccable manners. "Lead on."

"Right this way." I made an effort to hide my reaction, but I felt elated. The hard part was over. The Jinn weren't nearly as terrifying in person as the stories made them out to be. He'd even called Arie, our girl in rags, a lady.

"His name is Gideon," Arie said in a hushed whisper as she brushed past me.

My skin tingled where we'd touched, but I didn't reply. She was already five paces ahead on the road.

I gestured for this "Gideon" to go ahead of me, and waited until he turned his back before I signaled my men to follow.

We stepped into a small clearing just two blocks down on the outskirts of town, where no one would overhear our conversation. My men were careful to stay out of sight, peering out from buildings and trees. No telling if the Jinni might spook easily. I snapped off a piece of long grass from the side of the road, chewing on it out of habit.

"Now," Gideon faced me, placing his hands atop his cane. His quiet voice carried in the little clearing. He stared at me with those sharp blue eyes as if he saw more than I would like. "About my lamp."

"You mean our lamp," Arie corrected him, crossing her arms. I had to give her credit for her gumption.

"We're willing to part with it," I amended her statement smoothly. "For a price."

"I have graciously offered double what you paid." Gideon stood stiff and unmoving. Not a flicker of expression crossed his face.

"We have a slightly different form of payment in mind," I answered. Now was the moment of truth. "I'll give you the lamp for only half what we paid for it." We'd make the coin back. We always did. "If you agree to come with us to the kingdom of Baradaan. To bear witness to the prince of Baradaan breaking the Jinni code."

"Bear witness," he repeated.

Arie frowned at the phrase.

I'd picked it up in my inquiries. It was the Jinni's ancient term for observing an action and passing judgment.

Legend had led me to believe it was a common practice in Jinn, but Gideon narrowed his eyes. "So you lust for revenge?"

I hesitated. How did he know that? "The princes are abusing their Gifts," I answered after a long pause. I didn't want to spill my story to a stranger. "Across all the kingdoms. Someone needs to hold them accountable."

"You lust for revenge," he repeated, and it was no longer a question. I wondered how he'd deciphered something I'd kept so carefully hidden. When I didn't answer, he asked, "There is truly no other way I can convince you to part with it?"

"No." I didn't want it in the first place. I wanted his help.

"Then I'm truly sorry," Gideon said. He knelt, scooping up a handful of rocks and picking through them. He chose a simple gray stone barely larger than his thumbnail, more a pebble than a rock, smooth and round. He dropped the other stones, placing the gray pebble in his palm, and running his other hand over it in a smooth motion. Was that... Was he doing a Jinni spell?

He held it out, but he offered it to Arie, instead of me.

I gritted my teeth yet again, keeping my face smooth, and peered over Arie's shoulder to see it. There was a strange design etched into the previously smooth rock, a swirl that almost resembled a snail shell, intricate and detailed enough that someone could mistake it for an actual shell and not notice the uniqueness of the pebble.

"If either of you change your mind about selling the lamp, give my talisman a rub," he told us, pointing to the pebble. Arie's fingers curled around the talisman and she placed it within the folds of her dress pockets, making me nervous.

"We're not changing our mind," I repeated, emphasizing *we* to make it clear that Arie didn't have a choice. I felt desperate and hated it. "What can we do to change *yours*?"

"Nothing, I'm afraid." Gideon tugged his vest down as if to make himself presentable, though he was perfectly neat. Tapping his cane on the ground, he sighed. "I'm unable to spare time for your schemes, as I'm obligated to finish an urgent assignment of my own. Good day."

The air bent around him as if folding him into it like a blanket, and he vanished. One second he stood in front of us, and the next we stared at the tree behind him.

"Wait!" I shouted into the thin air he'd left behind.

But he was gone.

Chapter Thirteen

Kadin

"DO YOU THINK THE Jinni is gonna steal the lamp from the auctioneer?" Ryo asked without malice.

"No," I shrugged, barely seeing the dirt road in front of me as we trudged back into town. Everything had fallen apart. "The Jinn honor their code. They wouldn't stoop to stealing." The code of Jinn. What I'd hinged my entire plan on in the first place. What if I was wrong?

According to the code, there were three unbreakable rules:

1) Never use a Gift to deceive
2) Never use a Gift to steal
3) Never use a Gift to harm another

Every bone in my body had been convinced that all I needed to do was point a Jinni in the right direction—to Baradaan—and my little brother would finally receive justice.

I'd overestimated how important their code was to them. Something to keep in mind.

Arie walked beside me, lost in thought. Could the little Jinni-hunter find another Jinni as quickly as she had today?

She glanced up at me as I thought this. She tended to do that a lot.

I didn't think on it long though, as another idea struck me. What if Gideon was bluffing? What if he might be willing to help us, if we called his bluff? After all, he'd given us his talisman as a way to reach him...

"Well, what're we gonna do, boss?" Bosh asked, picking up his pace until he was by my side.

"We're going to return to the auction block and claim our lamp before the end of the week." I smiled at him as my plan clicked into place. "We'll just need a little more coin."

Bosh nodded, content to have another job on the horizon.

We would see if Gideon still turned me down when I held the object he so clearly wanted in the palm of my hand.

"What if the Jinni is still with us now?" Daichi whispered from the other side. The big man looked nervous. Not one to startle easily, he must be truly terrified.

The Jinni *had* appeared and disappeared into thin air.

For the second time that day I felt a prickly unease. I tried not to show it. "Then he should know we're serious." My voice rose higher than usual.

"His name is Gideon," Arie piped up from behind us where she'd slowly fallen behind and now trailed after the group. I'd forgotten she was there. "And he was perfectly nice."

I paused at the entrance to town, turning to face her. "Nice enough, but not very helpful."

"Well, maybe not everyone is interested in going on a little revenge assignment. I think I'd prefer not to go either, actually." She tossed some of that beautiful raven hair over her shoulder and skirted around me, continuing down the road into town. "It was very nice to meet everyone, thank you for letting me stay with you for a while. And good luck on getting your payback, whatever that might be."

"Not so fast," I called after her, picking up my pace until I walked beside her again. "I'll need that talisman before you go." I held out my hand.

"I'd like to keep it." So casual. As if she wasn't withholding the most precious item in all our possessions combined.

"I don't think so."

She clutched it tighter. She wanted the Jinni's help as badly as we did. But why? Had she ever meant to help us, or had she only joined our crew for herself?

When she just smiled at me, I dropped my hand. "Please." The word fell flat. "I need it to call Gideon back once we officially purchase the lamp."

"He gave it to me," she argued, not slowing down for a second. "How do you know it would even work for you?"

I considered that. Then considered stealing it from her. The idea of taking it by force made me uncomfortable. Glancing back, I found my men trailing us, wide-eyed at the girl standing up to the boss. Not something that happened every day.

"Unless you've come into a fortune recently, you can't go anywhere," I told her, grinning in triumph. "The auctioneer expects *you* to pay him by the end of the week for that lamp."

She froze mid-step.

"And it's strange," I continued, stopping beside her to cross my arms and tap my chin. "I don't know how I know this, maybe I have a Gift—but I feel fairly certain you don't have any coin to pay for it." I let my eyes drift to her clothing, ripped along the collar and by her feet, as if someone had hacked at it with shears, and dirty from sleeping on the ground at least once.

The men had grown silent behind me. Probably trying to fade into the background as Arie's glare burned up all the air in the space between us.

She took one menacing step toward me.

I stayed planted in the middle of the road.

"I don't *want* the lamp." She took a step toward me, and another. "I don't *need* the lamp, and I have *no* plans to pick it up, so why should I worry about paying for it?"

She stopped in front of me, less than a foot of space between us, hands on her hips.

"I hate to break it to you, but creditors aren't going to see it that way." I shrugged, whistling a tuneless song as I stepped around her now, gesturing for the others to follow. "As far as they're concerned, your bid means you bought it. No excuses, no changing your mind."

Over my shoulder, I spoke up in case she was too stubborn to follow just yet. "Illium, what do the creditors do to people who can't pay their debts?"

"Well, sometimes they'll enslave them," Illium answered in his deep voice, as serious and dour as ever. "Other times, they'll put them in a cell or cut off a hand." He shrugged. "Depends on the size of the debt, really."

I let that sink in for a moment, before I turned back to face Arie, where she still stood in the middle of the street. "I suppose you could try to go into hiding. But I can't guarantee that'll be very effective."

Ryo caught on to my tricks and backed me up. "Oh, they always find you." He shook his head. "It's terrible what they do when someone backs down on their word." He lowered his voice so she was forced to step up and join us as we walked on. "I've heard awful stories of them taking the payment however they can…"

"Aww, maybe it won't be that bad," Bosh tried to encourage her, not realizing my ploy. "How much did you bid again?"

When she told him, he whistled a high note that fell low and final. "Ah," he said, "Nevermind."

I smirked a little, but didn't turn around. "It's up to you," I shrugged, still not looking back. "But we're going to need that Jinni's talisman back, either way."

Chapter Fourteen

Arie

I'D WANTED TO FIND a quiet corner in the city where I could call Gideon back and make my request. I'd been rehearsing what I could say to convince him since the moment he'd vanished. But now... I clutched my skirts and squeezed, imagining they were wrapped around Kadin's neck. His cocky smile made me furious. After my brush with slavery just the day before, he knew I wouldn't risk that again.

But he *was* beginning to worry. *Is she going to follow?*

He and his men continued to walk, though Bosh broke the unspoken agreement between them and glanced back at me multiple times as the space between us grew.

Good. Let them stew a bit longer.

Why hadn't I just asked Gideon sooner? It had only taken me a few short minutes to work it out. I would start by appealing to his Jinni code, *I'm sure the Jinn dislike humans stealing their abilities.* And then, straight to the point: *I don't even want my Gift and would like to request a Severance...* No... maybe a bit more formal. He seemed to appreciate formality: *I would like to beg you to consider providing me with a Severance...* I could improvise that part... *In return, I'll sign the lamp over to you.* A willing subject asking for their Gift to be removed? How could he say no? But the only way it would work was if I could get away from the crew and it didn't look like Kadin was going to let that happen anytime soon.

"If I'm staying with you, I'm keeping it," I finally called out after them as I started to walk. I slipped my hand into my pocket, clutching the small pebble before I caught myself. Making every effort to avoid rubbing it, I carefully let go and pulled my cloak around me as if that would stop them from taking it. I could only trust Kadin's thought earlier would hold. He didn't want to harm me.

I stopped in front of him. "Gideon gave it to me."

We stood at a crossroads in the streets, literally and figuratively. I could tell he was frustrated, as much as he tried to hide it. The way those golden-brown eyes squinted at me. But I didn't back down.

"Fine," he said, after a long moment. He turned, leading us through the narrow passages between tall buildings, winding this way and that, until I was thoroughly lost.

The men kept me in the center of the group, and no one said another word until we reached the now-familiar green door of their small dwelling. They didn't trust me as much now. *We'll have to keep an eye on her at all times,* Naveed signed and they nodded agreement.

Everyone kept quiet as we entered, sensitive to the strange mood that had settled over us.

I didn't care.

I had nothing to say, so I stayed silent as well.

We sat down to the piping hot stew that Naveed had put together before we left. I sat on the far side of the sofa from Kadin. We ate in silence that grew more awkward the longer it stretched.

Why doesn't she want to help us? I tried to ignore Bosh's thought, holding my bowl out to Naveed and gesturing for a refill. I'd eat until I couldn't take another bite. At least then I'd have a full stomach when I snuck away later.

"Please, Arie," Bosh surprised me by speaking up. "I know you don't want to stay with us. But we're not all bad. We can be quieter and Naveed's food is really good and—"

"Shut it," Daichi growled. "She doesn't care about us."

Ryo smacked him across the head. "Not you at least, if you go around talking like that."

Kadin cleared his throat. "What they're trying to say, so poorly—" he lifted one eyebrow at the men and it disappeared under his long hair, "—is that we really need a Jinni's help. It's not right what these princes get away with. No one stands up to them. We just want justice."

I accepted the second bowl from Naveed slowly.

His eyes pleaded with me.

Glancing around the room, I saw that all of them hung on my reply. Daichi restlessly played with his doorknob, while Ryo chewed his lip. Illium scowled, even grouchier than usual; he'd already made up his mind that he didn't like me. Kadin wouldn't lower himself to beg, but his eyes implored me to reconsider, almost as if he knew what I was planning.

Lowering the bowl, I stared down at the food in thought, avoiding their gaze. I'd grown up with the princes and their foolish, power-hungry ways. At least I'd been somewhat protected, as a princess. What must it have been like for these men, for them to venture out on a quest for vengeance?

Glancing up again, I caught the men signing to each other, but whatever they were saying, it wasn't about me because the thoughts stayed a wordless hum. Bosh's head whipped back and forth, watching Daichi sign, then Illium and Kadin respond. Naveed joined in, hands moving faster than all of theirs combined. Bosh squinted, looking as confused as I felt.

My mind drifted back home, to the reminder of my own power-hungry, unwanted *fiancé*, King Amir. I imagined Gideon teaching him a lesson that would send him running back to his castle, leaving my father in peace. That alone made me reassess my decision.

Maybe it was possible to do both; to help them convince Gideon and to convince Gideon myself. I didn't really have anywhere else to go. No one was hiring. I didn't have any coin. Better to stay with this small group of people whom I half-trusted, where I could get a warm meal. If I helped them first, and asked for Gideon's help later, it would give me time to get to know Gideon too. That seemed reasonable.

"*If* I stay long-term," I began, and Bosh and Ryo cheered. "Then I get paid as a partner. Whatever the rest of you earn, that's what I'll earn too." I had no idea how much that might be, but judging by their clothing, they had to have *some* coin. If I was careful, I could save my pay and make it last. No one would steal from me again without serious consequences.

"Agreed," Kadin said. And this time everyone cheered. Except me.

I paused in chewing. "So how *are* you going to pay for the lamp?" I asked. "Because as you said, I obviously don't have enough."

Out of everyone here, I should've been most able to afford it. I ignored the urge to mourn the loss of my tiara and jewels once more. "Do you have some treasure hidden somewhere that I don't know about?"

"Don't worry about it," Kadin said, waving off my concerns with a smile. "It's something we know how to do."

Chapter Fifteen

Kadin

"WHAT ARE YOU DOING up so early?" I asked Arie, stepping out onto the roof. The morning sun still kissed the horizon and the light had a pure, shimmery quality to it, cool and refreshing before the heat of the day.

I tried to catch my breath as I approached. When I'd awoken, her door had been open—and though I wouldn't admit it to her, I'd run through the entire house searching for her, terrified she'd left in the night with the talisman.

She sat curled up on the sofa surrounded by pillows, wearing the same dress she'd worn the last two days. It occurred to me, belatedly, that she didn't have anything else. Didn't have a single bag or coin to her name. And yet, besides a hint of dark circles under her eyes, she looked beautiful and perfect. A blush rose in her cheeks as I admired her.

"Were the men too loud last night?" I pulled a chair over to sit by her, turning it backwards so I could straddle it and drape my arms over the back. I faced the colorful sky as well. "They aren't used to having a lady in the crew. Have we made you uncomfortable?"

"No." She shook her head, but didn't take her eyes off the sunrise. "They're fine. You're all fine. I just couldn't sleep."

"Are you worried about something?" I studied her out of the corner of my eye. "Something you want to share?" Ever since we'd told her our plans for the heist last night, she'd been quiet.

That got her attention. One perfect brow arched as she glanced over at me. "Something *I* want to share? How about you go first? It's not every day one meets six men preparing to steal treasure from a king. And not to keep, but to pay for a Jinni's services? All of which, everyone immediately changes the subject when I ask…"

I laughed. "Fair point." The men were just following orders. They had their secrets, and I had mine. The pink streaks in the sky were fading to a more normal blue. The men would be up soon if they weren't already.

"You're good at keeping secrets, you know that? You're impossible to… read," Arie faltered over the last word.

"Am I?" I smiled, liking the idea. When she frowned back at me, I chuckled. Oh, why not tell her a little? "You want to know about us? About how we started stealing from castles?"

She nodded. Swinging her legs off the sofa, she faced me fully, leaning forward.

"Where should I start?" I teased, tapping my chin. "Well, Illium, Ryo, and Daichi aren't here for the Jinni. They only care about getting paid. I caught the cousins fleecing travelers along the road for small coin almost two years ago. They're better at working together than they let on. Illium, we met even more recently; about nine months back. We'd heard rumors he was good with poisons, but he was selling sleeping tonics and other potions when we met. We went looking for him, since we needed someone with his talents for some jobs. He's a bit spooked by the Jinni though. I'm not sure if he'll stay with us." The thought made me pause. The older man could be dangerous if he wanted to be. I'd have to handle him with care and a generous send off.

"What about the others?" Arie's voice pierced the quiet. "And you?"

I held up a hand. "Settle down, I'm getting to that. The rest of us are here to find a Jinni. The heist is just a necessary part of our work."

Arie pressed her lips together, raising a brow.

"Naveed and I grew up together. He's been with me since we started. We want to find a Jinni for the same reason—and no," I added when her mouth opened, "I don't want to talk about it."

"But Gideon said it was revenge?" she said anyway. "How did he know that? Was he right?"

"You're stubborn, you know that?" I rested my chin on my hand as I half-smiled at her. I didn't want to think about it. "Does that normally work for you?"

"It does," she allowed the tiniest smile in return. "What about Bosh then? Isn't he a bit young to be running heists? What if he were caught? His family would never forgive you."

"He doesn't have any family," I replied, shrugging. "He wants to find a Jinni who can help him locate his father, who abandoned him in a village when he was a baby. But I think…" I hesitated. Why was I sharing so much with someone who was still a stranger?

She blinked, breaking my gaze. "I'm sorry. I shouldn't have asked."

"That's alright," I said. Something made me feel like I could trust her. "I think *we* have become his family in a lot of ways. He's been with us for four or five months now, but it feels like he's been part of the group forever. He doesn't have anywhere else to go."

"Oh…" she whispered.

We were quiet for a long moment. I didn't feel the need to break it.

The door to the roof burst open and Bosh stepped through first, followed by the others. Naveed held a tray of cups filled with tea and he set the tray down. Everyone took a cup.

"I was thinking, maybe now that we have Arie we could do the 'Dancing Chicken?'" Ryo said without preamble as they all came to sit with us, pulling up chairs.

Arie blinked at the strange name for the con, and I held back a laugh. We'd been planning the heist for weeks now; we already knew every second of how the job would go down tonight. But the men still liked getting a rise out of her.

"I vote we do 'Parade of Princes,'" Daichi chimed in, grinning, which made Ryo mutter about how he always disagreed with him.

I leaned back and stayed quiet. Let them get this nervous energy out of their system.

"Which one is that again?" Bosh spoke up, "Is that where they line up or the one where we—"

"We stick to the original plan," Illium interrupted, his deep voice carrying over the racket. He looked to me for confirmation and the others turned my way as well.

I switched the warm tea to one hand so I could lean on the other. "We keep the plan," I agreed. "We've had Ryo in place for almost two weeks now. He knows most of the kitchen maids. Among other things. Now that Arie's here, I have the perfect role for her." I'd come up with the idea last night, but hadn't told any of them yet.

"Me?" she said, biting her lip, which only drew my attention there. "What will I do?"

I mulled over how much I should tell her. Her eyes flashed to my face as if she could sense me holding back. I just popped a sugar cube in my mouth and smiled. "We'll need you to be our driver." That's all she needed to know for now. Keep it simple for her first heist. It wasn't technically the job I had in mind, but somebody had to drive the wagon. The men glanced at me curiously, but didn't say anything.

"Do you know how to drive a wagon?" Bosh asked her eagerly.

"Um... no?" Arie was frowning at me.

"She'll learn," I said as I took one last sip of tea and stood. "We only have a couple hours left to get ready." Everyone tried not to tense at that, but the nerves always came into play around this point.

"Naveed and Bosh, it's time for you to collect the horse and wagon. Illium will finish mixing his concoctions. Ryo, you'll go ahead of us to the castle and charm your way inside. Take Daichi with you. Teach him the ropes."

"But he'll get in the way," Ryo complained. "You can't flirt with a woman when someone's watching. It's just not right." He stood too, moving back across the roof.

Daichi bristled, following him. "What's not 'right' is the way you constantly lie and manipulate. Have you ever kept a promise you made to a woman? Hmm?"

"Absolutely!" Ryo huffed. "I phrase my words carefully so there's never any real lies. It's an art really. A skill."

"Teach him this supposed 'skill' then," Illium growled from his corner, still finishing his tea.

"Naveed's intel says we'll need two men to lift the bar for the back door," I explained calmly, interrupting the fight about to break out. "Unless you've been lifting tree trunks in your spare time, you're too weak on your own."

Ryo grumbled to himself. "C'mon," he said to Daichi, opening the door. "Let's go."

"I'm going to run an errand in town," I added before they disappeared. "Don't forget. Right before the dinner hour. You'll hear the cue."

"You got it, boss," Daichi said and Ryo nodded. The door closed behind them.

Our plan had officially begun.

Chapter Sixteen

Kadin

"THE PRINCES LIKE TO have guests to dinner to show off their wealth," I told Arie. We rode in the front seat of the wagon down the road toward the Aziz Castle.

She rolled her eyes, but was too focused on the road to come up with one of her usual fiery responses. Her fingers clenched the reins so tightly I thought they'd lose circulation.

I reached out and gently pried them loose, flipping her hands over and lowering them to rest in her lap so she could cradle the reins instead. "Don't worry, the horses won't rip them out of your hands," I teased. "We got the nice ones."

She snorted, but her posture softened slightly. "It's not the horses I'm worried about. I can handle any horse. It's this ridiculous plan."

She didn't even know the half of it.

Her frown deepened and no matter how much I teased her after that, she didn't lighten up. Earlier, when I'd gone out on an errand, I'd mulled over how there was something *off* about her. Usually I could read people better than a book, but it felt as if Arie was written in a completely new language.

"Don't worry about the plan." I waved off her concerns when she asked about it yet again. "We could do this in our sleep."

"Yeah," Bosh chimed in from the wagon bed as Naveed and even Illium nodded. "We're the best of the best. That's why Kadin picked us, right boss?"

"That's right." I grinned at him. He wasn't wrong actually. The kid could pick any pocket and pilfer any object. He could probably steal a spoonful of food directly out of a starving man's mouth without him ever noticing.

"King Gaspar is hosting a dinner party tonight for all the nearby nobles and neighboring royals, so he, his guards, and all the castle staff will be thoroughly distracted," I continued. "Naveed made sure to learn exactly how many guards will be on duty tonight. Illium came prepared."

I didn't need to check with him or even look back. Illium always came prepared. "Stop here."

Arie pulled the reins and the horses slowed until the wheels stopped rolling. I hopped down and held out a hand to her.

"What're you doing?" She didn't move.

"I'm trying to help you down."

"But, I'm the driver." She scowled, tightening her grip on the reins.

"And you drove," I agreed. "Now, you're a walker. It's the second stage in the master plan. Come on, trust me." I leaned over the side so my hand was just inches from her own.

For a minute, I thought she was stubborn enough to challenge me further, but she set the reins on the holder and stood, clutching her skirt in one hand and placing the other in mine, before climbing down carefully. Once on the ground, she let go.

I hid my disappointment, taking my bag from Illium.

"Your turn to drive," Illium told Bosh, not moving. The older man knew my plan and he was good with secrets; mostly because he didn't care. He and Naveed could fill Bosh in after we left.

Bosh hopped up into the front seat, eager to drive, while Illium and Naveed continued to lounge in the back.

"Good luck." I nodded to them as Bosh clicked for the horses to take off down the road once more.

"You too, boss," Bosh called back cheerfully, and they were off.

"Why aren't we going with them?" Arie asked me, frowning. "And why are they dressed like servants, but we're not? I'm not going any further until you explain."

"You have cute frown lines," I told her as we strolled down the road, unhurried. It was true. She also had a dimple in one cheek when she was trying not to smile. "They're going to need them to blend in once they're inside."

"Aren't we going to need to blend in too?" Her voice fell in disappointment as she added, "You're taking me off the crew, aren't you?"

"Not at all," I reached down to the side of the road to snap off a long piece of stiff grass. "You and I are taking the easier way in."

"Easier?"

"Mmm," I nodded, chewing on the prairie grass, an old habit. "Daichi and Ryo are going to unbar the door on the castle keep and drop a rope out the outer tower window. Naveed, Bosh, and Illium will all be scaling the wall to get inside. I figured you and I could just walk in instead." Unlike the other men, I was dressed in my finest. "That reminds me." I lowered the sack from my shoulder. "I got you something."

With a flourish, I tugged a huge pile of red fabric from the bag, struggling to find the top and botching the unveiling a little.

She gasped. "What's this?"

Feeling quite pleased with myself, I grinned and held it out to her. "Try it on. Humor me." I returned to the road while she stepped behind the trees on the side, switching her torn grey dress for the brand new one.

"How's this?" she asked, sounding breathless.

When I turned around I accidentally let the piece of grass fall from my mouth. "Very nice." She looked stunning. Her raven hair flowed down her back, free and wild, and the red dress made her look fiercely beautiful. "We're gonna need to do something about your hair," I said, clearing my throat. I stepped up to her. "I grew up with sisters. Trust me."

She frowned at the idea of my doing her hair, but didn't protest. The simple crown braid only took me a few minutes. Playing with her hair felt intimate. And absolutely nothing like doing my sister's hair. "There, done."

She touched a hand to the loose braid, brows rising. "I'm impressed."

"You should be. You look beautiful."

She blushed at the compliment—or possibly my gaze. "So. Walking in, you say."

"Only for another minute or two," I said, turning to glance behind us. "In fact, I think I see our ride coming now."

Chapter Seventeen

Arie

A NOBLEMAN'S CARRIAGE APPROACHED.

"What do you mean our 'ride'?" I hissed.

"Oh, didn't I tell you?" Kadin smiled at me. The gold flecks in his eyes seemed brighter in the light of the setting sun. "We're going to attend the celebration."

I scowled. "You know perfectly well you didn't tell me." How had he kept this from me? Was he so confident in his plans, he hadn't even needed to think about it? At least, he hadn't in my presence.

"You only just met me," I reminded him. I could *not* be seen at this dinner. What if we ran into guests who recognized me? "How do you know I won't betray you all?" Surely that would change his mind. "I'll have to sit this one out."

He only shrugged. "I think you'll be fine."

My mouth opened and closed as I struggled to find the right words. "What—how can you—why would you trust me?"

"I don't know," he said, scratching his chin where there was a shadow of a dark beard forming on his jaw. He pretended to consider me intently. "You have a very trustworthy face."

I snorted.

"Besides, usually when someone is running from something, they don't like to draw attention to themselves."

I froze in place on the road. "How did you know?"

"I didn't until just now." He stopped as well, grinning at the shock on my face, as he raised a hand to wave down the carriage that drew closer.

The driver pulled on the reins to stop and the nobles poked their heads out the window to see what the fuss was about.

"Hello there," Kadin called easily, smiling at them as he strode up to the carriage. I trailed after him. A local Shah, his wife, and their daughter peered out at us. I didn't recognize any of them and blew out a soft breath of relief.

"I do apologize for the inconvenience," Kadin was saying. "But our carriage broke down and we've been forced to walk to the party. It's terribly undignified. I don't suppose you'd have room for two guests? We'd be happy to compensate you for your troubles."

I raised my brow at Kadin's sudden fine manners, so composed and believable.

Despite never having heard of him, they immediately accepted his explanation, inviting us in, and within moments the carriage was moving again.

I sat next to the parents, while Kadin sat across from me, perched on the edge of the seat beside the daughter with his hands on his knees like the perfect gentleman. His clothing was as fine as theirs, but the way his hair fell in front of his eyes and that five-o-clock shadow made him seem just the tiniest bit wild and out of place.

He asked their names, which I promptly forgot, and acted as if we were all good friends who'd known each other for years. I was thankful he charmed them with a steady stream of small talk, because I couldn't say a word.

I studied Kadin as he chatted away amiably. Who was he really? He didn't fit the mold of any man I'd met before.

Less than an hour ago, I'd volunteered to go to the horse gate to stay with the animals while the men gathered their things. The poor horses had stood in the heat along the side of the road, attached to a cart, heads drooping, too tired to move.

"They're working you too hard, aren't they boy?" I murmured to the closest horse, rubbing the soft white spot on his muzzle. He closed his eyes at the attention, soaking it up, and I moved to scratch the soft fuzz on his shoulder and neck, missing my steed back home.

The other gelding was a soft brown color with dust patches all over from neglect, while my stallion back home was a deep inky black that shone from daily brushing. "You like that, don't you?" I smiled at them, as I pet them both, relaxing for the first time in a while. The first horse nuzzled me back. "I like you too."

"You've said nicer things to those two in the last five minutes than you have to us in the last two days," Kadin teased from behind me.

I whirled around to face him, swallowing. "Animals are better than people. They deserve it."

"People aren't that bad," he argued, crossing his arms casually. When I finally glanced up, those golden eyes pinned me in place, studying me curiously.

"They are, actually," I said. No malice, just the truth. I stepped around him. But I only took a few steps before I heard his fascination with me. I sighed.

Before I could think about it, I paused to look over my shoulder at him. "Don't."

"Don't what?"

I turned to face him fully, crossing my arms just like him, although admittedly a lot more defensive. "Don't be interested in me," I said, raising my chin and keeping my tone cool and self-assured, though I didn't feel it. I'd never called a man out like this before. It felt good, so I added, "You're just like every other man, admiring my body and my face."

"Yeah," he surprised me by agreeing immediately, a slow smile spreading across his face. "I definitely am."

Despite my frustration, I blushed.

"A man can like more than one thing, you know," he added, still wearing that smirk. "I was also admiring your way with animals and how you're a bit prickly in the mornings."

"Well," I faltered. "Don't."

He just stared at me, one side of his mouth twisting up in that crooked smile. He took a step closer until he was nearly toe to toe with me.

I tried to swallow but my mouth was dry.

"Don't tell me what to do," he said with a smile. And this time, he stepped around *me* to climb up into the wagon.

The rest of the crew approached as I stood in the street, confused.

I hid my red face in the horse's neck. "What just happened?" I whispered to the beast, but he was too busy falling asleep to pay me any attention.

Now I sat across from this enigma in the carriage, and I couldn't help but admire him. Not only was he handsome and intelligent, but he seemed kind. Was it a façade or was it real? I couldn't tell.

"The Lady Dusa and I are grateful to you both for rescuing us," Kadin said, pulling me out of my thoughts. Had he picked that specific name intentionally? Dusa was a common name, so maybe it meant nothing… but it also meant 'sweetheart.'

"We've been looking forward to this event for ages." Kadin switched to the next subject, without even a glance in my direction. Maybe I'd imagined it. "When was the last time you visited the Aziz castle?"

The conversation continued on around me, but my ears had caught on that one word and stayed there.

We.

I'd officially become a thief, just like the rest of them. I wasn't ready to admit it to Kadin yet, but it sent a tingle down my spine. I was playing an important role in the heist. I was valuable. As the carriage rolled up toward the grand castle, I admired it with them, murmuring my delight for the coming celebration, slowly coming into playing my part.

I rather liked it.

Chapter Eighteen

Kadin

WE SLIPPED INSIDE THE castle with the other arriving nobles without incident, walking up the steps alongside Azadi-Shah, his wife, and their daughter, who kept sneaking jealous glances at Arie.

Despite her reticence, Arie drew everyone's attention like a fire on a dark night in her vivid red gown. Even as we entered the grandeur of the castle with its vaulted ceilings, ornate sculptures, and brightly painted décor, I found myself admiring her more than anything else.

She gripped my arm as if it was the only thing that kept her from drowning, and kept reaching a hand up to hide her face.

"You look beautiful." I caught her hand and drew it down. "Stop worrying. You'll stand out far above everyone else."

Instead of reassuring her, her brows drew together and her hand flew back up to her face. "I don't want to stand out. I shouldn't be here. You don't understand..."

I was at a loss. Was it the heist? Was she having second thoughts? "Help me understand then."

"It's nothing." We passed through the enormous entrance into the grand dining hall where the tables were laden with a feast that could feed a thousand.

"It's obviously not nothing," I murmured under my breath as I smiled at those around us, searching the room for my mark.

"It's nothing, because there's nothing you can do," she replied, lifting her chin. "Why have you brought me here?"

I let her change the subject. A distraction would help her get over the nerves. I leaned closer to explain as we walked, "Each night, the Captain of the Guard gives the men who stand guard over the treasury a code that only they and the King know. They guard the treasury at the end of a long hallway with an arrow notched and ready to point at anyone who tries to approach without this code. If we can learn tonight's code, Illium can get close enough to use his sleeping powders on the guards. Without it, we may have to shoot them to keep them from raising the alarm. I'd like to avoid that if at all possible, which is why you and I are looking for the Captain of the Guard."

Arie groaned.

I paused, turning to study her. She was pale and shaking now. Steering us through the crowds, I led her out onto the balcony, and found a corner sheltered by a potted palm where we could talk in private. "What's going on?"

She pulled away, crossing her arms. "I just don't want to be here. It makes me uncomfortable. This sounds like something you could do on your own."

I stared her down. She was hiding something. I crossed my arms as well. "I originally planned to get the Captain alone and force him to tell me. But I thought if you were here, you could sweet talk him into giving up his secret, the way you charmed Gideon. And then we wouldn't need to hurt anyone." I shook my head as I spoke. "Never mind, it was unfair of me to expect that of you without asking. Go meet the others instead. I'll handle the Captain."

I turned to go back inside, but Arie's hand on my arm stopped me.

"Wait."

Chapter Nineteen

Arie

I AGREED TO IT on one condition: Kadin had to let me
talk to the Captain of the Guard alone.

She's embarrassed, he thought as he agreed.

And I let him think that, leaving him standing on the
balcony as I moved indoors. He couldn't know I'd met Captain
Tehrani during my visit here last summer. Or that the Captain
would recognize me on sight. Not to mention dozens of others.
I'd already spied the king's son across the room and made
note.

Is that Princess Arie? The thought struck me like a
physical blow over the hum of other shapeless murmurs.

I nearly choked.

Only a few paces away, a girl with a mass of curls caught my gaze and waved. Her silver dress shimmered with a hint of expensive Jinni magic.

I flashed her a smile and a wave before turning sharply in the other direction, only to bump into another familiar face.

"Arie?" Someone touched my arm to stop me. I turned to squint at him, vaguely remembering him as a Shah from one of my first courtship tours. "I hadn't heard you were visiting? When did you arrive?"

"I—um—today actually," I replied, stepping backwards, trying to keep moving.

But he wasn't having it, he matched me step for step, as if we were crossing the room together. "I as well," he said, "I would've thought we'd have crossed paths." *Is she avoiding me? Was she keeping her visit a secret? What does this mean for my...* the thought trailed off as he stopped thinking of me, though he smiled into my eyes as if infatuated.

His obsession with his own importance irritated me. With the nobles, every word carried layers of meaning, always weighing what I said, what they said, what each of us really meant, like a dance... But now, confronted with his false smile, I decided to try Kadin's direct approach. I stopped walking. "Have you seen Captain Tehrani?"

The Shah blinked at the blunt question, probably searching for hidden meaning that wasn't there. "I... haven't... but, I'd assume he's stationed by one of the main doors...?"

"Thank you." I smiled, turning on my heel and leaving him to stew in confusion over my strange behavior and what it might mean for him.

I felt oddly elated.

Striding across the room to the only other entrance, I couldn't help but grin as a new realization struck me: the people here might recognize me, but they didn't know I'd run away.

Of course they didn't. It made sense. Amir would never make it public; it would raise too many questions. And if my father had any say in it, he wouldn't risk my life falling into the wrong hands.

Even more reassuring: both my father and King Amir were a full day's journey from here. Although there was still the matter of Amir's guards... My heart fluttered at the possibility they'd remained in Aziz—would they have stayed at the castle? I couldn't be sure, which dampened my mood for a moment. But no, a couple of lowly guards would never be invited to a party like this.

As long as the royal family didn't notice me, everyone else would just assume I was here visiting. By the time they learned otherwise, I'd be long gone.

I was safe.

The room bustled as everyone searched for someone of importance to talk to. Women tried to be seen; men tried to see them. Finally, by a smaller side door, I spied Captain Tehrani.

Swallowing, I strode up to him. Using Kadin's tactics yet again, I skipped all preamble and dove straight into what I wanted to know.

"Captain Tehrani," I whispered as I stepped up beside him and touched his arm to get his attention, leaning in and leaving it there. His thoughts immediately zoned in on it and how close I stood. "I've just heard the most fascinating rumor. You must tell me, is it true that the king has a code for the men who guard his treasury?"

The captain startled. "Where did you hear that?"

I let my lips curve in a mischievous smile and pressed even closer, lowering my voice as an excuse to do so. "I can't reveal my source. But I'm dying to know, what is it? What's the big secret?"

He coughed to cover his surprise and stayed still, his thoughts revealing he was too concerned about offending me to move. "I can't say."

This wasn't the reaction I'd hoped for. "Oh, come now, you can tell me. What would a girl like me ever do with that kind of information anyway?" I laughed, rolling my eyes at the absurdity, making him chuckle as well, though possibly just to humor me.

He was growing suspicious. I needed to make this more believable.

"Oh, alright, it was that guard by the entrance," I said, guessing my way through. "The one who's kind of lazy, you know? Looks right through you…"

Captain Tehrani scowled. "I know just the one."

"But, now my curiosity is piqued," I whined, batting my eyelashes and hoping it came across more flirtatious than ridiculous. "Just whisper it in my ear. I'll never tell a soul." I pressed my hands to his chest in earnest, drawing his gaze there.

"I know you wouldn't do anything…" he trailed off, considering it. *I can't tell her. If King Gaspar found out she knew, I'd lose my head.* His eyes raised to mine. "Sadly, rules are rules."

That truly was unfortunate. "What if I guess correctly, hmm?" I ran a finger along my lips thoughtfully, drawing his attention there. He made it too easy. It was times like this where I understood why men feared my Gift. Before he could argue, I began guessing. "Is it the King's name?" That would be horribly egotistical. And completely like King Gaspar.

He smiled, but refused to answer. *She'll never guess.*

"Mmm, something other than a name maybe." I watched him carefully for a sign that I was getting closer. "Maybe his favorite food…" no reaction, "or a pet…" still nothing, "or… something to do with the treasure itself…"

How did she—no, don't respond, she'll give up if you don't let her know how close she is.

This I could work with. "Maybe it's… the number of coins in the treasury?" I sincerely hoped it wasn't or I'd be here guessing all night. "Or maybe a painting… or, oh, is it jewelry?" I trailed off, running out of ideas. "Maybe a weapon of some sort?"

He was scowling now. *This isn't possible. If she guesses jade dagger, I'll need to interrogate her to find out which soldier leaked the information.*

I sighed, slouching a little in defeat. "I give up. It's probably something impossible like a secret lover's name, isn't it? This isn't nearly as exciting as I'd hoped. If you'll excuse me, Captain, I'm off to find dessert."

"Yes, of course," he replied, and his relief was palpable.

I listened for his thoughts as I turned away to find Kadin, hoping I hadn't been too obvious. Not a single one about me. Because after all, what would a girl like me ever do with that information?

Chapter Twenty

Kadin

THE WAITING WAS THE hardest part. Arie met me on the balcony right at sunset and swore she'd learned the code, but refused to tell me her methods.

"Jade dagger?" I scrunched my nose at the surprising choice. "Are you certain? I thought for sure it'd be his niece or a favorite pet."

Arie shrugged. "So did I."

"I don't know why I trust you," I told her honestly as we strolled to the ledge to admire the view of the open sea. "I barely know you."

Her eyes narrowed. "If you put me through all that just to say you don't trust me, I swear on a Jinni I might hurt you."

"Only one way to find out, I suppose." I grinned and changed the subject. "Can I just say how pretty you look?"

She rolled her eyes and faced the water, leaning on the edge of the stone wall, but a hint of red touched her cheeks. I faced the sea as well, trying to focus on why we were here. It should begin any moment now.

When the trumpets sounded from inside the great hall, I knew it was finally time.

"Everyone, please come to the balcony for a surprise," the King's voice boomed over the crowd.

Everyone already on the enormous balcony began to murmur in excitement.

"Come," I said softly, pulling Arie away from the edge, pushing against the flow of people. I regretted staying on the balcony so long. We only had from now until the final dinner course.

The volume and chaos of the great room transferred outdoors and rose to new levels as they crowded each other, trying to get the best position. Arie pressed closer to me as we approached the King and his son, ducking behind me out of sight as they passed, and then returning to my side once indoors.

I didn't say a word. Whatever her secrets might be, they could wait until this was over.

I stuck to the sides of the room, slipping into the hall at the first opportunity, keeping a slow, meandering pace for appearances as a distracted couple strolled by and busy servants glided past. "Not long now," I murmured.

Sure enough, the first boom sounded behind me. The castle shook.

Arie's eyes flew open and she gripped my arm.

I patted her hand, grinning. "Don't worry, it's just the fireworks."

* * *

We met up with Naveed, Illium, Bosh, and Ryo in the far tower. Naveed signed to Bosh, who frowned as he tried to follow, while Ryo outright ogled Arie in her finery. Illium's scowl deepened, causing his dark skin to wrinkle.

I held the door open for Arie and entered behind her, waiting until it was closed to whisper, "Where's Daichi?"

Ryo rolled his eyes. "After we unbarred the door, he followed some girl out of the kitchen. Haven't seen him since."

My jaw tightened.

They looked to me with brows raised, to see if they should be worried or not.

I was, but they didn't need to know that. "He knows the plan," I said, waving them onward. "Let's go."

We circled the tower stairs to the ground floor. A quick pick of the lock and we were in, following the mosaic patterns along the floor toward the Keep.

The Keep held the treasury. And also the dungeons.

If Naveed's reports were accurate, this part of the castle should be very quiet, with everyone in the kitchen and dining room on the other end of the castle, or in the guard house by the entrance.

"Illium," I whispered, gesturing for him to take the lead. "You're up." As the authority on powders of all forms, our demolitions expert could flatten people as easily as buildings. Before our departure, I'd watched him grind up a special formula that would render any man unconscious within seconds of breathing it in.

According to Illium, one simply needed to blow the powder in their direction. But we all preferred him to do the job. What if we inhaled by accident? Most likely, we'd wake up on the dungeon floor. Better to let Illium do what he did best.

He led us down the halls until we reached another turning point. The guard on the other side was down before I rounded the corner. He'd been posted alone. No one else to raise the alarm.

We dragged him inside the stairwell, and Illium stripped him of his armor, putting it on over his own clothes for the next stage of the plan.

The tiny arrowslit window in the tower barely let in the light of the moon. As the hallway door swung shut, Naveed lit a match and held it to the wick of his small candle, before lighting the rest of ours.

We continued to follow Illium in his armor down the hall, bunching together, no longer worried about appearances this deep within the castle. No average servant would be caught wandering here.

Our shadows crept along the walls as we reached the Keep.

Another guard down.

A set of stairs that led to the basement of the castle. Dank and dark. Now our candles were our only light.

Halfway down, the stairs split in two. The red carpet continued on down the staircase to the right, while the one on the left was bare and plain.

Everyone paused to check with me.

I nodded to the red carpeted option. If our choices were treasury or dungeons, I doubted they'd put a fancy runner on the path to the dungeons.

The stairs curved as we crept down.

A light at the bottom made us slow.

Illium stepped into the hall and into their line of vision.

"Halt!" We heard the guards call immediately. "What's the password?"

"Jade dagger," Illium's deep voice rung out.

A long pause.

"Come forward," they called, less strident now.

I waited, picturing Illium calmly drawing out his powders and blowing them in the guard's faces.

Moments later, a thud sounded, followed by another, as the guards dropped to the floor, unconscious.

Though Illium insisted the powders would only reach his intended victims, I still drew the collar of my shirt up over my mouth and nose as we stepped into the hall and passed the two armored guards sprawled helplessly on the floor, out cold.

This time, I nodded to Ryo, my escape artist. Able to get in and out of a tight squeeze, he could always see all the angles. He would stay outside and rearrange the soldiers to concoct a believable scene.

With two it could be trickier. It'd be difficult to convince someone that two guards fell asleep at the exact same time.

Since our aim here was to be invisible, Ryo had sketched a few different options. He pulled a small hammer and chisel from his toolbelt, which meant he'd gone with his favorite choice. He intended to chip away a few large bits of rubble from the ceiling and rearrange them around the guard's heads, to make it look like a small earthquake or shift in the castle structure had caused debris to fall from the ceiling and knocked them out.

Grinning, Bosh pulled out the key to the lock that he'd swiped from Captain Tehrani in the midst of the feast upstairs.

Once the bolts clicked open, he swung it wide for us with a smirk and a bow.

Naveed led the way inside, and we followed, leaving Ryo to his work.

We'd broken into many castles before, but this treasury was definitely on the larger side. The vast room stretched what had to be almost a third of the castle above. We held our candles aloft.

King Gaspar had an enormous work table front and center, currently piled with gold bars, leading me to believe he often came down and counted. We wouldn't touch those. Along the walls were different cases set up to display a wide assortment of jewelry and weapons, which all gleamed in the light.

Arie lit one of the main lamps before I caught her and the room burst into light.

"Stop," I hissed before she lit another. "We leave no trace. That includes everything down to the dust on the table and the oil in the lamps." I twisted the key to extinguish the flame in the lamp, which caused the room to fall into a deeper darkness than before, almost sinister.

"You should've told me," Arie mumbled.

"This is how you learn." I grinned and bumped her elbow to show her no harm was done. "Now spread out, touch as little as possible, and look for things that won't be missed right away. Things we can sell fast before the king starts looking for them." Everyone nodded and steered away from the obvious gold bars lying on the table, which were stamped with the king's face.

I moved along the wall, studying the delicate designs on the sword in the glass case nearest me, specifically the jewels lining the hilt. Carefully opening the case, I lifted the weapon, turning it over. There were just as many jewels on the other side—but not for long.

With one of my smaller tools from my bag, I managed to dislodge the jewels along the backside with ease, dropping them into my bag, before replacing the sword on its stand inside the glass case. No one would be the wiser unless they also took the sword out, which I highly doubted would happen anytime soon.

"Here, boss," Bosh handed me a bag full of coins. "These were in a trunk."

Naveed stepped up behind him and gave me a string of pearls, a jeweled bracelet, and a small pin crusted with diamonds.

I dropped all the items into the bag. They clinked together in the quiet room.

"Keep going," I called softly. "There's enough here to pay for the lamp plus a couple months in a new town."

Bosh glanced over at me, pointing to a large gold statue with eyes of pure emerald and the belt covered in the same.

I shook my head. "Too noticeable."

We continued to make our way through the room, searching for valuables that could be overlooked until we'd filled my bag and the other two we'd brought along to the point of bursting.

Just as I was about to call it quits, I opened a drawer and found a silver dagger with a wicked curve and a small jade jewel inlaid in the handle. It wouldn't fetch a high price, but I took it on impulse. A little souvenir of our successful raid on yet another high and mighty king.

"That's enough," I said to the men as I placed the dagger in my boot. "Let's go."

Once everyone filed out, I held my candle up high, studying the room, making sure we'd left everything in sight the same as before we entered. With a nod, I closed the door, taking Bosh's candle so he could lock it up again behind us.

"Illium, lead the way," I said as I gave Bosh's candle back.

We set off, circling the guard's bodies and the strategically placed rubble.

Ryo dusted off his hands proudly and took up the rear.

So far, so good.

Back up the tower's circular staircase, we left the Keep behind and passed the chapel without any problems, reaching the tower landing where we'd originally met.

"Alright," I handed my bag full of treasure to Bosh. Naveed and Illium carried the other two. "This is where we split up. You three," I nodded to my men with the treasure, "Leave the way you came."

They obeyed, slipping out the door one by one at Naveed's cue, unseen, just like we'd planned.

"Ryo, go find Daichi. He needs to help you bar the door behind them. If you have *any* problems, come find me, understand?"

"You got it, boss." Ryo slipped out of the room after the others, headed down a different hall back toward the kitchen where I sincerely hoped he would find Daichi lazily lounging with one of the women just like he suspected.

I wished Naveed were still here so I could have someone to complain to. Of course, Naveed would only shrug. Though the cousins had been with us for a few years now, this wasn't the first time one of them had gone on their own path. I shouldn't be surprised.

I sighed. It was just me and Arie now. "You ready to go back to the party?" I asked, putting on a smile. "We'll ooh and ahh over those fireworks with the rest of them and then exit right out the front door."

"But what about dinner? I'm starving," she whispered as we stepped out into the hall. I tucked her hand in my elbow once more. "And what about a carriage? The Azadi family won't be leaving for hours yet."

"We'll borrow one." I winked, striding confidently back to the party.

We slipped through the great hall and each took a drink, clapping politely at the back of the audience just as the last few fireworks sounded. Another benefit of Arie's presence: no one would suspect anything of a young man and woman slipping away to be alone together.

We cheered as loudly as anyone else, and began slowly making our way toward the exit as everyone found their seats for dinner.

"Halt," King Gaspar shouted over the buzz of conversation. "No one leaves!"

One glance at his red face, turning shades of purple from fury, and my instincts kicked in.

Something had gone wrong.

"Hurry," I whispered to Arie, ignoring the king's command. I pushed through the crowd toward the door. "I think we've been made."

Chapter Twenty-One

Arie

IT HAPPENED SO FAST. The guards stopped us at the door, merely holding up a hand for me to wait, but yanking Kadin to the side to search him.

They found a blade in his boot.

"What's this?" a guard's voice rose.

King Gaspar strode over to us, snatching the dagger.

Though the king's gaze was glued to Kadin, he was only a few short strides away from me. One glance in my direction and everything would be ruined. I shrunk back, but the guards held me in place.

I kept my gaze on the king, and resisted the urge to react when I heard the first thought about me rise above the wordless hum of the crowd. *Princess Arie… it's the princess…* Glancing out, I saw multiple fingers pointed my way.

I was furious with myself for agreeing to this plan. I should've told Kadin no. Soon enough, word would get back to Amir.

"Where did you find my father's blade?" King Gaspar's formidable glare didn't seem to phase Kadin.

"I'm not certain where your father's blade is," he lied smoothly. "But that blade is mine."

King Gaspar growled at Kadin, holding the dagger as if he might put it to Kadin's throat. "Is that so? Then why does it have an inscription on the handle with my name on it?"

"Ah," Kadin said, glancing at me as he shrugged. "I missed that."

"Take him to the dungeon," the king said. "I'll interrogate him after the party."

They began to drag Kadin away.

"Your Majesty," one of my guards spoke up. "They were together."

One glance over his shoulder had the king spinning around to face me. "Princess Arie? It can't be…" his voice rose. "What are you doing with that criminal? Does your father know you're here?"

As he spoke, the voices in the room rose and the thoughts about me doubled in intensity, making me wince.

A light came into the king's eyes. *King Amir's guards were here searching for someone just a few days prior.* "Detain her," he said aloud to his men, "I'll deal with her shortly." *As soon as I find out why they were looking for her.*

The guards tugged me after Kadin, down the same halls we'd just trespassed earlier, but this time we turned down the stairs toward the dungeons instead of the treasury.

As the guards unlocked the massive door to the dungeon, we caught up to Kadin and his captors, where they were shoving him inside a cell.

The dank stone and cold, wet air reeked of stale urine. It was pitch-black except for small crevices lit up by a torch here and there. I was thrust into the cell on the opposite side.

The door creaked as it closed. Keys jingled in the lock as the bolts clicked into place.

The light faded as the guards left, until only the tiniest sliver of light slipped in from a far away torch. At the top of the stairs, the heavy door crashed shut, sealing my fate.

I shivered.

"Is it true?" Kadin's soft voice spoke into the darkness. There was a pause. "Are you really a princess?"

He'd overheard after all.

I gripped the bars of the cage. Did it even matter now? King Gaspar would undoubtedly send me home. I'd never see Kadin again. So why did the sound of betrayal in his voice hurt so much?

"Kadin?" another man's voice sounded from a nearby cell. "Is that you?"

"Daichi, you're in here too?" Kadin's voice rose, almost cheerful, as if we weren't reuniting with him in a cell. "We were worried about you."

An oomph sounded as one of them ran into the cell bars between them, followed by hands clapping each other on the back.

I moved carefully through my own dark cell, until my fingers brushed the opposite wall. I slid down to sit on the floor and lean against it.

"There was this pretty girl," Daichi mumbled. "I'm sorry. I wanted to impress her, you know—I didn't say anything I swear! But then they threw me in here, and they were asking so many questions. Don't worry, I told them I was alone!"

Kadin's sigh reached me. "Did they ask?"

Daichi paused. "No... but, I thought that's what they meant—wait, did they not know that already? I'm sorry, boss! This is all my fault, I didn't mean to give you up—"

"It's okay," Kadin cut him off. "Everyone else got out. We'll be out of here soon too, don't worry."

"Do you really believe that?" I snapped from the corner. Nobody broke out of prison. I'd been a fool to come here.

"Maybe the better question is, do I believe I've been in the presence of royalty all this time?" Kadin's voice challenged me, and I regretted speaking up. "You never answered me, *Princess* Arie. Is it true that you're the daughter of a king?"

"No," I lied, sighing and shrugging before I remembered he couldn't see it. "I think he was just trying to turn us against each other. To see if I'd give you up." I wondered if that sounded as weak as Kadin's 'found it on a table' excuse earlier.

"That's brilliant," Daichi's voice floated over to me in awe. "You know, you could actually be a princess if you wanted to be. I saw you from the kitchens—you looked like one."

I couldn't help but smile. "Thanks, Daichi."

He accepted my words immediately and his thoughts turned from me to something else, likely how we would escape these small cells. But I could almost feel Kadin's eyes on me in the dark.

"It's funny really," I added for good measure, ridiculing the idea with a small laugh. "I'm no princess."

In the silence that followed, Kadin's thoughts whispered, *You are, though, aren't you?*

Even though he didn't know of my Gift, it felt as if he was thinking directly at me.

My words hadn't fooled him in the slightest.

Chapter Twenty-Two

Kadin

ALL THIS TIME, I'D been mocking a princess. I couldn't decide whether I should even worry about it, considering our present circumstances. Daichi was easily spooked and Arie might be acting tough, but I heard the tremble in her voice. They didn't need to know I was terrified too.

I'd never been caught before. We'd gotten lazy. How long would it take Naveed to realize something had gone wrong? Any amount of time was too long.

Staring aimlessly into the blackness of my small cell, I scratched at the dirt underneath me with my fingernails, thinking.

My eyes slowly adjusted to the deep darkness; there must be a torch lit somewhere down the hall out of sight, but everything in my cell was in shadows.

One difficult situation at a time, I told myself, letting go of the dirt and dusting off my hands. Arie and I could have a very specific conversation once we escaped. Preferably before the king found my men waiting in the wagon just outside of the city walls with three bags full of treasure.

"If I'd packed some of Illium's powder, I could've knocked those guards out when I was discovered," Daichi was saying.

"Don't worry about it," I reassured him. "We'll do better next time."

Standing, I checked the cell door again, though I'd already checked it twice. Still locked.

"I wish I'd taken my tools," I muttered. Of course, that was foolish. Even if I had, the guards would've removed them from my person as fast as they'd taken the dagger and my own small blade.

As I paced the room, I tried to get comfortable with the space. Two steps, turn, two steps, turn. They fell silent, listening. I paused by Daichi's shadow in the cell next to mine. "Any chance anything in your pockets might help?"

I could just barely make out his head as he shook it, posture slumping, even more dejected now. "They confiscated everything."

I sighed, returning to pacing. Maybe we could adapt 'Three Tickets to the Theater' to somehow trick the guards into letting one of us out? Not likely. Even in the streets that one only worked half the time. Then again, we had nothing to lose…

"What if we did 'Pigeon Down?'" Daichi said, he scrambled up onto his feet to come closer to me and whispered, "We might not be able to get the girl out, but it could work for you and me."

"We're not leaving her behind." I hoped she hadn't heard. "And 'Pigeon Down' would only help one of us anyway."

"Oh... even if we played dead one at a time?"

"I think they'd catch on." I rubbed my temples, trying not to snap.

Daichi dropped back to the floor.

We were quiet for a long time.

I wracked my brain for another con—something that had a better outcome.

But nothing.

Daichi lay down to sleep, but I couldn't.

At least a few hours later, Arie's dress rustled in the quiet as she stood. "I have an idea!" An outline of her form appeared at the door of her cell, and I could just make out her arm as she stretched it through the bars, holding something out toward us.

In the palm of her hand was a small dot.

As I squinted, the dot turned into a rock and triggered my memory even as she spoke, "Gideon's talisman!"

Chapter Twenty-Three

Kadin

ALL THREE OF US stared at the Jinni's stone. That small gray pebble held our future in the balance. Would Gideon even come to a prison cell? And who was to say he would help us if he did?

"What have we got to lose?" Arie asked as we all just stood there, ogling the rock in silence. Before we could argue, she rubbed it. At first gently between two fingers, the way one would feel a coin to test its purity, barely visible in the gloom. Then more aggressively, holding it in her palm, while scrubbing at it with her other hand—first the thumb, then the butt of her palm.

"A little patience, please," a voice said from the opposite corner of her small cell, "I got your message when you first began. Why in the name of Jinn is it so dark in here?"

A light appeared behind Arie and she turned to face the owner of the voice.

Gideon stood tall and pale as ever, eyeing her cell warily with those sharp blue eyes. He held a ball of white light in the palm of his hand. It flickered and cast shadows on the now brightly lit walls. "This is quite unusual," he commented with a frown.

"Greetings, Gideon." Arie sank into a deep curtsy. "With respect, we're in a bit of a situation and we're hoping to ask for your help." Her ability to shift into formal speech and the ridiculous curtseying made sense now, knowing where she came from.

"Name it," he said, but not in a generous way, so much as just impatient.

"I would like to once more request the same bargain as Kadin offered you," Arie began. "I would like to see you bear witness to a Gifted prince for a day. And then we will give you the lamp for half what we paid for it."

Gideon eyed us. "You don't appear to have the lamp in your possession," he said finally.

"We were on our way to claim it," I took over, a half-formed plan in my mind. "My men are waiting with the coin outside the city walls, but we've been unfairly detained. The lamp is yours if you can get us out of here."

"And to our horse and cart as well," Arie said.

When I shot her a look, she added. "What? I'm assuming Gideon is quite skilled."

"The question isn't whether I *can* accomplish your request," Gideon replied. "Rather, are you truly being kept here outside of the law, or did you possibly do something to deserve this cell?"

That blasted Jinni code was going to stop him from helping us!

I acted on a gut-feeling. Leaning toward Arie, I stage whispered through the bars, "I don't think he can do it."

Thank the stars, she was quick. She even turned away from him before she whispered to me, "You might be right. Well, I guess the lamp will just have to wait for us to pick it up."

I nodded, then shook my head tsking, "It could take weeks for us to get out of here."

Arie turned back to Gideon, as if he hadn't heard our discussion, saying to him in a normal voice. "It's such a shame we won't be able to get the lamp to you sooner then. But of course, we understand if you're unable. We will contact you again once we're rightfully released." And she bowed low in dismissal.

"I'm perfectly capable of getting a hundred men and horses outside the castle," Gideon snapped. He cleared his throat, straightening his jacket. "Since you would eventually be released, I see no harm in making it sooner rather than later."

With one snap of his fingers, the cell shifted, turning into the forest outside of the castle—outside of the city entirely. The lights twinkled in the distance.

Even though I knew rationally that I had moved, it felt as if everything had materialized around me. It threw me off balance, making my head spin and my stomach react.

"Your wagon and men are waiting alongside the road, just a few short paces from here," Gideon told us in a bored tone. The light of the moon was strong and I could make out his face clearly.

"Many thanks," I told him, and Daichi echoed my words.

Arie stepped forward, stopping to press her hands together as if she'd been about to hug him. "Truly, Gideon, thank you. We couldn't have done it without you."

Gideon nodded in response, but even in the dim light, I could see his cheeks darken. Was he blushing? Maybe the Jinn were more human than I'd thought.

"I'll take the lamp now," Gideon said to me, clearing his throat and straightening his vest and jacket once more. "Shall we drive to the auction block to collect it, or shall I meet you there?"

"As soon as you honor the bargain with Arie, we'll give it to you," I replied, nodding.

Daichi began to back away from us, paling at the mention of the deal changing. "Did you say they're—the men—the others are, um, around the corner? I'm just..." He pointed behind him, disappearing around the bend behind the trees. Coward.

"I do believe you changed the agreement," Gideon argued, ignoring Daichi's retreat and growing quite still. "You stated it would be mine if I brought the three of you outside the castle."

"But I didn't say *when,*" I reminded him. "It was no change to the original agreement—I was simply saying we couldn't get you the lamp while still inside the castle, could we?"

Gideon's mouth fell open. "Why, the audacity... you thought to fool one of the Jinn?" Was it my imagination, or was he now turning an almost ashen-gray, like a storm cloud about to release a tempest.

"Never!" I was quick to protest, wide-eyed. "I think you read into it." It was daring to accuse him of being at fault. But I held my ground with a look of innocence. "My sincerest apologies, of course."

"Of course," he muttered, seeming unconvinced, but his normal color began to return as he calmed himself. He squinted at me, straightening his vest with a sharp tug. "Do not think to pull something like this so easily in the future. When the lamp is in your possession, contact me again."

And before any of us could answer, he vanished.

Chapter Twenty-Four

Arie

I GRINNED AT KADIN. In his excitement, he picked me up and whirled me around. "We did it!"

I laughed, forgetting my annoyance for a moment.

We.

He'd included me in that word, again. It was an odd sensation, to belong after feeling so alone these last few months. It bloomed in my chest, hopeful and proud. Quite addicting.

When my feet touched the ground, I plummeted back to reality.

He let go and stepped back, shifting into a more somber deference I recognized.

"It's not everyday I rob a castle with a princess," he said, raising a thick brow. His dark hair fell across his eyes, making me want to brush it back. "I don't even know where you're from."

"Hodafez," I whispered, throat tightening. That one word alone could give away everything if he asked the right questions of the right people.

Before he could ask anything further, I turned and ran around the bend to where Gideon had said the men would be.

Sure enough, they were lounging around the wagon and horses, waiting anxiously. Daichi must have filled them in. Ryo and Bosh whooped softly at the sight of me and Kadin, who clasped Naveed's hand, then patted Bosh's back as the young thief jumped up and down.

"I looked *everywhere* for you!" Ryo punched Daichi in the gut out of nowhere, making him double over in pain.

I gasped, but the men only chuckled as Daichi wheezed, and Naveed held him up so he didn't completely buckle over. When he finally got his breath back, he only shook his head as he straightened. "I deserved that."

They laughed again, and I found myself laughing with them as Daichi and Kadin described how we'd gotten out of the dungeon.

"You're so smart," Bosh praised me as Kadin checked the wagon bed. The clink of the bags knocking against each other seemed to reassure him. "For thinking to call Gideon, I mean. That was brilliant." His adoration made him the butt of jokes as we all climbed into the wagon.

I chose a spot near the back, furthest away from Kadin, as he took the reins and clicked his tongue for the horses to move forward.

We set out along the dark road, toward the auction house.

Nerves from the heist still thrummed in our blood. No one spoke as we watched Illium rearrange his powders in a way that made sense only to him, and then, despite the darkness, he returned to whittling something that was beginning to look like a pipe.

"I thought we were gonna get caught when we were climbing over the wall, and the guards were right there below us," Bosh spoke up in a giddy whisper.

The others laughed, nodding at the memory.

I shook my head at the way near defeat entertained them; I'd never understand how men's minds worked.

"I thought it'd be when you told the cook the food was cold," Ryo taunted him. "Good thing the other girls backed you up. If they'd gotten suspicious, they would've started asking who you were and why you were there."

"They *did* get suspicious," Daichi mumbled, crossing his arms. "Maybe it wasn't my fault, maybe it was Bosh's fault..."

"We need to be on the road within the hour," Kadin said over his shoulder, interrupting the debate. "Or sooner. The moment the king discovers our absence, he'll have the guards out searching for us. We need to be long gone before then."

I wrapped my arms around my legs, staying quiet and letting the men forget I was there as they re-told the stories from each of their viewpoints.

Even an hour felt too long.

If King Gaspar found Amir's guards, and they found me here... I shivered in the cool morning air.

The sky grew lighter as we entered town through the main gate, nodding at the guard as we passed by.

It'd be dawn soon.

Once we were out of hearing range, Kadin pulled the horses to a stop beside the wall, climbing into the wagon bed to join us, all business now. "Arie, Naveed, go pay for the lamp." He handed Naveed a bag full of coin.

Though he didn't waste time thinking on his decision, I still knew what it meant. He didn't trust me to go on my own yet. I supposed I deserved that.

I stood to climb down after Naveed, accepting his hand. Though he couldn't speak, his smile was encouraging; at least his opinion of me hadn't changed.

"Illium and Ryo will take the wagon around the bend," Kadin continued, "and pull off into the foliage to wait for us."

The older man nodded, but didn't stop whittling. Ryo jumped into the front and grabbed the reins. "You got it, boss."

Kadin hopped down onto the road, landing softly on the stone beside me. "Daichi, Bosh, you're with me. We'll gather everyone's belongings and meet at the wagon."

I nodded along with the others.

"No mistakes this time," Kadin added. Without another word, he turned away from me, leading the big man and the gangly teen off into the narrow streets.

Naveed took us to the auctioneer and gave me the coins. Though the auctioneer yawned at the early hour, complaining we'd pulled him out of bed, he was quick to give us the lamp and take our payment.

My fingers wrapped around the simple green-glass lamp, expecting to feel a sense of its magic or power of some kind, but it felt like any other oil lamp with cool glass that warmed to my touch.

I handed it to Naveed even as we walked out the door, hoping to earn some trust if he told Kadin later.

The only true difficulty was pretending not to understand Naveed right away, even though his thoughts were so transparent to me. *Let's go to the wagon now.* He pointed toward the city gates, miming what he wanted.

"Um, I'll just follow you," I said, as if unsure.

When we reached the wagon, the others were already waiting.

Ryo clicked for the horses to take off and we were bouncing along the road out of town only seconds after climbing in.

I settled onto the same bale of hay in the corner where I'd been before, watching Naveed hand the lamp to Kadin.

The men fell into conversation, and I relaxed as the sun rose, enjoying the rarity of no one thinking about me, until I felt Kadin staring. *Not bad at all.*

When I glanced up, he gave me a small smile. Even though he didn't mean for me to hear the thought, I still felt heat rise in my cheeks until I was sure I was bright red.

For a split second, I imagined what it might be like to live like this—free to do whatever I wanted. Be whoever I wanted.

But it didn't last.

The road behind us stretched off into the distance, reminding me that I was only traveling further and further from home and the people who needed me.

Pressing my lips together, I swore to myself that the next time I saw Gideon, I would find a way to ask him for help. My Gift was a death threat and Amir's was a weapon; Gideon could solve both problems.

"It'll be two days before we reach Baradaan," Kadin spoke up. His thoughts revealed that the men already knew, but he was telling them again for my sake. He was uncomfortable with me now that he knew my secret, but was trying not to let on.

He turned back to face the road and whatever lay ahead of us.

I took a deep breath. Just being near him made me feel slightly unhinged. If he was this uncomfortable over my heritage, what would he think if he knew the whole truth? If he learned of my Gift? Part of me wanted to tell him, but the more rational side refused. Who was to say he wouldn't leave me by the side of the road?

Naveed signed something that caused the men to burst out laughing and Daichi to shout curses; I assumed it was a joke at his expense.

I shifted on the hay bale, when Bosh got up and plopped onto the bale beside me.

He dug into his pack, pulling out a smaller one.

My heart skipped a beat. It was my stolen bag!

"Um, Kadin says this is yours," he mumbled. His face was red as if he was embarrassed.

Had Kadin told him my secret? Fury fought against the panic, making my pulse leap. I listened intently, but Bosh's thoughts didn't indicate anything unusual.

He slid it over to me; the others didn't notice. "He says you stole this before me, and we don't steal from each other... anyway, I didn't see you that day, but he says he knows it's yours, you know, because of what's inside. Sorry. Now that you're one of us, I figured I should give it back."

"That's... alright." I took the bag, resisting the urge to open it there in front of everyone. He thought I'd stolen the things inside?

"The, um, the food was all gross, so I threw it out... and I owe you a ruby, but the rest is there... you can check if you want..." he mumbled the last bit as he stood to go back to his seat.

I touched his arm. "Thank you." For more than he knew.

His face lit up and he nodded, returning to his spot. Easy to please, that one. And easy to fool.

I forced myself to wait until nightfall when Kadin got each of us a room in a small town for the night, before I opened the bag in private. I shoved the jewels aside.

There, at the bottom, was my crown.

Safe.

I didn't have to stay with the men anymore, if I didn't want to. As soon as I could convince Gideon to help me, I could place my crown on my head and ask the nearest royal family to take me home.

I should have been ecstatic. Things were looking up.

So why did I feel so sad?

Chapter Twenty-Five

Kadin

EVERYONE WAS QUIET IN the early morning dawn, still waking up after spending the night in a small inn on the way to Baradaan.

I drove the wagon while everyone else lounged in the back. It didn't take much focus. The animals plodded along, following the road, and the reins weren't even necessary except for at the occasional crossroad.

I slipped the small lamp from my bag and held it in the palm of my hand. The green glass was smooth and thick, surprisingly sturdy and not nearly as fragile as it had seemed from a distance. I couldn't help but wonder what this Jinni wanted with it.

Carefully, I re-wrapped it in the cloth, and placed it back in my bag for safekeeping. We might never know.

All that mattered now was that we'd finally found a Jinni to bear witness; Prince Dev was about to receive the justice he deserved.

All these years he'd gone about his father's kingdom doing whatever he wanted and getting away with it. I couldn't wait to see that smirk wiped off his face. No doubt, Naveed felt the same.

When I pulled my gaze from the road again to glance back at my friend in the bed of the wagon, my eyes snagged on *Princess* Arie instead.

I hadn't found a way to bring up her secret again. Though I'd made Bosh return her crown the moment I'd pieced together that his latest haul belonged to her, I'd pretended not to notice the way she'd clutched the bag to her ever since.

The whole situation frustrated me more than I wanted to let on, because I should've guessed. Of course she talked like a queen—she was destined to become one. But at the same time, it didn't fit the Arie I'd come to know. She was so normal. Not at all like the ruling class I'd known my whole life, who flaunted their Gifts and authority. She was just... Arie.

I wasn't familiar with her kingdom of Hodafez. All I knew was what I could glean from a map. It was almost three days east of Baradaan, where I'd grown up. Where we were headed now.

I'd visited many kingdoms in my travels with Naveed. He'd been my closest friend since we were children running around naked in the streets. When we first left Baradaan, it was just the two of us. We'd added to our crew along the way until we grew to the size we were today. But I'd never been to Hodafez. And I hadn't been home either. Not since I'd left four years ago.

Bosh's voice pulled me out of my thoughts. "Should we call on the Jinni soon or wait until we arrive?"

Naveed signed to me and the others. *Do we even know how he travels? Does he need time to reach us?*

I translated for Arie—and Bosh, who was still new to us and learning to sign. "Does our little Jinni-hunter know?" I asked Arie, though I suspected even more now that this title was a ruse.

She pulled out the Jinni's talisman and we all stared at the little gray pebble like it might come to life. She shook her head. "I'm not sure."

"We've already traveled a full day and then some," Ryo spoke up. "What if they can only do that little zip from one place to another if they're close by? We'd better call him now so he has time to catch up."

Illium chimed in. "What if it's nothing to him? You want to risk pissing off a Jinni? Be my guest, but let me off first."

"Yeah," Daichi agreed, standing even though the wagon hadn't stopped. "Let me off too."

"Don't worry," Bosh said from the opposite corner. "We will. No one wants to see you wet your pants when he shows up."

Daichi lunged for him, and both Naveed and Illium held him back while Ryo laughed with Bosh. Arie shifted to another hay bale to avoid getting run over.

"Only one way to find out," I said, and they quieted, turning to face me. I gestured for Arie to go ahead. "If it takes him a while to arrive, then we'll know."

"And if it doesn't?" Illium asked, but Arie had already wiped her thumb across it, ever so gently.

The horse carried on down the road, but we all stayed frozen in a semi-circle, staring down at the pebble in silence.

When nothing happened, I opened my mouth to suggest she try rubbing it a little harder.

I hadn't even begun when Gideon appeared. He sat at the back of the wagon on one of the hay bales, plucking a stray piece of hay off his trousers. "You certainly choose unique places to meet."

Daichi yelped and jumped a whole hay bale over before catching himself and growing still.

Illium's skin had gone ashen. As the oldest member of our group, he had grown up with stories of the Jinn terrorizing humans. Despite nothing really happening over the last few decades, he hadn't forgotten, and had made sure we didn't either, but I leaned forward, more curious than afraid.

"Thank you for coming," I began, straddling the wooden divider between the driver's bench and the bed of the wagon to face him, still holding the reins. It was uncomfortable, but I tried not to let it show on my face.

"Of course." Gideon gave up removing the straw and placed his hands casually on the elegant cane he carried but didn't seem to need. "It is a strange place to bear witness, but I'm ready to begin whenever you are."

"Of course," I imitated his polite manners, swallowing. His piercing eyes and my complete lack of knowledge about his abilities brought Illium's stories back to me. "We'll arrive in Baradaan around dinner time tonight. Since we—Arie—has your word you'll bear witness for a full day, I was thinking we could officially start tomorrow morning?"

"Why, praytell, did you summon me now then?" Gideon said, tapping his cane on the wagon bed, drawing my attention to the elegant walking stick. Did he have a limp? I hadn't noticed one. And if he did, why didn't he cure it? Couldn't the Jinn cure anything? Questions plagued me, but I didn't dare ask and risk offense.

"Our sincerest apologies," Arie answered before I could. "We thought you'd appreciate knowing the plan." Such a diplomatic response. I tried not to smile.

Gideon softened a bit, though his features remained solemn. "I do appreciate that, thank you."

"Would you like to stay and have dinner with us?" Bosh chimed in, fearlessly. "If you're traveling all alone, it might be nice to have company."

I glanced at the others, especially Daichi and Illium, both of whom sat stiff and anxious, watching Gideon like he might explode any moment.

"Only if you want to," Ryo interjected.

Naveed nodded vigorously.

I held my breath and waited as Gideon considered us.

Bosh would get an earful from me later. He hadn't been around for some of Illium's more chilling stories. Though I didn't necessarily believe everything I'd learned about the Jinn, I knew there was some truth to the rumors. Most of us had grown up on the legends of the Jinn before they'd withdrawn to their lands.

They were enough to terrify a teenager, much less a young child who'd just wanted a bedtime story. I'd spent more than one late night lying awake in fear that a Jinni might come snatch me from my bed.

Bosh blinked in confusion at the men's glares. As an orphan, he must have missed those bedtime stories.

The worst of it was, I didn't know how to separate fact from what parents told children in order to scare them into obedience. When a Jinni appeared, were they really coming from a place outside of our realm? That seemed a bit far-fetched. But then again, so was the whole appearing and disappearing, and that had turned out to be true. What about the other myths? Could the Jinn really steal your soul?

Gideon's eyes snapped to me at the thought. Had he—no. No, it couldn't be. Had he *heard me*? Quickly I sorted through the stories, feeling a distant memory of a Jinni who could read minds—did Gideon have this Gift? Immediately I threw up mental shields, imagining walls twice as high as a castle and ten times as thick, in the feeble hopes I might be able to protect myself.

Gideon tilted his head slightly and blinked at me, before returning his gaze to Arie, who was speaking to him.

"I'm guessing a traveler so far from home must be lonely," she said. "I'm new to this group myself, but they're mostly good company. Besides Kadin, of course," she teased. Gideon didn't react. "Anyway, you're very welcome to join us, right Kadin?"

Normally I'd have a good comeback, but the fact that she and Bosh had just invited one of the Jinn to spend the evening with us—not to mention the whole day tomorrow—I could barely think, much less formulate an excuse.

There was no way he'd say yes. But now that they'd offered, I couldn't say otherwise. "It's up to you," I told him after an awkward pause. "It won't be anything fancy. Just dinner at the Red Rose, one of the nicer inns in town."

One of the only inns in town, to be specific. Baradaan's two villages flanking the castle were both small. That was part of why Prince Dev had found a way to personally terrorize nearly every single villager. It was also why it'd be the perfect place for a Jinni to bear witness to the crimes of the princes. In a town that size, there was no way he'd miss it.

Gideon sat more still than any human being, thinking. Then he surprised me by saying four words I'd never expected to hear. "Very well." He nodded to Arie, Bosh, and the rest of us. "I accept."

Chapter Twenty-Six

Kadin

I FELT LIKE I'D held my breath the entire afternoon. My chest hurt from the effort. I'd fixed my eyes on the dirt road and blue skies ahead of us, but my crew kept asking Gideon the most inappropriate questions!

"Where are you from?" Bosh had begun hours ago.

"Hush," Illium hissed before he'd even finished.

"It's alright," Gideon waved a thin hand in the air smoothly, managing to look like it was part of a dance. "I have traveled much of the world, but I hail from Jinn, like most of my kind."

"But what made you come here?" Arie asked, just as innocent and wide-eyed as Bosh.

Stop bothering the Jinni, I thought at her as hard as I could, though of course, she couldn't hear me. Gideon surprised me again, by turning those pale eyes in my direction, studying me the way a bard might examine a new instrument. Once again, I imagined throwing up all manner of mental walls in an effort to shield myself, though for all I knew, they could be as impenetrable as water.

"I'm terribly sorry," Arie said in the silence when Gideon paused. "I didn't mean to pry."

"Not at all," Gideon's lips stretched in a thin but genuine smile as he turned back to Arie. "It's quite a long story, but suffice it to say I'm on a mission to find a small number of lost objects."

"Like the lamp," Bosh interjected, and he grinned when Gideon nodded. Ryo, Naveed, and even Daichi were warming up to the Jinni, less anxious now. Illium, on the other hand, had resorted to a sullen silence on the far side of the wagon— although he let them pester Gideon, since the Jinni had made his wishes clear.

When they asked if there was any significance to the lamp we'd purchased, Gideon simply said, "There is."

Naveed's eyes darted to mine more than once, whenever a question veered into unsuitable territory, which nearly all of them had, and I frequently glanced back at him. What had we gotten ourselves into? I could only hope the next day and a half would pass quickly.

The scenery changed as we traveled. Trees and undergrowth thinned out until they disappeared entirely. Eventually only scorched, rocky land stretched empty and infertile for miles in every direction, except for the occasional rock formation. In the rainy seasons, the valleys filled with water, but now it was dry as a bone.

"Keep an eye out for dragons," I told everyone over my shoulder.

"What?" Bosh squeaked. "You didn't say anything about dragons!"

"They're rare in Baradaan," I reassured him. "Very unlikely."

"Is that so?" Illium growled, pulling out his pipe.

Only seen a few in my life, Naveed signed. *They almost never come this far south.*

I nodded, glancing at Gideon who simply observed. Did they have dragons in Jinn? He didn't seem concerned. "It's just good to be prepared."

"Prepared how?" Bosh asked, ready to jump. "What do we do if we see one?"

"Not much you can do, except spread out," Ryo said with a smirk.

Daichi nodded gravely, and Bosh paled.

After that, we had no shortage of eyes on the sky, no matter how much I reassured them.

Normally the open spaces relaxed me. Cities were so claustrophobic compared to the desert. This was my home. But the comfort was ruined by the tickle of a Jinni's eyes on the back of my neck.

We passed another towering ridge of rocks bleached almost white from the sun; they blended into the sand, creating the sense of wandering through a strange maze that was missing half of the lines.

The city was visible long before we reached it. Built directly into the stone of the mountain, the homes and even the castle were all the same desert sand and rock color that made them nearly invisible if you didn't know where to look.

The others had never been here. Only Naveed and I, and not since we'd left four years ago. Since we'd lost everything.

When our wagon drew closer to the mountains, the homes carved into the face of the cliffs began to take shape. The city stretched all across the base of the mountain with the castle on the far side, higher up and more protected.

We approached the Red Rose at the edge of town; it was close to the road and the simple cave-like entrance made it appear deceptively small, though I knew from experience it tunneled back deeper and above into a second story as well.

I jumped out in front of the sandy stone building before the wagon even came to a stop, landing hard on the packed dirt, desperate to get away and work through my concerns with the men without the fear of Gideon overhearing my thoughts. "We'll meet up for dinner in one hour," I told them, mainly for Gideon's sake. "I'll get us all rooms for the night. Ryo can take care of the horses."

I paused. Now it was my turn to ask an awkward question, and I found myself wishing it had already come up. "Gideon, can I, ah... get you a room, as well?"

"Yes, thank you," he replied as the wagon stopped fully and everyone stood to dismount after me, following me inside. The tension in my shoulders made my headache ten times worse.

I'd finally found a Jinni to bear witness to a Gift being misused, I reminded myself. After tomorrow, everything would be different. That's what mattered.

I booked a room for everyone, plus paid for the horse and cart as Ryo came in from the stables. It depleted a small chunk of our new funds. We were burning through them faster than I liked. But it would all be worth it. Once we received our rooms, Gideon left us for some time alone. The others waited until he'd climbed the stairs and disappeared around the corner, before they each followed suit; I caught Arie's hand. "Can we talk?"

"Sure," she replied, brows drawing together, wary.

"Not here," I said. "Let's find some place quieter."

The Red Rose had a tavern on the main level. Only a couple patrons occupied the large room, day-drinking. The sun shone in through a simple, wide-open window carved into the rock, which wafted delicious smells during meals, drawing in crowds.

Ignoring them and the space, I led Arie out the front door instead. I needed to put some space between us and the others. Especially Gideon.

Everything was built with the sand-colored rock, which made it easy for newcomers to get lost. Even so, nothing had changed. I found my way easily down one narrow street and the next, turning here, then there. We reached the other side of town in no time.

"This way," I said, the first words either of us had spoken since we left. I pointed to a small crevice in the rock formations that the city had been built up against. "I used to come out here as a boy."

I led her inside the narrow cave. Ducking to avoid hitting my head, I entered the darkness without hesitation.

Arie didn't follow.

I poked my head back out. "Just trust me, would you?" I laughed. "I promise you'll like it."

Her brows rose in disbelief and she hesitated.

I tried to see it from her perspective. We were still nearly strangers, after all. Without thinking much about it, I reached out my hand, palm up. "I promise you'll be safe."

She slowly accepted, curling her fingers around mine.

I gently led her through the tunnel, which curved into darkness in one direction, then back in the opposite direction, shrinking down until at a certain point we had to get down on our knees and crawl, which was likely the only reason it'd gone undiscovered by anyone else because an adult would never think to keep going.

As children, Naveed and I had discovered this place, but we'd never shown it to anyone before; for some reason, I found myself wanting to show it to Arie.

In the dark of the tunnel, she clutched my hand but didn't complain.

As we stood on the other side of the pinch point, light trickled in and I led her toward it.

A small oasis opened up before us, walled in on all sides by steep rock walls that from the outside were too sheer to scale. But inside the small space was a small, quiet pool, soft sand, and the sun shone down cheerfully on us.

Arie gasped, stopping in the tunnel entrance.

"Told you." I smiled at her over my shoulder. I didn't need to hold her hand anymore, but I didn't let go just yet.

Though she tried not to smile, her lips twitched, and she let me lead her on.

"Right here," I said, letting go of her hand and stepping to the side to let her go ahead of me.

We followed the beaten path Naveed and I had created as children, rounding the deep pool to where a boulder made a natural seat on the other side.

Up close, the pool was too deep to see the bottom, kept constantly full by some internal spring even in the heat of summers, except for one side where a shallow ledge was visible and the deep blue water turned nearly clear, showing the bleached rock beneath.

Instead of joining me on the boulder to sit formally, Arie dropped to the ground by the shallow side of the pool, pulled off her boots, lifted her skirts up to her knees, and stepped into the cool water with a happy sigh.

I blinked. This felt so much more intimate than I'd planned. But the water did look refreshing. I hesitated before joining her, removing my shoes as well and rolling up my pant legs.

As I splashed into the water, it caused ripples that slowly faded the further out they went.

"It's so beautiful," she whispered reverently, as if a normal tone might disturb the sanctuary.

Dropping onto the dry ground at the edge, leaving my feet in the cool water, I leaned back, content to stay silent and enjoy the moment.

Arie was still taking it in with awe and wonder written all over her face.

I patted the ground next to me, and she sat closer than I expected, not even noticing when our arms brushed together.

"This is heavenly," she breathed.

"My secret paradise," I replied with a smile, staring at the water instead of her. "Well, mine and Naveed's. We grew up here, you know."

Arie was quiet for a moment before she put two and two together. "*This* is the kingdom where the prince cut out his tongue?"

I nodded, not really wanting to dwell on that day. We'd truly thought we would lose him. So much blood.

Her soft hand slipped over mine. She'd never touched me intentionally before. I lifted my eyes, happy to be distracted. Her pretty face was just a foot away from mine. Those warm brown eyes and soft lips distracting as she said, "I'm so sorry."

I shrugged. My throat grew too tight to speak and I looked away. For a long minute, we stared out at the water and didn't move. I needed to change the subject. I said the first thing that came to me. "I think Gideon can read minds."

Arie pulled her hand away in surprise. "He spoke directly into your thoughts too?"

"What? No—" I spun to face her. That chased away all thoughts of how her dark hair shone or how her cheeks were tinted red. "He did that with you? When?"

"At the auction." She bit her lip and averted her eyes.

"I wish you'd told me." I blew out a breath, running a hand through my hair. "It's not right. I'm glad the Jinn left our land. If only they would've taken all the Gifted with them." I turned back to the water, tossing a pebble into the stillness. The little rock smashed through the sense of peace there, which was exactly how my mind felt at that moment. Mind reading was such an unfair advantage. It was abuse. Anyone with an ability like his should be avoided at all costs. "Do you know the extent of his abilities?'

Arie shook her head. "No. But we could ask him?"

"No!" I turned to face her. "You and Bosh both need to be more careful about what you ask a Jinni. Haven't you heard the stories?"

She just laughed. "You mean the Jinn who steal away naughty little children? You know those are just bedtime stories, right?"

When she put it like that, I felt foolish, but I persisted. "Think about it. All stories come from a place of truth. If Jinn really do have even a few of the Gifts the princes have, we're completely at their mercy."

She shifted uncomfortably, pulling her feet out of the water now as if chilled. "But everyone knows they have a code of honor. That's the whole reason you brought Gideon here in the first place, to uphold their principles?" Her statement turned to a question at the end.

"I sure hope so." I pulled my feet out to dry as well and we sat in silence, staring at the ripples still disturbing the pool's calm surface.

It was time to bring it up.

Past time really.

"So. You're a princess, hmm?" I elbowed her lightly to take the edge off my words. "When was that going to come up?"

"I was thinking right after never," she joked, grinning back at me. But then she grew more serious. "No one can know. Please."

"I promise to keep your secret," I said, "if you tell me why." It was underhanded. A good man would swear a solemn oath and never ask again. But I wanted to know.

"I can't," she protested, clutching her dress so tightly I thought it might rip. "If they ever found out where I am, they'd make me come back, and I… I just can't…" She swung around to face me. "Please, Kadin."

I liked the way she said my name. Those dark brown eyes were wide and pleading, drawing me closer. "Please, just promise me you won't tell anyone."

She sounded so desperate, I felt guilty. "Don't worry. I wasn't going to."

"Promise me."

"I swear on a Jinni's Gift," I agreed. She relaxed somewhat, but the mood was ruined. Life as a princess must not be so great after all. I tucked it away to think about later, when I was alone with my thoughts. But that just made me think of Gideon. Would I ever be alone with my thoughts again?

Chapter Twenty-Seven

Kadin

BY THE TIME THE first light touched the room, I gave
up on sleep. Between thoughts of Arie and of the day to come,
I had too much to worry about. Rolling out of bed, I threw on
my boots and headed downstairs. Breakfast and a strong cup
of coffee would wake me.

In the doorway, I stopped. There was only one other
person at the breakfast bar.

Gideon.

The staff at the Red Rose clearly recognized a Jinni when
they saw one. They tiptoed around him, wide-eyed.

I nearly turned around to go back to my room, when he
turned to face me.

"Good morning," he said, as polite as ever.

"Morning," I replied, my voice raspy from waking up. Uncomfortable, but not sure what else to do, I pulled up the stool next to him, slouching over the bar. I should've stayed in my room. As soon as the thought came to me, I shoved it into a dark corner of my mind and told it to stay there. "Coffee, please," I said to the bartender.

"How... did you sleep?" I ventured, struggling to find an appropriate topic of conversation for a Jinni. Did such a thing exist?

"Very well, thank you," he replied. "And yourself?" There was a slight twist to his lips that made me feel like he was laughing at me.

Not well, I thought impulsively. *I kept thinking about how you read minds.*

And that kept you up?

I leapt out of my seat, the stool falling backwards, hitting the floor with a crash. This was far worse than I'd imagined. Gideon looked over his shoulder as I crouched near the door.

"Goodness," he said, "I didn't think you'd be so easily spooked."

I cleared my throat, just blinking at him for a moment. "I wouldn't call this easily spooked at all," I answered after clearing my throat again. "This definitely falls into justifiably spooked."

He wasn't using any other abilities that I could tell. But it would be wise to be cautious. "How do I know you won't use any Gifts on me?"

"It's against the Jinni code," he said simply, shrugging. "I cannot use them to steal, manipulate, or cause harm."

"But I have no way of knowing you'll honor that." I straightened, dusting off my clothes, feeling like I'd slightly overreacted. "It's just not right."

"It's not entirely fair," Gideon admitted. "But there are ways for the children of men to block some Gifts. Concealing thoughts for instance. You have a strong mind. You can learn."

Picking up my stool, I gingerly sat next to him again. I needed to know more. But I found myself leaning away even as I tried to act natural. "Is it... Can you teach me?"

"You've already begun teaching yourself," he said, taking a bite, only half his attention on me.

I accepted my coffee, taking a big gulp. I needed to wake up. He wasn't making sense. "What do you mean?"

"The mind has many natural defenses. You can train it just as you would train yourself to not think on something—say, a pretty girl when she's nearby. Or the opposite, train it to think overly long on a subject—such as, say, a particular vendetta."

"That's not training," I argued, forgetting for a moment my wariness when it came to his kind. "It's impossible not to think on it—you don't understand because you don't know what happened."

"Enlighten me," Gideon said, pausing at his meal for the first time since we'd begun our conversation.

"I'd rather you bear firsthand witness," I mumbled. I didn't want to relive that day. Not again. It had haunted my dreams for months afterward.

I'd been only fifteen-years-old, but old enough to have been taking care of my siblings for many years already. I was like a second parent to them while my father worked and my mother drank.

When I left my little brother, Reza, with my mother to pick up a bit of extra work, he'd crawled into the street, as Prince Dev paraded through town with three neighboring princesses.

In his desire to show off for them, he suggested a race. Though the women declined, he took off anyway on his newly broken stallion.

Some blamed the horse, said it was out of control.

But I came out just in time to see a hoof crush my little brother's skull. The agony I felt in that moment had barely faded, even now, nearly five years later. Though I'd only thought of it for a split second, I blinked away tears.

"Was it an accident?" Gideon asked softly.

I cursed myself. Of course he'd eavesdropped on my thoughts. "What do you think?" I snapped. Everyone always sided with the prince. How could they not?

"I want to hear what you think," he replied, still in that soft, but unyielding tone.

Against my will, I remembered staring up at Prince Dev's face that day for the ten-thousandth time. Shock crossed his face for a brief second followed by a look of revulsion, and then a sneer.

Witnesses gathered at the scene, whispering, but no one came forward to help.

"Someone clean that up," the prince commanded his guards, reining his horse around the body, readying to move on.

That's when I'd found my voice. Roaring, I raced out into the street, falling to my knees at my dead brother's side and screaming at the prince, *"My brother! That's my brother!"*

My choked screams roused the crowd, who began to murmur in dissent.

For the first time, real concern crossed Prince Dev's features.

Naveed, a year younger than me but slightly taller, had stepped out in front of me and my little brother. *"You* killed him!" he'd shouted at Prince Dev in a strong voice that carried his accusation out to any who may have wondered. "You *murdered* him!"

"Silence!" the prince yelled, waving for the guards to move on us. "One week in the stocks!"

Naveed dodged them easily, screaming insults at Prince Dev through the crowd. *"You're* the one who needs to be punished! Murderer!"

"Arrest him!" Prince Dev screamed, red-faced. He was shaking in fury.

They caught Naveed, and I watched through tears as they dragged him out of the crowd.

"All the Jinni-forsaken luck on your bastard head!" Naveed continued hurling insults even as they hauled him in front of the prince. "May your father and mother despise the day you were born! May they–"

"*Enough!*" Prince Dev's voice cracked as he yelled. "Cut out his tongue!"

Next came the blood.

Days of wondering if my friend would make it.

Mourning my baby brother, while comforting my other siblings.

What had Gideon asked?

Was it an accident.

"I don't know," I whispered honestly, since he could read my thoughts anyway. "Probably." My voice cracked a little. "But does it matter?"

Gideon didn't answer right away. "You called me to bear witness to a Jinni's Gift being misused." His blue eyes seemed especially pale this morning. "I haven't noticed it in your memories. Does this prince have a Gift?"

I toyed with my uneaten food, moving it around with my fork to avoid his gaze. "He does," I said, but my mind betrayed me. He'd never used his Gift that day. He hadn't even discovered his Gift until after his 18th birthday.

"Mmm," Gideon murmured, as if I'd told him more than I'd meant to. I supposed I had. "And what is his Gift?"

I tried hard to keep my thoughts in check. "He can speak any language," I mumbled.

Gideon's brows rose. "Is that so."

I nodded, but kept my mind blank.

"Has this prince ever used his language Gifting for vile purposes?" Gideon probed.

"That's what we're here to find out," I said, straightening to face him, pushing away from the bar to stand.

But Gideon stopped me, placing his hand on my arm. His touch wasn't ice like the stories. It was warm like any other man's.

But I still shivered.

When he didn't speak right away, my mind drifted to his last question, but I stopped it and did my best to throw up mental shields like I had before.

"Very good." Gideon nodded, just once. "You're a quick study."

I took that to mean I'd successfully kept him out of my mind and felt the tiniest sliver of relief. "Thank you," I said in response.

His hand was still on my arm.

"Is there anything else I can help you with?"

"When do I begin bearing witness?" he asked in that calm, quiet tone, releasing me.

"How does an hours' time sound?" I asked. Everything in me was focused on that mental wall, keeping him on one side and my thoughts on the other.

"Very good," he replied, watching me closely.

I bowed quickly and left the room, putting some distance between us before he heard the truth: I didn't know if Prince Dev had ever abused his Gift.

I hoped he had.

And I was ready and willing to provoke him into doing so today, if necessary.

Chapter Twenty-Eight

Arie

KADIN HAD THOUGHT ABOUT kissing me for a split second last night. My toes curled at the memory as I lay in bed. It hadn't been a thought, so much as an emotion, but I'd felt it. I turned the feeling over, examining it. It was different with him. Because for the first time I wanted it too.

I sighed at the sun streaming in through the window. All I wanted to do was stay under the covers and go over each moment from the night before, one at a time, savoring them.

We'd talked until sunset, long past dinner, making our way back as dusk settled over the land. Shadows crossed Kadin's cheekbones and hooded his eyes. But whenever he looked over at me, he smiled. How could someone who'd been through so much, be so lighthearted?

He'd had four siblings. And he was the eldest. The way he described growing up, watching the younger children, always looking out for them, feeding them, tucking them into bed at night. And then... how his whole family had died four years ago...

It made my heart ache for him.

Though I'd been too afraid to tell him my story, it was impossible not to think what might be happening back home. I told myself for the thousandth time that my father was okay. Amir had no power over him or Hodafez if I wasn't there. Sooner or later, the king would have to go home.

This was for the best.

I rolled over and shut my eyes. Better not to think about it.

But my conscience wouldn't let me close the door so easily this time. A little whisper asked, *What if I'm wrong?* Each day that worry grew louder, more persistent.

As tempting as it was to stay with these men and never look back, I couldn't do that to Baba. I was all he had.

My chest tightened. I couldn't go home, and I couldn't stay. Neither one would do.

I sighed, climbing out of bed and putting on the red dress Kadin had given me, and the brown cloak over it. Heading downstairs, I focused on the question that plagued me above the rest: *how would I convince Gideon to help me?*

Under my cloak, I clutched my small bag. I carried it everywhere I went, now that I had it back. Perhaps between my share in the heist, the jewels, and my crown, I could convince Gideon to travel to Hodafez for just one day.

I bit my lip. He was so impatient already; would it be enough? Would he even consider my offer once he had his precious lamp?

I felt a headache forming even before I entered the common room. Dozens of stranger's thoughts slipped into my mind uninvited and unwelcome. I loathed this ability. Pinching the bridge of my nose, I struggled to focus as I wove between the tables to find a seat.

Gideon sat at the breakfast bar on one side of the room, while at least a dozen other guests occupied the tables on the opposite side. Though Gideon sipped his tea with his usual unwavering composure, I couldn't help but wonder if he was lonely. Traveling so long and often must be isolating. He couldn't be more than a few years older than myself—or was age deceptive for the Jinn?

This was my chance. I tried to rehearse what I would say along the way, but the pressure of thoughts following me across the room shoved all rational thought from my mind.

"You just missed Master Kadin," he told me when I greeted him.

Kadin's name put a few extra butterflies in my stomach. I sat and accepted a breakfast plate from a server, piled with food, before turning to Gideon.

"Tell me," I began as I took a bite. "How long have you been away from home?" The food here was flavorless, but my stomach growled and I continued.

When he frowned, I paused, feeling guilty. "I apologize, if that was insensitive…" Had I already offended him? Why did I have to be so stupid?

"Not at all," he said. So formal. He touched the napkin to his lips before folding it in his lap. "I suppose I'm not used to conversation. Most people fear my kind."

"I've noticed." I took another bite. "I don't get it. You seem perfectly nice."

A small smile tugged at the corner of his mouth as Gideon turned back to his food as well, and there was a comfortable silence. "To answer your question," he began, "I've unfortunately lost my ability to return home. I'd prefer not to discuss the circumstances."

I nodded.

He sipped his coffee, before continuing, "It's my hope that the lamp you possess might help me return. I've lived among the human kingdoms for the better part of a year now."

I slowed in my chewing. He couldn't go home? We had more in common than I'd realized.

Gideon tipped his head once, almost as if in a nod. Had he overheard?

I cleared my throat, feeling vulnerable, and said the first thing that came to mind. "Can I ask what brought you to our lands?"

As soon as the words were out of my mouth, I knew I was prying. Would he take offense? But Gideon's expression didn't change. He lifted his cup to drink again. Only after finishing the glass and setting it down did he answer. "I've been... tasked with finding ancient artifacts."

"I see. They must be important?" I wanted this conversation to be over. It'd been a mistake to think I could make my request while in a public place; I couldn't hear my own thoughts above the noise, much less form an appropriate question. I set down my spoon.

"Very." He nodded, carefully folding his napkin and placing it on his plate. "Artifacts all enhance or add to a Jinni's Gifting."

"Enhance..." I had to ask. "You mean it makes Gifts stronger? Or better?"

"Both." He turned to face me. "In some cases, they provide a new Gift altogether."

"Do the artifacts work on humans too?"

Gideon didn't confirm or deny it, only staring at me with those unblinking eyes.

Understanding bloomed at the secret I'd just uncovered. I whispered, "They do, don't they? That's why it's not common knowledge. They must be terribly powerful."

Could an artifact give a half-Jinni like me some sense of control? Help me muffle thoughts in a crowd so I didn't feel like I was losing my mind?

Gideon turned away without a word, still not denying it, and pulled out coins from his pocket to pay for his meal.

"Even if humans did find the artifacts," I spoke my thoughts aloud since he could hear them anyway, "they wouldn't know they had something of such value. And if they did, they wouldn't know how to work it. I mean, with the lamp, I'm sure it's not as simple as merely lighting it…" I trailed off, watching him.

He paused in the middle of setting some coins on the table before he stood.

"Or… I suppose it could be that easy."

He still didn't answer.

"Gideon," I pushed, standing as well. "What does the lamp do?"

He only shook his head, picking up his cane and moving toward the door without using it once.

"I'm not going to light it," I teased. "But you wouldn't want to risk my using it by accident, would you?" I followed him out of the room.

The pressure of thoughts lifted as we entered the hall. I flashed him one of my most charming smiles. No prince alive had ever resisted.

Gideon, as otherworldly as he was, was no different. He smiled back at me slightly. "It isn't a violent Gift," he admitted, now that we were out of earshot from the others in the common area. "I suppose there's no harm."

I smiled, ducking my eyes for a brief moment, before staring up at him in rapt attention, going for irresistible. "No harm at all," I encouraged.

Gideon tucked his cane under his arm, leaning forward to speak, "The lamp is for traveling." We were conspirators, he and I, and I could tell he wanted someone to confide in. "For a Jinni who can already travel, such as myself, it increases our distance considerably. On my own, I'm not powerful enough to get home, but with the lamp, I could reach the gate to Jinn."

My mouth fell open. "That's incredible," I whispered. I could see why he would want it so badly. "What would it do for a human?"

His eyes narrowed and he straightened, shrugging. "I don't honestly know."

We were no longer accomplices; I'd made him suspicious.

"It's never been tested, to my knowledge."

Before I could find the words to appease him, Kadin's thoughts intruded and he spoke up from the staircase behind me, "Ready to go?"

I faced him, clenching my teeth at the interruption. His men followed behind him, joining us at the base of the stairs.

Was it my imagination or had Kadin's face lit up at the sight of me. When he grinned, I couldn't help but smile back.

Gideon and I greeted him at the same time, and as a group, we left the inn.

At least one of us might get what they desired today.

It was finally time for Gideon to bear witness.

Chapter Twenty-Nine

Kadin

I'D THOUGHT THROUGH EVERY angle of my plans.

Except this day.

I'd avoided this day like a fool. Because I couldn't allow myself to think about what might happen if we failed.

Though I loved to visualize Prince Dev suffering, the path from this morning until the hour he faced justice was unclear. I'd let myself hope that any misstep on Prince Dev's part, related to his Gift or otherwise, would be enough. But it seemed I'd been wrong.

We strode down the narrow streets in pairs, winding along the side of the mountain, climbing toward the castle ahead of us. Built into the rock, it wasn't designed for beauty but to be impenetrable, blending seamlessly into the sandstone around it.

The windows were long, narrow slits that rose high above our heads, too high to scale and too thin for anyone but a child to enter. The enormous arch of the entrance stretched wide and dark, ready to swallow us.

The men joked and taunted each other behind me, relaxed enough to include Arie and Gideon. None of them knew how unlikely this plan was to work. Except Naveed.

My childhood friend walked beside me. I didn't speak and he didn't sign; we didn't need to. Not a day had gone by since we left this place four years ago that we hadn't thought of it.

Neither of us had gone home to visit. Naveed's only family had been mine.

And mine were gone.

After my brother's death, Prince Dev had tried to silence all protests. It was only because Naveed and I had been in hiding, planning our revenge, that I was still alive.

Glancing over at my friend, he nodded tersely. Even if he still had his voice, he'd never tell them how Prince Dev might not misuse his Gift at all today.

After speaking with Gideon at breakfast, I'd found Naveed and pulled him aside. "If Prince Dev doesn't explicitly use his Gift, I don't know if Gideon will lift a finger."

Even if he breaks other laws? Naveed signed. The Jinni were supposed to be such sticklers for the law.

Lips thinning, I shook my head. "Even then. It *has* to be related to his Gift. So. Think on ways to make that happen." There was no way we'd let him go free of consequences for even one more day.

Grimly, Naveed had nodded, and now here we were, stepping out in confidence, putting on a show for Gideon and the others.

First and foremost, we needed to gain entrance to the castle. Prince Dev's father held hearings for his people in the mornings, while the prince held parties that lasted all day. That's where we would start.

The homes surrounding the castle were small, tucked away into the rocks, built in layers along the sides of the cliffs, but the castle itself stood on its own, separate and above, strong and spacious. It was a good hike, enough to make you out of breath on arrival.

Naveed stuck close as we ascended the path to the castle. "Any ideas?" I whispered to him.

He shook his head.

"Do you think it would count if the prince told a lie?" I hissed. "Or maybe if he spoke Jinn? Is that a crime?"

Though Naveed's brows rose hopefully, a single thought from Gideon came through. *No.*

I sighed, shaking my head. "I guess not." Naveed frowned at me, but I didn't explain. Instead, I built up those walls in my mind, making them ten times thicker, so I could think of a better plan in peace.

Yet, by the time we reached the castle, where it rose, tall and imposing, with a guard on each side of the open drawbridge, I had yet to think of anything.

Standing in line to speak to the king, we watched for Prince Dev. He didn't show. Likely, the man was still in bed with a hangover. Though we'd left early that morning, we still had to wait an hour in line, making our way slowly around the courtyard as each person had an audience with the king.

Finally, we reached the castle entrance, through the enormous double doors, entering the throne room. Though I encouraged Gideon multiple times to roam the castle and search for the prince while we waited, he insisted on staying with us. Everyone clammed up at the color of his skin. A shell of silence surrounded us, making my scheme much more difficult.

Once inside, Ryo slipped away from the group. I scanned the room full of petitioners and the tall sand-colored ceiling while I waited for his signal. When he appeared at the entrance, I nodded confirmation and he entered the hall.

"Naveed, you're next." My friend melted away from the group. Only moments later, he signaled from the door. Another success.

"Alright Daichi." I waved him off.

Before the big man had gone far, Gideon spoke up, "What exactly is taking place here?" His voice carried in the quiet.

"Nothing." I signaled for Daichi to wait, but he wasn't paying attention. Too late to call him back now. I watched him make the grab and hoped no one else noticed.

As he pocketed the paper and turned back toward us, Gideon snapped his fingers and the corner of the document where it poked out of Daichi's pocket disappeared.

It reappeared in Gideon's hand. He held it up to study it.

"What did you…" Daichi searched his pockets and came up empty. "How'd you do that?"

"An invitation?" Gideon ignored him, looking at me over the bridge of his nose.

"Everybody needs one if we're going to spend the day here," I muttered. Getting caught was so rare. Twice in just a few days? Was this a new streak? "To be allowed in for tonight's dinner."

"Why didn't you say so?" Gideon smiled, sharp blue eyes glinting with mischief. He and the parchment disappeared.

Everyone around us gasped.

Whispers and pointing fingers directed our attention toward the throne.

Gideon had flashed into existence on the raised dais between the King and the current petitioner. The guards belatedly raised their weapons as the King stiffened. Before they could react further, Gideon bowed low.

"What's he saying," Bosh hissed.

"If you can't hear, what makes you think we can?" Illium snapped.

I couldn't help but be irritated as well. I hated when things didn't go according to plan. As much as we tried to eavesdrop with the rest of the crowd, we couldn't make out a word they said from this distance.

When Gideon disappeared in a flash once more, I tensed, waiting.

"Here are your invitations," Gideon spoke from his original position. He waved seven of the formal parchments that we'd intended to steal. Just like that.

"What—how did you—" I flushed as everyone around us stared, including my men.

"I asked."

Of course. Who would refuse to give an invitation to a Jinni? The King would have to be a fool to risk his ire. In fact, he probably assumed he was being honored by the presence of a group of Jinn and hoped to be showered with Jinni favor all night.

I gritted my teeth together in a forced smile. "Thank you." It was foolish to be angry about this. I shrugged off the discomfort, gesturing toward the opposite side of the castle, where we could now enter the great room with a genuine invitation. "Lead the way."

As we left the line, we passed a tall fireplace and approached the double doors to the great room, where two guards stood stiff on each side.

Gideon simply flashed the invitations—and the guards opened the heavy doors wide. The first thing my eyes landed on were tables filled to the brim with food.

As I surveyed the crowds of people, some seated, others dancing or talking, the muscles in my jaw tightened. I barely reined in my rage at the sight of him.

Prince Dev.

Blood pumped in my ears, making the merriment around me almost inaudible.

My fingers curled and I clenched my fists at my sides, unable to move.

Do not start a fight, I reminded myself. *Not here. Not yet.*

The prince was taller and more muscled than I remembered, but he had the same unruly brown hair and smirk. Seated on yet another raised dais, he was surrounded by food and drink, as well as a large group of men and women. Their boisterous laughter carried across the room.

We made our way around the outer edge. "Split up," I said. "Get some food. We'll meet by the pillars at midnight." I pointed to the massive white stone pillars marking the main entrance.

Everyone dispersed, except Arie and Gideon.

I scratched my neck. "I assume you have a method for bearing witness..."

Gideon half-smiled. "Don't worry about me, Master Kadin. I'll be watching." He slipped away into the crowd before I could ask if he meant watching the prince, or me.

"Shall we?" I turned to Arie, leading her to a table with two open seats. Normally I didn't waste time in places like this; not like these nobles who spent their entire day enjoying entertainment and filling their mouths. I forced myself to unclench my fists and focus. We only had the day to make this work, so we had to work smart and we had to work fast.

Chapter Thirty

Arie

KADIN BARELY SPOKE THROUGHOUT the meal. The muscle in his jaw ticked and he chewed as if the feast was a job and the sooner he finished, the better.

"It's good, isn't it?" I pointed to a dish of Ghormey-Sabzi. "This one is delicious."

He scooped some onto his plate and chewed without expression, staring at the prince across the room.

I gave up on conversation.

"Excuse me." I pushed my chair out. "I'll be back in a moment."

He didn't blink.

I searched for Gideon and found him seated on a gold sofa in the corner, where he had a good view of everyone.

The surrounding sofas were empty. Finally, we could speak alone.

I stood taller and approached the circle of seats, pushing a smile onto my face. Resting my hands on the back of a sofa, I stood behind it like a shield. My instincts screamed at me to walk away, but I cleared my throat and spoke, "May I ask you a question, when you have a moment?"

"I am free now," Gideon said, waving toward Prince Dev, who stepped down from the dais seating and walked toward the washrooms. "Since I'm not following the young Prince Dev to use the toilet, as much as Master Kadin might wish it."

I paused, then laughed. "You're making a joke!"

"It happens once a decade or so," Gideon replied, lips twitching. "Please, sit."

I settled onto the sofa across from him, too tense to lean back against the pillows. Which problem should I bring up first? Where to start?

"How about the beginning," Gideon said, but his voice was gentle, patient.

His calm reminded me of Kadin, even though he was light-skinned where Kadin was dark, his raven hair slicked back instead of falling across his face, and crystal-clear blue eyes instead of Kadin's warm amber gaze, like molten sunlight. Why was I thinking about Kadin right now?

I cleared my throat. "I have two requests actually…"

He waited for me to continue.

"First…" I licked my lips and launched into it, words spilling over once I let them free, "Once you're done bearing witness for Kadin, I was hoping you might be willing to spend just a few short days in a nearby kingdom as well, where another king is also misusing his Gift and—"

"No. Next." Gideon leaned back, crossing one leg over the other.

"Please, if you'd only reconsider—" I slid to the edge of my seat, hands clasped, begging.

He interrupted once more, waving a hand. "I understand. But I'm afraid time is of the essence. I can't afford to waste even one more day before I use the lamp to return home."

I sat back at that. I'd had my hopes pinned on convincing him. Without his help, I would have to resort to my original plan of waiting for Amir to return home as a jilted fiancée.

"You mentioned a second request?" Gideon's voice interrupted my thoughts.

"Yes," I said to my hands, afraid to look at him as I spoke. "Ever since that first day, I could feel—could sense—your Gifting. And so, I assume… that you could sense mine as well?"

Suddenly I was afraid *not* to look at him.

When I lifted my chin to meet his sharp gaze, there was no sign of surprise. He only nodded.

I lowered my voice even more, as I continued. "I'm sure you're also aware it's against the law for women to be Gifted. Throughout the kingdoms a Gifted woman is required to be put on trial, before being judged as a danger to themselves and to others."

"It's my understanding those trials are a bit of a farce."

I lifted my chin. "If you mean the results are always the same, then yes. It's supposed to be a fair trial." I waved a hand. "But the women are always sentenced to have their Gifts severed. And they usually die within a month. I think—" I leaned forward, lowering my voice even more, "—I think someone kills them."

Gideon shifted in his seat, no longer lounging casually, but leaning forward, tense. "Why did you bring this up to me?"

Another deep breath. I had considered this moment for ages, but once I spoke the words, I wouldn't be able to take them back. "If they ever discover my Gift, they'll put me on trial. And if they put me on trial, it's a death sentence. I don't want to die. But I can't keep this Gift hidden forever. Either way, it's killing me. I want you to remove my Gift."

Chapter Thirty-One

Arie

"NO." GIDEON SAT BACK again, this time as if the conversation was over, signaling for a servant to bring him a drink.

I waited until he took it and the man left. "Why not?"

"Tell me," Gideon said, swirling the drink before taking a sip. "Has any Gifted woman survived a Severance, to your knowledge?"

"No. But as I've said, I think it has to do with the trials." I pursed my lips, trying to find the right words. "The deaths always take place within a month of a Severance. They try to make it seem random, but I *know* they're killing them. That's why I've come to you instead."

He shook his head.

Scooting to the edge of my seat, I clutched my hands together. "Please Gideon," I begged, "I can't live with this Gift anymore. You don't understand what it's doing to me. I can't control it. I can't go home. I'm not safe anywhere." *I'm an abomination.*

"You are not," Gideon's soft voice crept into my thoughts. I'd forgotten he might be listening.

"I am," I whispered back, tears filling my eyes so that he was only a blurry image when I looked up. "Please. I just want to be free of it."

"You misunderstand. You cannot be free of it, because your Gift is a part of you," Gideon told me. His eyes burned with intensity. "You can no more remove it free of consequences than you could remove an eye or a limb. The women do not die because someone murders them, they die because they can't live without it. So, do not ask me again. No Jinni in his sane mind will ever agree to do this for you, do you understand?"

My hopes fell and a pit formed in my stomach, growing dull and bitter as I nodded. "I understand," I whispered.

He gave me a moment to stare at the blurry floor in silence, before standing with a sigh and sitting on the sofa beside me.

"What exactly does your Gifting entail?" he asked.

"It's hard to describe," I said, swallowing my disappointment and blinking tears of frustration away before he could see them. "I can hear… well, not *everything* people are thinking, but I always hear when a thought exists, like the way you'd hear waves on the shore or the buzzing of an insect. And then, when they're about me, I hear…" I glanced around to make sure no one was nearby before I whispered, "I hear every single word."

Gideon didn't move. He didn't blink or react in any way. Only stared at me.

I dropped my gaze.

It appeared he'd spoken too soon. I was a disgrace after all.

"What was your mother's name?" he asked, out of nowhere.

"Hanna," I said, frowning. "Why do you ask?"

He didn't answer, only took a deep breath, slow and steady. Was he surprised? I remembered the note I'd found in the book that had insinuated my mother might be a Jinni... "Did you know her? My mother?"

"It's hard to say." Gideon's expression didn't reveal a thing. "But the Gift of Intuition is very rare. It's certainly not something to be ashamed of."

The name caught my attention. Intrigued, I turned it over in my mind. "Is this your Gift as well?"

"One of them." He nodded. Before I could ask what his other Gifts were, he added, "You can control it." He rapped his cane on the floor to punctuate his words. "With time and practice."

He lifted his cane to point toward a mouse scurrying along the edge of the wall. "Imagine each thought is like a mouse. Right now, the mice are running around in chaos."

I nodded vigorously at the mental image.

"Close your eyes," he continued. "Imagine picking up each thought like catching one of the mice, and placing it in a jar."

When I struggled to picture it, he only said, "Take your time."

As I picked up each squirming thought by the tail out of the mess in my mind, dropping them into an imaginary glass jar, the noise surrounding me didn't change. Was it working at all? I kept going, laboring over them, until my imaginary jar was full.

The chaos of thoughts washed over me, as overwhelming and muddled as ever. Even more so now that I was paying attention to it.

"It's impossible... there's too many." I blinked back tears.

He gave me a small smile. "It will take some time and practice. Now, put a lid on the jar, and screw it shut."

Closing my eyes again, I tried to picture a thick lid for the glass jar, twisting it hard, locking them in. The din instantly softened. My eyes flew open in surprise. "I did it!"

"Well done," Gideon said, and it felt like high praise. "Once you've mastered this, you can begin to open the jar, taking out one thought at a time whenever you choose."

A lump rose in my throat. "Thank you. Truly. I didn't know this was possible. I didn't even know my Gift of hearing thoughts was called Intuition." He nodded in response, turning to look out into the room where I assumed Prince Dev had returned.

I took that as my cue to leave and stood, enjoying the regular everyday noise of conversation with only a soft hum of thoughts—one in particular stood out. Gideon's method of singling the thoughts out had made them feel more tangible, more like the person they belonged to. This one felt close by. Familiar.

I turned and my eyes met Kadin's. Just two steps away.

Staring at me.

All the thoughts I'd so carefully placed in the jar exploded out into the air as I lost control, but I didn't need to pick his out of the crowd. From the disbelief written all over his face, I had no doubt he'd heard everything.

Chapter Thirty-Two

Kadin

I STARED AT THEM both. Gideon, the Jinni I was using to fight those born of the Jinn. And Arie, the girl I'd been falling for, who was one of them.

One of the very people I hated more than anything else in the entire world.

Arie reeled back, as if I'd slapped her.

Gift of Intuition, she'd said, *hearing thoughts.*

I took a step back.

How *dare* she read my mind. I threw all my willpower into envisioning walls thicker than a dungeon around me, imagining pouring the cement myself, thickening it with every bit of my resolve.

"Kadin, let me explain," she began, pressing her hands together, pleading with her eyes for me to listen. Was that a trick too? If she was one of the Gifted, I couldn't be sure.

I spun on my heel and pushed through the crowd, aiming for distance. *How far can she reach?* I asked myself, feeling my usual calm slip away completely.

No one answered, and I realized I'd half expected Gideon to, but maybe my walls were working.

I couldn't believe I'd been harboring a Gifted girl for so long without knowing. How had I not seen it?

I gritted my teeth as I remembered how every time I would enter a room, she seemed to know. Even if her back was turned.

I'd been flattered. Thought it meant we had a connection. I wanted to punch a hole in the wall.

Shoving my way through the crowd, I curled my fingers into fists. Something in my expression made those who saw me move out of my way.

"Kadin, wait!" Arie yelled, and people turned to look.

She was drawing too much attention.

I pushed through a closed door, not caring where it led.

She followed me through. "Please, Kadin."

Oh, for the love of Jinn, she sounded like she was going to cry. Was that real? I felt a twinge of guilt at the thought.

The hallway wasn't empty.

Stopping, I turned to face her. "Not here." I tried not to feel anything, think anything, as I took her elbow and guided her down the hall, searching for a quiet corner. A small alcove ahead, just large enough to hold a short sofa and a few plants.

It would do.

The space was tucked away, meant for meetings just like this. Except nothing like this.

"You've been lying to us this whole time," I hissed, and it wasn't as without feeling as I'd hoped. My voice almost broke and I cut off.

"I can't help my Gift," Arie said, ripping her arm from my grasp. I was eager to let go, stepping back. She pulled back as well until we stood on opposite sides of the small room. "Do you think I *want* to be this way?" Tears welled in her eyes, but she refused to let them fall. I crossed my arms and stared at the marble walls as she continued, "Do you think I have a choice? I couldn't tell you." She gestured to me. "You would've reacted just like this."

I stiffened. "Reacted to an unfair advantage where I have no control? Absolutely."

"Not everyone is like Prince Dev. I don't know what he did to you to make you hate him so much, but it wasn't *me!*"

Her voice rose and I held up a hand, reminding her to keep quiet.

Of course it wasn't her. She never would've done that to my little brother. Part of me understood why she'd kept it secret… but I'd trusted her. And she'd betrayed that trust. "You're all alike." I refused to think, to let her overhear anything further, but my voice was unsteady. "You *use* people."

"No," Arie shook her head. She took a half-step toward me, but stopped when I recoiled. A tear escaped, although she dashed it away before it reached her cheek.

"You used me." Quiet opened up like a canyon between us. I cleared my face of expression, pretending a calm I didn't feel. "You were only with us to find a Jinni. You're just like all the other Gifted."

"That's not true—"

"There's no space for you in my crew," I interrupted. "Take your things and go. I don't want to see you when this day is over." I stormed out of the alcove, but I couldn't outrun the soft sound of her weeping.

Chapter Thirty-Three

Kadin

IT WAS NEARING MIDNIGHT. Our deadline. I'd spent the entire day avoiding Arie. "Bosh, can you keep her busy? I need to focus." He'd been more than happy, and I knew she wouldn't bring up her Gift around him. But then I'd spent the night feeling rotten for placing him in that position. He didn't deserve to have his thoughts overheard any more than I did.

They watched a snake charmer on one side of the room. I kept to the opposite end of the vast hall, listening to the man beside me tell a dull story about farming. In any other situation, I would've left. But I forced myself to watch the prince. Watch him laugh. Watch him pick his teeth. Watch him drift off during the storyteller's fable. Watch, as nothing happened, and all my efforts over the last four years were wasted.

Naveed dropped into the seat beside me. *Is something wrong?* he signed. *Have we been discovered?*

I shook my head, sighing as I ran a hand through my hair. I couldn't tell him. It wasn't my secret. Even the fact that I would consider keeping it made me furious. It'd been hours since we'd spoke, but my anger hadn't faded.

Arie had a Gift.

All this time, I'd thought the secret written across her face was her noble heritage, only to find it was a different heritage altogether: Jinni blood.

"Let's focus on framing Prince Dev," I answered finally. "Any ideas?"

When my friend shook his head, I rubbed a hand across my face. "We're almost out of time."

He clapped a hand on my back.

What would I do if this failed? I'd lived every waking hour of these last few years focused on finding justice. Everything hinged on this plan succeeding. But there was less than an hour left before Gideon's time with us ended.

And Prince Dev was so drunk he'd fallen asleep in his chair.

I raised my head to check on him.

No change.

My eyes landed on Arie. Despite my best efforts to ignore her, I couldn't look away. She was slumped in an extremely un-lady-like posture, staring at a spot on the floor.

Bosh appeared at my side. "Boss, I'm gonna take Arie back to the inn, okay? She says she's not feeling good, but she doesn't know the way back."

Shame washed over me. I'd been so angry, I hadn't even considered that she was stranded here because of me. I nodded and Bosh scurried back to her. When she stood to leave, I tried to catch her eye, but she didn't look back.

The Gifted can't be trusted, I reminded myself. Standing in a huff, I strode to the corner where Gideon still lounged on the gold sofas.

Prince Dev might be sleeping sitting up, but he was still all the way across the room. I should've expected a Jinni to side with his own kind. "You look like you've definitely found something," I goaded him, dropping onto the sofa beside him.

"I'm beginning to think this is a waste of time," Gideon replied. "The Prince-ling does not display any signs of misusing his Gift." Those blue eyes flickered as he added in a dangerously soft tone, "Have you ever considered that perhaps the Gift isn't the problem, but rather, the person who wields it?"

How dare he judge me? "Whatever the outcome, it's the agreed upon payment," I snapped. Taking a deep breath, I added in a calmer tone, "We still have until the end of the day." Which, of course, ended in a handful of minutes.

The prince roused enough to call for another drink, leaning into the women around him, whispering in their ears. They giggled and batted their eyes at him.

A serving woman pushed through the crowds, causing a wave of annoyance as she strode toward the dais and the royals. Her thick, roped hair reached her knees and marked her as a foreigner from Chimigi. When she spoke, the torrent of foreign words confirmed it. She wailed and carried on in a language that meant nothing to me, tears streaking down her face, as she pointed at the prince.

"I believe this poor woman is requesting you to translate," the king said to his son in a bored tone.

Prince Dev had shoved the other women off his arms, and while he pretended casual attention, the blush of wine in his pale cheeks seemed to have faded. *Was he nervous?*

"Of course," he said with a grand smile that he cast out to everyone except the woman in distress. When he faced her, his tone turned sharp. We waited, glancing back and forth between them, listening to the babble.

The king's foot tapped impatiently after a few moments. "What does she want?" he cut in when the prince didn't seem inclined to share.

"Ah, well," Prince Dev paused their discussion, turning from the woman to his father.

I watched his thoat bob and my suspicions grew. What if this was the moment I needed, finally, but none of us knew it? I clenched my teeth. Glancing over at Gideon, I hoped against hope that he might speak this foreign tongue, but he remained as expressionless as the rest of us, waiting for the translation.

"She does indeed want me to translate for her," the prince began slowly. "Apparently, some scoundrel has taken advantage of her. Now she's pregnant."

Gasps sounded across the room as all eyes turned to the woman, lowering to her stomach. She placed her hands over her belly as only a mother does, all the while glaring murderous daggers at the prince. She lifted a finger, no longer weeping, but pointing directly at him and declaring something no one understood.

"She, ah," Prince Dev cleared his throat and raised his voice to speak to the whole room. "She has asked me to help find the father." He replied to her in her native tongue. His tone sounded dismissive, and the pregnant woman sneered.

When she spoke again, he didn't bother to translate, calling instead for one of the castle serving women. "Help this poor woman to a spare room so she can rest. We will begin the search in earnest in the morning!" He waved them away.

The serving woman obeyed, tugging the arm of the young mother, who called out another string of words, eyes circling the room, begging one of us to understand her, only to meet blank stares. Finally, she followed the other woman out of the room with shoulders hunched in defeat.

I glanced at Gideon again. He stood, still impassive, staring at the departing prince.

The day was over.

Gideon had borne witness, but found nothing. If this last situation wasn't enough to sway him, nothing would be.

I felt my own shoulders curve inward in disappointment. All those years of searching for nothing. Justice would never come. Prince Dev would never be forced to face his crimes.

I opened my mouth to call the others, but Gideon clamped a hand on my shoulder. His sharp blue eyes met mine, and a cold fury burned within them that I hadn't noticed. "I have borne witness," he said in an icy tone I'd never heard before. "And I have seen enough."

Chapter Thirty-Four

Kadin

THE WORLD FLASHED AROUND me in a dizzying fashion, and my stomach revolted. I focused on not throwing up on the scuffed wooden floor. Wood? The castle floors were marble.

The room spun as I looked up and my confusion only added to my nausea. We stood in a small, cramped room with one tiny window. The sandstone color of the carved-out walls and ceiling reminded me of the Red Rose. Was this—I glanced around to find the bed on one side, a table and chairs on the other—yes. This was Gideon's room.

Groans came from my men where we all hunched over the floor, except Gideon.

He must have caught Bosh and Arie before they left the castle; they both crouched in front of me.

Bosh held his stomach with one hand and his mouth with the other, while Arie leaned against the wall.

Traveling was much worse when you weren't expecting it.

My thoughts must've given me away. She glanced up and our eyes met.

Staring at me, she pursed her lips, not saying anything.

I ripped my gaze away.

That's when I saw Prince Dev.

Gideon stood unmoving in front of the prince, who was bent over on his hands and knees, eyes squeezed shut, groaning.

The others registered our surroundings with wide-eyes, gazing at Gideon with a new reverence. It only grew when Gideon began speaking to Prince Dev in the same harsh language that he and the pregnant woman had spoken.

I licked my lips, leaning forward on my toes. Across the room, Naveed met my gaze. His eyes glowed with the same fervor as mine.

But Prince Dev ignored Gideon, standing with a groan as he frowned at us and the strange room. He fell onto the bed. "I have a wicked headache," he mumbled. He leaned back as if to go to sleep, mumbling to himself, "This is a wild dream. I must've had too much to drink…"

Though Gideon kept a calm front, those cold eyes narrowed. His tone was so soft it was nearly a whisper, "Tie him to a chair."

Every single one of us leapt to obey.

Ignoring Prince Dev's protests, we dragged him off the bed and threw him onto the small wooden chair. Daichi produced ropes from our bags. We wrapped and knotted them around the prince's arms and legs.

"Remember me?" I whispered in the prince's ear, yanking the ropes tighter, pulling back so he could see my face. "Remember what you did to my family?"

Prince Dev paled. "What're you doing?" he howled, fighting the restraints. "Release me at once!"

I stepped back to join the men and Gideon. I wanted to smile at the justice finally being meted out, but instead my blood boiled hotter. It wasn't enough.

"What right do you think you have to hold me here?" the prince demanded, as haughty as ever. "You'll pay for this!"

"You have broken the Jinni code," Gideon answered with that deceptive calm.

"I've done no such thing," Prince Dev argued.

All of us watched Gideon. Though we knew the Jinn took their code seriously, none of us knew how they punished criminals who broke it.

"You were the only one who could speak Chimigi with that woman," Gideon settled onto the edge of the bed across from the prince. "Or so you thought."

Prince Dev blinked and swallowed, pulling at his restraints again as if he couldn't help himself. His face glistened with sweat.

Gideon continued, "You used your Gift to keep the truth of that baby from everyone." A drop of sweat rolled down the prince's face as Gideon leaned forward. "Would you like to tell them the truth now?"

Prince Dev shook his head, and his curls stuck against his face. "I don't know what you're talking about." But his shirt was drenched and his voice trembled.

"He is the child's father," Gideon announced.

How had I not guessed? No one said a word, including myself, until Gideon filled the silence. "You stand in judgment. How do you plead?"

The prince scoffed. "I don't have to justify myself to any of you. Who do you think you are that you can just drag me from my castle and—" though his mouth moved, his words vanished.

Gideon held something small and pink between his thumb and forefinger. Was that a... tongue?

The prince's eyes grew huge. His mouth opened and closed like a fish, making strange gurgling noises.

"I will ask again," Gideon said, as if they were carrying on a polite conversation. He released the strange object between his finger and thumb, and it disappeared.

Lowering his hand, he dusted off the top of his cane before tilting it on its side, gripping the top of the cane and pulling. A sharp sound of metal on metal pierced the room as a wicked sword appeared out of the sheath, revealing the cane to be hollow inside. Gideon set the base of the cane on the bed and ran his finger along the thin, gleaming blade absently. "How do you plead?"

The prince twitched slightly, rolling his tongue over his teeth and lips before speaking more cautiously. "What I did is nothing compared to King Amir of Sagh."

I crossed my arms to keep from punching him. Even his efforts to be respectful came across arrogant and offensive.

"Oh, haven't you heard?" He sneered, even as he tested his restraints, which held fast. "He's sent out a message to all the kingdoms to attend his wedding to the princess of Hodafez over Summer's Eve, but if you know the right people, you'd know there's rumors that say the girl is in hiding and he's holding her father prisoner. He'll kill the king if she doesn't return and no one will stop him."

Arie gasped.

At first, I tried to ignore her. As a sheltered princess, this conversation probably opened her eyes to a whole new world. But something about that name, Hodafez, triggered a memory. When it came to me, I lifted my eyes to Arie, finally letting myself look at her, and it confirmed my suspicions.

Pale, she stared at the prince, trembling.

"According to the rumors, people obey every word King Amir speaks. He could tell King Mahdi to kill himself on the rocks and then declare himself the new ruler, and not one person would question it. At least, not while close to him." Prince Dev settled back, shrugging as much as he could while bound to a chair, and continued. "Compared to that, my dalliances are trivial. Like a sneeze, or a misstep." He raised his brows and smiled.

My fists clenched, despite my slow, careful breaths. I wanted to knock that smirk off his self-righteous face. I might have if Arie hadn't stepped forward.

Chapter Thirty-Five

Arie

MY PULSE POUNDED LIKE I'd been running. Prince Dev had said it so casually.

"What else did you hear?" I demanded. I barely held back from asking if my father was still alive.

When the men frowned at me, I added, "Gideon needs to hear the whole story. Prince Dev is right, he's not the only one using his Gifts to an unfair advantage! King Amir is misusing the Gift of Persuasion. That seems far more dangerous than languages—maybe Gideon should bear witness to his crimes!"

I risked a glance at Gideon to see if it had swayed him at all. Instead, my eyes were pulled to Kadin's like a magnet. His thoughts were somehow inaudible to me—had been ever since he'd discovered my Gift—but I could see him putting the pieces together as his eyes narrowed. Even so, I had to know. I whirled on the prince. "Speak!"

Dev barely glanced at me, before he wrinkled his nose. "Don't you dare address me that way, woman."

Before I could react, Gideon stepped forward. In that soft voice, somehow more menacing than a yell, he leaned over Dev's seat and said in his ear, "You will tell the *lady* what you've heard." Like a lion eyeing his prey, he stepped back slightly, still looming over the chair with that razor thin blade.

"Ah, alright, well…" Dev struggled to keep an air of calm. His nostrils flared and his fingers twitched. "I told you everything I know. There might be a lovely wedding or there might be a hostile takeover. I, for one, have bets on the latter."

My throat seized up.

Knowing they were watching, I kept my face smooth and turned away. I couldn't pressure him for any more information without raising suspicion. But when they turned back to Dev, I slipped out of the room.

Hurrying downstairs, I raced toward the bartender, trying to keep an outward calm. "When is Summer's Eve again? I've… been out of town and lost track of the days."

"You lost track?" He stopped cleaning and stared at me. "Lost track. I've never met a young girl who lost track of Summer's Eve before. All the dancing and ribbons and boys. My own daughter's been talking of it for nearly two months now."

Blushing, I held my ground. "So, it's in a few days then?"

He shook his head and snorted. "It's tomorrow. Well, today really, considering the time."

My lips parted. Today. We were at least three day's travel from Hodafez… How was I supposed to get home in time?

"You gonna order anything?"

When I shook my head, he disappeared into the back.

I could scream with frustration. I had to get home. A half-formed plan budded in my mind. I sprinted back up the stairs.

King Amir would pay for this. He thought this would get me to marry him? Shaking with rage, I rehearsed what I would say, stopping outside Gideon's room to stuff my feelings down until I felt numb—burying every stray thought and emotion that might give me away—before I turned the handle.

Chapter Thirty-Six

Kadin

ARIE SLIPPED BACK INTO the room and I exhaled. Gideon's interrogation was thorough; the smallest details labored over, actions questioned, memories recalled. The Jinn didn't take judgment lightly.

After pacing the room for a while, Gideon had told us to be still or leave. Now my men and I lounged against the walls, chairs, and bed. Illium even snored softly in the corner. I'd perched in a chair near the door without thinking much about it until Arie showed up.

As soon as she closed the door, she approached me, eyes on the ground, and whispered, "May I speak with you privately? I only need a moment…"

Despite my intentions to ignore her, I agreed, fighting the guilt that plagued me for how I'd treated her earlier.

We stepped out into the dark hallway. The rest of the inn had gone to bed long ago and it was quiet.

She still didn't meet my eyes, crossing her arms.

I swallowed, fighting to keep my mental walls up. I'd been harsh earlier. Maybe I should apologize. And tell her she could stay with us a few more days if she needed. I could handle a few more days, right?

"I'm so tired," she said, before I could form the right words. Yawning, she rubbed her eyes. When she finally lifted her gaze, it radiated sadness that tugged at my emotions. "My room is right next door and that awful prince is so loud." She pulled out her room key, fiddling with it. "Would it be okay if we trade rooms for the night so I could get some sleep?"

I blinked. I'd been expecting her to bring up her Gift. Maybe she was as nervous to mention it as I was. I reached into my pocket without thinking, exchanging my key for hers. "Of course." Just because I didn't fully trust her, it didn't mean I wanted her to suffer.

Swallowing again, I tried to figure out how to tear down the walls in my mind, so she could see my confusion, but she turned to go. "Thank you Kadin. Goodnight." Her tone was solemn.

"Goodnight," I called after her. We could talk in the morning. My mind shifted back to Prince Dev, where Gideon was listing every torturous thing the prince had been up to since Naveed and I had left town.

Hours passed in the tiny room, before Gideon finally spoke the words I'd been waiting to hear for years: "It's time to pronounce judgment."

My men sat up. Naveed bumped Illium's arm to wake him, and we all turned to Gideon.

"Prince Dev of Baradaan, I pronounce you guilty of misusing your Gift," Gideon began.

"That's not tr—"

Gideon snapped his fingers and once again held a wet, pink tongue while the prince roared wordlessly, struggling against his restraints. This time, Gideon ignored him, moving toward the window where the first hint of dawn crept in, filling the room with a soft light.

"It seems fitting that a punishment for misusing the Gift of Tongues, would be the removal of the offensive organ," Gideon continued, and we all gaped at the tiny piece of the prince in Gideon's palm as he stretched his arm out the window and waited patiently.

An enormous bird with a wingspan as large as my horse swept down and snatched the tongue from Gideon's hands in its cruel talons, swooping up and away as suddenly as it had appeared.

Prince Dev cried out. *Can he still feel his tongue?* The bird rose into the skies to devour it, unseen.

As I turned to look at the prince, he fainted.

I glanced at Gideon, and pictured my mental shields lowering. *Thank you.*

He nodded, once.

Naveed stared at the prince as well, tears in his eyes. This was our justice. The prince who'd stolen his tongue would finally know how it felt.

A fitting punishment in more ways than one.

But I felt numb. Why didn't it feel like enough?

Chapter Thirty-Seven

Kadin

THOUGH I DESPERATELY WISHED for a bed, once Gideon sent the forever wordless prince back to the castle with a snap of his fingers, I knew it was time to pay the price: one ancient lamp.

As my men filed out of the room to find their own beds, I paused at the realization that Arie was sleeping in my room. "I'll be back shortly," I told Gideon.

At the opposite end of the hall, I tapped on the door to my room, hissing, "Arie."

No response.

"Arie, wake up. I need to give Gideon the lamp."

No answer.

I knocked a bit louder.

"Pipe down!" a male voice called from another room. But as far as I could tell, not a single sound came from the other side of Arie's door. She was a sound sleeper.

Embarrassed, I returned to Gideon's room, which he opened before my fist connected with the wood.

"My apologies," I began, "The lamp is in my room, but I let Arie sleep there… the noise," my excuses sounded weak. "Anyway, she's still asleep, but I'm sure she'll be awake in a few hours and then the lamp is yours, I swear." I tried my best to expose my thoughts, not sure if it was working. "I'm good for my word, you can read my mind if you need to…"

Gideon's head tilted to the side. "I suppose it would be good to rest a few hours." He nodded. "Come back with the lamp at midday."

A few hours of sleep sounded heavenly. Shuffling downstairs just long enough to ask someone to wake me before noon, I used Arie's key to slip into what had been her room, noticing she'd brought her belongings with her as I fell into bed. Even with the sunrise peeking into my room, sleep hit me like a boulder.

I felt as if I'd only just closed my eyes when a knock roused me. Was it already noon? I rubbed my face, eyes burning.

Forcing myself out of bed, I dragged my feet to the door. The hall was empty. I trudged to Arie's room, knocking as I yawned.

No answer.

I knocked louder. If people weren't awake by now, it was their own fault. But even when I pounded on her door, Arie didn't stir.

I began to worry.

Jogging down the stairs, I asked for a spare key.

"We don't just go around giving out keys," the older woman minding the bar told me. The wrinkles etched in her forehead deepened. "If you lost it, you pay for it, and you don't get another one."

"I didn't lose it," I tried to reason with her, though I'd already explained once. "I paid for all the rooms, and I gave that key to another member of my group. But now I need to get into the room."

"Why?" she scowled.

"None of your business," I snapped. But when she raised her chin at me, I sighed. "I'm worried, alright? I just want to make sure she's okay."

"She?" The woman slapped her rag down on the bar. The wrinkles lifted, growing deeper still. "I see how it is. You want to sneak into the poor lady's room? I'm not going to help you with that, and I'm considering having you thrown out just for asking!"

"No, no," I backpedaled, frustrated with the direction this conversation was going. "No, listen. It's *my* room. I gave her my key, but I need to get something from my luggage."

"Mmmhmm," she said, crossing her arms. "There's always *something* with you men, isn't there? I thought you wanted to make sure she's okay. Now you need to get something?"

I groaned. "I do, and yes! Why don't you come with and make sure I behave. How's that sound?" When she hesitated, I pressed harder, "Please. I'm worried. Just help me check on her—then I promise I'll go away."

Though she huffed, the woman turned to the kitchen and called out, "Arman, I'm checking on a guest. Be right back."

"Thank you," I said, dropping some coin onto the table, hoping it'd make her move faster.

She pocketed the coin before wiping down the rest of the bar. She stopped to fiddle with a ring of keys. Only once she was satisfied they were all there did she finally push through the door to join me on the other side of the bar, tromping up the stairs without looking back.

I hurried to catch up.

She knocked on Arie's door, even though I reminded her I already had.

Just like earlier, Arie didn't answer. That girl slept like a rock.

The employee frowned and inserted her key, calling out as if Arie would somehow hear her voice when she hadn't heard the knocking, "I'm coming in, miss."

With a twist, the door swung open and we stepped inside.

The bed was empty.

And made.

Like no one had slept in it.

I didn't see Arie anywhere. Had she risen early?

Puzzled, my eyes settled on my bags. They were open, and the contents were strewn about the floor. My heart beat faster. Moving toward the bags, I ignored the babbling of the woman who'd let me in.

It couldn't be.

The lamp was missing.

Chapter Thirty-Eight

Arie

AFTER LEAVING THE INTERROGATION earlier that night with Kadin's key, it hadn't taken me long to find the lamp. Moonlight poured into the room as I dug through his other bags until I found some flint as well.

I stopped in the middle of the room with the oil lamp in one hand and the flint in the other, stalled.

There was no oil.

On the other side of Kadin's room, by the window, there was a table with a single chair and a small lamp. Praying I'd be so lucky, I crossed the room and made out a dark liquid in the bottom of the other lamp. When I picked it up, a thin layer sloshed around inside. It barely covered the bottom. I hoped it would be enough.

Setting the ancient green lamp in the middle of the table, I carefully transferred the oil from one to the other, preparing to light it.

I paused.

Kadin would never forgive me.

Not to mention Gideon.

The Jinni had made it clear that once he had the lamp, he was leaving immediately. But if my plan worked—and if he didn't murder me first—then maybe, just maybe, I could not only get home, but draw Gideon to Hodafez after me... and once he was there, he could stop King Amir from abusing his power.

It was risky.

Gideon was honorable, but there was an urgency to his plan I didn't understand.

Either way, I had to stop King Amir, or at the very least, rescue Baba. There was no time to waste. Summer's Eve festivities began in just a few hours.

Still I paused, Kadin's face etched in my mind. To betray him twice in one day... There was no way he'd forgive me after this.

Should I leave a note? Did he even read? This was silly. I didn't know him well enough to know if he could read, so why should I leave him a note?

Even with this sound argument, I couldn't make myself move. *Gifted people use people.* His words reverberated in my thoughts, the way they had all day. But instead of urging me to light the fire and leave him behind, the memory only made me feel even more guilty. I stared out at the moon, as another memory hit me.

When he'd turned back to the interrogation, opening the door, I'd heard his thoughts about Prince Dev.

Not one of them had been about me.

Yet, I'd still heard him as clear as day.

Had I imagined it? Was there some whisper of thought related to me? I didn't think so...

I shook my head. This wasn't the time to worry over Kadin's thoughts, not the ones he had now or the ones he would have in the very near future when he found out what I'd done.

Swallowing hard, I set my bag on the table and loosened the drawstrings. I pulled out my crown. Even in the moonlight the diamonds glittered. It might cost more than the lamp, but I knew it still wasn't enough.

I chewed on my lip. Was there any way Gideon might follow me? And if he did, would he let me ask for help before he punished me?

Turning to Kadin's bag, I set the crown inside where the lamp had been. It would serve as both a note and a payment for my theft.

Picking up the flint, I lit the lamp.

My father needed me. If I didn't get home soon, his murder would be my fault.

I wrapped my fingers around the base of the lamp.

Nothing happened.

Was I supposed to say the place I wanted to go? Picture it? I opened my mouth, thinking back to where I'd left my father's kingdom, which had just happened to be at the mouth of the ocean—

Splash!

Cold water engulfed me and the scenery shifted from the warmth of Kadin's room at the inn, to pitch-black darkness. Still gripping the lamp, I lifted it above the water, which came up to my chest.

Struggling to find my bearings, my eyes began to adjust. The moonlight danced on the water all around me. Ahead the lights of Keshdi twinkled.

It was the exact place I'd crawled out of the ocean almost an entire fortnight ago.

I groaned, wanting to smack myself. I'd intended to transport myself directly into the palace.

Wading out of the water to the shore, I held up the lamp, squinting. Was there any oil left?

Though something sloshed around, I couldn't be sure if it was oil or saltwater. I knelt, setting the lamp on the packed soil, reaching into my pocket to pull out the flint—but it wasn't there.

I moaned again.

I'd set the flint down on the table. Back at the Red Rose. Almost three-days travel from here.

Without any way to light the lamp, I gripped it desperately, closing my eyes and picturing my bedroom. "Take me to my room," I whispered. "*Please*, take me to my room."

But, of course, I didn't move. Dawn was breaking and the dark sky was turning gray with a hint of color on the horizon, lighting up the shoreline and the path that led to the road.

Sighing, I stood, tucking the lamp into my dress pocket and brushing the sand off my wet hands.

I would have to walk.

My cold, wet skirts clung to my legs, making me shiver. I wrung them out as much as possible before I began the long hike to Hodafez.

"Where can I get some of those?" A female voice spoke up behind me.

I whirled, heart thumping.

Before me stood a stark-naked woman with nothing on her except a seashell necklace, and a few other strategically placed shells.

I gaped at her.

She stood with her knees braced together as if she might fall and gestured to my clothes. "That whole ensemble would be nice. How can I go about getting something like that for myself?"

She sounded like a raving lunatic.

"What happened to you?" I asked even as I reached up to unclasp my cloak, pulling it over my shoulders. "Were you hurt? Did someone do this to you?" Fury rose in me. I swung my cloak over her thin shoulders. "Here, put this on, quickly now." I brushed her long, auburn hair out of the way, securing it in the front.

Stepping back, I expected a thank you, or an explanation, or both, but she only held out her arms, making the cloak swish open and closed. "How lovely. This will do very nicely." Glancing up at me, she grinned and finally added, "Thank you."

"Ahh..." I cleared my throat at the flashes of skin. "No, no..." I gripped the edges of the cloak and pulled them back together. "Keep it closed, like this, until you find a dress to put on underneath."

She acted like a child. I listened for her thoughts, but a void surrounded her. Total silence. Was I accidentally repressing them, like Gideon had taught me, or was she truly thinking nothing at all?

"Listen," I began walking. There wasn't time to get sidetracked. I aimed for the road to Hodafez, calling over my shoulder, "I need to go. Keep the cloak." I paused, glancing back. "You *do* have a dress you can put on, don't you?"

She shook her head, still grinning, and followed me, matching my pace. "Could I borrow one from you?"

"Borrow—you—" I faltered, then began to walk faster. When she kept up, I gestured to myself. "I don't have a spare dress with me." Sarcasm dripped from my voice, but she didn't seem to notice.

"That's okay." She tripped over nothing and caught herself.

"Have you been drinking?" I asked. That would explain the complete lack of clothes. Well, *explain* might be stretching it.

"Drinking what?" she asked. "Ooh, I've heard of drinking, could we try it?"

I slowed my pace, eyeing her. "What's your name? Where are you from?" Another glance as we walked and this time I was the one who tripped, as my eyes widened. "Are those *gills* on your neck?"

"Yes," she said simply, tripping as well, but smiling as if it were some accomplishment. "And my name is Grand Tsaretska Marena Yuryevna Mniszech." Her tone inferred this title should mean something to me.

"Are you a Jinni?" I asked in hushed tones, stopping in the middle of the road.

She whirled to face me, cloak flying open. "How rude!"

"I'm… sorry?" I resumed walking. It'd been a foolish question. She was nothing like Gideon, besides her fair skin. Instead of blue eyes, her's were a greenish color with flecks of blue, and even—was that, did I catch a hint of purple? It was impossible to tell while walking, with her facing the road. But while Gideon's hair was as dark as a moonless night, her red hair grew more fiery every second as the sun rose. Where Gideon stood tall and strong, this girl was diminutive. Waif-like enough that a heavy wind could likely carry her away.

"I'm from Rusalka," she said, as she struggled to keep up with me. She made walking look like a difficult task.

Rusalka was in the depths of the ocean; a place humans had never and would never see.

"You're a… Meremaid?" I trailed off, staring openly now. "I've never, that is, I—" I stumbled over my words, searching for a respectful way to ask what in the name of Jinn had made her leave her watery kingdom? "It's not everyday I meet a Meremaid. In fact, I don't believe I've ever had the pleasure…"

"That's because the Mere can't stand humans." She shrugged, smiling. "And don't get me started on the Jinn." She made a strange trill of disgust that sounded distinctly dolphin-like.

Even as she spoke, all I sensed around her was dead air.

Not a single thought.

Not about me, or even an inane one about what a lovely day it was or how perfect the weather.

I slowed. Memories resurfaced from my training growing up. It was rumored the Mere were immune to Jinni's Gifts—

something to do with the bad blood between the two races that led to the Mere creating protection spells and boundary lines, withdrawing to the sea over the last few centuries.

I wanted to tell Kadin. What if they would share their protection spells with the humans? Could they be convinced to share if they hated our kind so much?

I tensed, wondering if she could read my mind like Gideon, but she only kicked at the edges of the cloak as she walked, engrossed by the way it flung out with each step.

"Where's your tail?" I blurted out. Once the words left my mouth, I cringed. I'd been away from court etiquette for too long, the crew's honesty had rubbed off on me. I shrugged off the thought, uncomfortable with the way it made me miss them.

Fortunately, she only laughed, touching her shell necklace. "We have spells for everything."

On the road ahead, a farmer's cart approached, distracting me from the strange girl and reminding me of my mission. "Keep your cloak closed," I hissed. "If he sees what you're wearing—or rather, not wearing—he'll have questions. I don't have time for that."

"We don't?"

"*I* don't," I repeated, emphasizing the singular. She was *not* coming with me. "If you want someone to see you in your birthday dress, be my guest, but I'm in a hurry."

"I don't own a birthday dress," she replied, keeping up with me even when I picked up my pace, stumbling less and less. "Where can I get one of those? And why are you in a hurry?"

I resisted rolling my eyes. After this was over, it would be wise to be on good terms with the Mere. I needed to tread carefully. "I have to get home. My father's in trouble."

"Where's home?" she asked, obediently pulling her cloak together as the farmer drove by on his cart.

Did he notice her bare feet? Whether he did or not, he didn't stop.

I let out a breath, pointing to where the Hodafez castle nestled on one of the mountains in the distance. "That's it right there."

"That's far. How long will that take us?"

I half laughed, but her face was solemn. "I do apologize," I said, summoning up a politeness I didn't feel. "But I'm afraid I have to make this journey alone."

"Why?"

My mouth opened and closed. How to tell her I planned to sneak into my own home? "I just have to."

"But you promised me a dress."

"I didn't—you can't—" I threw my hands up. "I'm not going through the front gate, okay? I need to keep my presence a secret. Having company would make that ten times harder." There. Straightforward without being rude.

"I love secrets." She grinned at me. "Don't worry. I'm very good at keeping them." The Mere didn't seem to understand subtleties. "How long until we reach the castle?"

I blew out a breath. Glancing up at the mountains again, and the long road that stretched out across the distance, I murmured. "It'll take all morning just to reach the town. Maybe longer." I stopped in the road to face her. "Listen. *If* we reach the castle without incident, and *if* I manage to find my way inside, and *if* we actually reach my rooms without anyone discovering us, I will give you a dress if you swear not to tell a single soul."

"I suppose I can spare a morning," she said, as if she was doing *me* a favor. "Very well, I agree."

Chapter Thirty-Nine

Kadin

I'D SAT HOLDING THE crown for hours. Just staring at the diamonds encrusted all across the delicate circlet. The men had given up trying to reach me. Naveed had brought me the noon meal, but I hadn't touched it. Somewhere around mid-afternoon, Illium had said his goodbyes. "Was here for the treasure, not the Jinni," he'd said, standing in the open door of my room, fiddling with his bags that held his potions and his take from the last heist. "Gonna go back to working alone. Prefer it that way."

I'd only nodded. I wasn't surprised.

If anything, I was baffled the others stayed. We'd accomplished what we set out to do. Four years of hard work culminating in one night of justice. So why didn't it feel like enough? Why did it feel so empty? And why was I worrying about a girl who embodied everything I'd spent so many years detesting?

They checked on me throughout the day, confused as to why we weren't planning the next big heist. Except Naveed. He understood.

Oh, and Gideon, who didn't understand at all.

He'd been furious.

When Bosh had wandered through the door earlier and found me staring at the crown, and the missing lamp, he'd called the others in.

"Arie stole the lamp!" he'd hissed as they filed into the room. "Why would she do that, boss?"

I hadn't had an answer for him.

The others stared at the crown and empty pack. "Why'd she have a crown?" Daichi asked.

"Don't ask me," Ryo answered with a shrug.

Naveed tapped my shoulder and signed, *Why?*

"Good question," I replied. I tried to be logical, but it hurt. Arie had betrayed us without a second thought. Maybe I'd been right about her all along. Gifted people used people.

"She stole it," Bosh repeated the lie I'd told him a few days ago. "But I told her we don't steal from each other—she wouldn't take… she'll bring the lamp back, right?" His voice squeaked with emotion. "I don't understand how she could just take it!"

"Excuse me?" Gideon's soft voice came from the corner.

Oh, Jinni save me.

I raised my head to find him standing by the table.

His knuckles were white as he gripped his cane, his movements graceful, yet dangerous, like a panther. "Where did she go? Why would she take it?"

"I don't know," I said flatly. "I don't know why *you* want it. I don't even know what it does."

"She said nothing else?"

The way Gideon asked made me feel inferior, as if I should have noticed. "No. I can't read minds like you," I snapped, losing it.

My men gasped.

It occurred to me that I'd kept secrets too.

A heaviness filled the room, as Gideon's face darkened and those clear blue eyes clouded. "You've lost track of my payment. I would watch your tone if I were you."

Bosh shrunk back against the wall. Daichi and Naveed glanced between us, while Ryo pushed off the door frame, looking ready to run if necessary. But I was no longer afraid of Gideon. He had his code to follow, after all.

"Take the crown, then," I snapped, holding the offensive piece out to him.

Instead of answering, he'd vanished.

And now here I sat, still on my bed, hours later. I'd pieced together where Arie was headed. I just didn't understand how she thought she could reach Hodafez—at least three day's ride from here—by sunset? Even now, the sun made its way across the sky toward the horizon.

Naveed brought dinner. The others trickled in with their meals as well, not saying a word, keeping me company.

I picked up my bowl to eat without tasting it. "We'll stay here another night," I began, but cut off as Gideon materialized in front of us.

"There's no sign of her within miles of here," he said in a terse voice. "I *must* get that lamp. You know her better than I, where would she go?"

I shrugged. "I know where she wants to go, but there's no way she could get there. Not for days at least."

"Don't worry about travel," Gideon said, unblinking. "Tell me where she went."

I spoke on impulse. "If I tell you, you have to swear you'll take us with you." I checked my mental walls, wishing there was a way to flex and make them even stronger.

"Why would we go after her?" Ryo asked, frowning.

"Because no one steals from us." I set down my bowl, no longer hungry.

And? Naveed signed.

He knew me too well. I sighed, running a hand through my hair. "And I think she's upset. She might need our help."

Daichi tsked. "Ah yes. You mean when Gideon took the prince's tongue. That had me unnerved as well."

"It's a bit bigger than that." I shook my head, glancing at Gideon. The color had returned to his pale skin, more obvious in the shadows, an ever-present reminder that he was something other. Something beyond my understanding. Listening to my every thought. He hadn't responded to my request. "What does the lamp do, anyway?"

Gideon didn't speak for a long moment, crossing the room to stand by the window. "It imitates the Gift that many in Jinn possess," he said softly, staring out at the setting sun. "It takes you wherever you want to go in a heartbeat."

"Ah." I raised my brows. The missing pieces of Arie's plan fell into place and I knew exactly where she was. I stood. "In that case we'd better get going. We have a wedding to stop."

Chapter Forty

Arie

WE HIKED THE DIRT road that twisted up the side of the rocky mountain toward Hodafez. The Mere girl admired the castle where it loomed ahead of us, a glaring white in the sun.

But when we slipped through the city gate, I guided her away from it, down narrow dirt streets that led parallel to the castle, keeping my distance. There was no telling where Amir may have posted guards, or how many. A few villagers noticed us pass, but most were too busy heading to Summer's Eve celebrations, or at home sleeping through the heat of the day.

We rounded the outskirts of the city, sticking close to the wall as long as possible. I held up a hand when we reached a dead end.

On our right, the wall curved with the line of the cliffs and the sea beyond and now blocked our path, with dwellings built up against it. Retracing our steps, we finally began to move deeper into the city, toward the castle.

"This is so thrilling," the Mere girl said. I'd forgotten her name already. I'd told her only my first name and that my father was inside the castle, nothing more.

"If thrilling to you means risking our lives, then sure," I replied, keeping my attention on the castle wall ahead and the guards posted there. They were my father's soldiers, marching along the wall as usual from one post to the next. It was possible they were still loyal to me. Far more likely they were touched by Amir's Gift. Better not take any chances.

The main castle entrance yawned open and inviting below them, but it was too visible, with a guardhouse beside it. A smaller gate for the stables was also open, and much closer to us; this was the gate I hoped to use. I halted in the shadows, pulling the girl back.

"Listen, Zarena Marena... whatever your name is..."

"Call me Rena." She laughed.

"Mmhmm, whatever you say," I agreed, still watching the guards. "When I say go, we're going to run for the stables, got it?" Eyes trained on the guards as they walked, I waited for them to reach the far end of their track. This would be their blind spot, but it would only last a few seconds. "Now!"

I ran across the courtyard, ducking into the back of the stables. As my eyes adjusted, I peered around to make sure I was alone. Nearby, I heard the clank of metal on metal, and a couple horses nickered, but I didn't have time to greet them.

I turned to find the Mere girl—Rena—staggering across the space with arms flying wildly as if she'd never run in her life.

I supposed she hadn't.

She lurched inside and I held a finger to my lips, listening. When no one called out, I waved for her to follow me through the quiet stables. A hum of thoughts came from the far side of the room, not audible enough to make out, but enough to avoid running into their owner.

We crept to the far end of the stables, where the stalls had been converted to store grains, saddles, bridles, and other equipment. Entering quietly, I shut the stable door behind me, peering over the top of it to make sure no one had seen us before I crept to the back wall.

I lifted my hand to a brick, but paused to meet Rena's gaze. "You must never speak of this to anyone, do you understand?"

She made a fist and hit her chest. "On my honor or you can feed me to the sharks."

I blinked and opened my mouth, but had no words. Instead, I faced the wall and pressed on the brick. It was smoother than the rest and if you looked closely, the mixture surrounding this brick was lighter in color—a soft clay instead of mortar, with a spring behind it. As I let go it sprung back into place while the wall began to shift and open beside it.

"Wow," Rena gasped, green eyes wide. "I've never seen anything like it."

"Neither has anyone else here," I muttered as I stepped into the dark tunnel, waving for her to follow. "And I'd like to keep it that way, if you don't mind."

I pressed another piece of the door and it slowly swung itself back into place until it latched shut, locking us inside the pitch-black tunnel.

I felt along the wall for the lantern that hung there, wishing I'd thought to pick it up while I could see.

"What is that?"

"Nothing," I mumbled, pulling the lantern down by feel and then running my fingers over the shelf where it'd sat to find a match.

"What're you doing?" she asked.

"You'll see."

I struck the match and she gasped. "There's some strange magic attacking your fingers!"

"It's just fire." If this were any other time, I would've laughed, but I couldn't summon the feeling now. I lit the lamp and blew the match out, tossing it to the ground.

"What is fire for?"

I sighed, pinching the bridge of my nose with my fingers. Was it really a relief to not hear her thoughts if she spoke every single one of them?

"Fire is good for a lot of things. Keeping warm, being able to see at night." I explained, moving into the tunnels at a slow pace, making sure I didn't stumble on the uneven floor.

"But it's so much easier to see without it," she whined.

That piqued my curiosity. "You can see in the dark?"

"Of course, can't you?"

I glanced over at the strange girl, shaking my head as I finally let out a small laugh. "Um… No."

She followed me through the winding tunnels, as I led us through one corridor after another, climbing a set of stairs before reaching a long, rectangular dead end. On the other side was the mirror to my bedroom.

It seemed like years since I'd wandered these tunnels with Havah.

There wasn't a peep hole, for privacy's sake, so I set my ear to the crack along the wall. Was there anyone inside?

I stood there for a full five minutes to make sure, holding my finger to my lips when Rena tried to speak. That, at least, she seemed to understand.

Finally, I pressed the latch that opened the secret door. The mirror swung out into the room on silent hinges.

No one was inside.

We entered my chambers, and I swung the mirror back against the wall, latching it before I crept to the closet, the bath, and the outer room, checking each one to make sure we were alone before I spoke. "It's safe. Let's get you dressed."

Inside the closet, I pulled the first gown I could reach off the hook—a simple dark green with a modest neckline. The girl was smaller than me, both in height as well as in the hips and bust, so I doubted it would fit her perfectly, but it would do. Anything was better than what she currently wore.

When I held it out to her, she shook her head. "That's a drab color. What about this one!" She plucked a bright blue dress from where it hung on the other side. "This looks like the ocean when you swim near the surface. And the jewels are like when the sun shines down and makes it sparkle."

I shrugged. "I guess it kind of is."

She tossed the cloak I'd given her to the floor and began to struggle with the dress.

"Here, let me." I carefully untied the strings at the back and helped her step into it before lacing it up.

"Oh, stop it this instant," she squealed as I tugged the laces. "I can't breathe!"

"Women aren't supposed to be able to breathe," I said with a small smile, but I tied them more loosely.

"Humans are so strange." She held up her long sleeve to admire the way the extra fabric draped, nearly touching the floor when she lowered her wrist.

"I suppose we are." I stepped back to admire my work. "Nonetheless, you're much more likely to blend in now that you're not running around..." I trailed off. "You know... as you were."

"In my birthday dress," she said with a grin.

"Ah. So you got that after all." I half-smiled before turning toward my bedroom. "Listen, I need you to stay here. There's something I need to do."

"What is it?" she asked.

I'd grown so used to her questions that I barely heard her. By my bedside I found my regular oil lamp, where it usually was, and peered inside. It was full. I pulled the Jinni lamp from my pocket and set it on the table as well.

Transferring the oil, I avoided touching the Jinni lamp, in case even a drop might transport me elsewhere.

I filled the Jinni's lamp halfway, stopping when I spilled a bit on the floor.

"Can I help?" Rena piped up when I didn't answer.

"No. I'm sorry. I have to go alone." I stopped when I saw her face. The way her shoulders slumped. "You can... help yourself to my jewelry box," I offered, gesturing toward the table. Whatever it took for her to look away.

"I suppose I can wait for you here." She trailed a finger along the bed frame and moved toward the jewelry box.

I took advantage of her distraction, stretching out my hand to grip the base of the lamp as I firmly imagined the place I wanted.

The room flashed around me, shifting into my father's chambers. He wasn't there. Where else would he be? My mind pictured another place. I hoped I was wrong, even as I gripped the lamp and imagined a space I'd only seen a few times before. A deep darkness surrounded me, only penetrated by the tiny light of my candle. Swiveling around, I worried that I'd chosen wrong, when my foot bumped something behind me.

"Baba!" I cried, barely remembering to keep my voice down. Kneeling beside him, I brought the lamp close to see his injuries, but couldn't make out the details through the blur of tears. "What happened? How did you get in here?"

He groaned and mumbled something I couldn't make out. His eyes opened. "Arie, you're alive!" His excitement made him cough, wheezing as he tried to catch his breath. "I was so worried!"

"I'm so sorry, Baba." I took his hand, feeling the guilt press down on me like the entire mountain sat on my chest.

His eyes fluttered shut as if he couldn't keep them open.

"I thought I was doing the right thing. I thought Amir would leave you alone. This is all my fault." I pressed my hand to his forehead. He was burning up. "You have a fever," I told him, even though he wasn't responding. "Don't worry. I'm going to get you out of here."

Squeezing his hand, I gripped the lamp in the other and envisioned the main street in town where I thought a healer lived.

The landscape shifted around me once more. I found myself kneeling on a quiet street.

Alone.

"No!" I cried out. The night sky was full of stars and the quiet, clear road mocked me.

Without thinking, I clutched the lamp and pictured my father's cell. The scenery flashed and I was in the dungeon once more. My father hadn't moved.

I set the lamp down on the damp stone floor, not wanting to travel again without meaning to. The infuriating object allowed *me* to travel… but no one else.

Staring at the flickering light, I wanted to scream. I could try to send my father away with the lamp. But he didn't look well enough to make it on his own. Would he even wake up? I could leave and come back with help. But what if something happened to him in the meantime? I would never forgive myself.

I shook my head, settling back on my heels and pressing the palms of my hands to my eyes. Who would help me? Who could resist Amir? Only I knew when he used his Gift; everyone else fell under his power. Maybe Gideon could've helped, but I'd left him behind.

The light sputtered.

Startled from my thoughts, I leaned forward to look at it. The oil was low. All my traveling back and forth must've used up quite a bit. Did I even have enough to return to my room? If Amir found me here, there'd be no explanation.

From inside this cell there was nothing I could do. I would lead Rena back out of the castle—better to have her roaming the village streets than the castle corridors, in case she broke her word and told someone I was there—and then I'd find the keys to the prison and come back for Baba.

Shaping the image of my bedchambers in my mind, tears dripping onto my father's prone form as I let go of his hand, I gripped the candle and let it whisk me back to my room.

Rena wasn't there.

Instinct made me hide the lamp in the secret tunnels before I moved through my bedroom into the outer room that led to the hall. I paused at the door. Why was I going after the girl? She wasn't important right now. I needed to save my father.

I slipped into the hall, determined to steal a key to my father's cell and get him out of there.

"Just where do you think you're going?" a man's voice rang out. I knew that voice.

I walked faster.

"Guards. Detain her." The familiar sense of a Gifting washed over me.

I ran.

"Stop!" The Gifting wrapped itself around my feet, making them sluggish as if wading through water. "You don't want to be rude to your guest, Princess Arie," King Amir called. His voice drew nearer. Footsteps sounded on the marble floor. One set sounded like the slapping of bare feet. "Come back and chat with us for a moment. Your little friend says you snuck in, but won't say how. Maybe you'll tell me…" A steel undertone lined his voice. Despite my wishes, my feet turned to obey, and I met them in the middle of the hall.

"I didn't know you were getting married!" Rena clapped her hands as we came face to face, shaking her head. "I don't know why you kept it a secret—your fiancée is so charming!" I frowned, confused. Weren't the Mere immune to a Jinni's Gift?

Amir smiled over at her and winked. Ah. She might be immune, but she couldn't spot a lie to save her life.

"She's just shy about my seeing her on our wedding day," Amir purred. He turned toward me, and I felt the full force of his Gift as he added, "Aren't you?"

Gritting my teeth, I nodded like a puppet.

Chapter Forty-One

Arie

KING AMIR SUMMONED A man who'd been standing unnoticed a few feet behind the king with his guards. I startled when my eyes landed on him. He was a Jinni!

Violet eyes and pale skin, tinted with a faint blue just like Gideon's, his hair was tied back and he stood just a bit taller, but they could've easily been brothers. He carried himself like a soldier.

"This is my friend, Enoch," Amir said, clapping a hand on the Jinni's shoulder, who didn't react. "And you are safe here with us. Your father is resting now, but he'll be excited to see you when he wakes."

Despite everything I'd just seen, a sense of peace stole over me and I believed him. Of course, we were safe. And my father was comfortable. King Amir would never hurt him. My body relaxed and my mouth tilted into a smile. I bit the inside of my cheek. Hard. The pain snapped me out of it, back to reality, as I tasted blood.

"I'd like to see him," I managed to say, hating the way my voice trembled.

His eyes narrowed. *She has a strong mind.*

I should've pretended to be more confused. He studied me as I stood there. My father's men did nothing. Their loyalties had shifted.

"You don't need to see him," Amir told me, still using his Gift. My mind stretched, fighting it but struggling. "You've a wedding to plan, doesn't she, Enoch?"

His syrupy voice was nothing compared to Enoch's response. The Jinni placed his hand on Amir's shoulder, and spoke for the first time, "Yes, you do, Princess."

Everything else faded.

"I've never seen such a happy bride." Amir's words made my ears pound. Excitement flowed through my bones, coursing through my blood and making my heart beat faster.

I grinned and clapped my hands like a little girl with her first pony. "I can't wait!" The feeling of joy was powerful, surging over me like a wave. "How long do we have?"

"Just a few hours." Amir smiled back. He wouldn't be so bad to marry. I wondered what my dress looked like. "See," the king turned to Rena, who was blinking between us, fascinated. "She's a joyous bride. I'd wager she would be thrilled to have one of the Mere as a bridesmaid, if that would interest you? You could wear as many jewels as you'd like."

His words drew my eyes to her neck and hands, which were covered in gold necklaces and rings, glittering with diamonds and jewels. She'd definitely been enjoying my jewelry box.

She stepped forward and took my hands, beaming, "It's settled then. I'll do it!"

"This way, my dear," Amir said to her with a smile. "We'll find someone to take care of you." He left as quickly as he'd arrived, with the strange, silent Jinni and Rena on his heels.

And they were gone.

Normally, I could shake off Amir's Gift within minutes. But this time, as I woke from my stupor, I found myself standing on the dressing room floor with Havah cooing over me as she drew a bath. While she described my wedding dress and elegant hairstyle options in detail, it slowly dawned on me that this happiness wasn't real. It took even longer before I remembered why.

Whatever the violet-eyed Jinni had done when he'd placed his hand on Amir's shoulder had amplified the king's Gift a hundred-fold.

Everything felt numb and distant as the truth of my circumstances finally reached me. My eyes filled with tears. I had to fight this. Somehow. But if I thought about it for one more second, I'd break.

Chapter Forty-Two

Kadin

WE SUFFERED THROUGH THE twist of traveling impossibly fast, standing in front of the Red Rose one moment, then in the forest beside a road the next. It was a vast distance to cross in mere seconds and my body rebelled, shivering and sweating simultaneously.

Bosh groaned, while Daichi outright heaved in the bushes. My own stomach felt unsettled, but I ignored it. "Where are we?"

"This is just a short walk from Hodafez," Gideon replied, pointing behind me.

I swung around. The peak of a mountain stood before us with a small city surrounding a beautiful white stone castle. Whisps of clouds brushed the tips of its towers.

I cleared my throat, searching for a diplomatic way to ask Gideon, "Why didn't you bring us closer?"

"If we were to appear at the front gate it would be very unsettling." Gideon stepped onto the road and began to walk, not waiting for us.

"Obviously." I resisted rolling my eyes as my men and I followed. "I meant, why didn't you bring us somewhere inside the castle, out of sight? Save us the walk?"

"That's breaking the rules," he replied, swinging his cane more like a walking stick.

I stared at his back. "What? To appear in the castle without an invitation?" I asked. "You just did that a few days ago!" The dirt road was steep and I was already out of breath.

"That's different. I had an invitation," Gideon replied. It was hard to read him by the back of his head.

"How so?" I demanded, picking up my pace until I walked beside him.

"Because you called for me."

I groaned. "I'm sure Arie would call now, if she could."

"That's not the same," Gideon said without looking at me.

"You care about her too. I know you do. She could be in trouble." Running my hands through my hair, I struggled to find some other form of logic to convince him. "What if they catch her? What if they kill her father? If your stubbornness keeps us from helping her, it will be your fault."

At my words, Naveed signed, *Don't be stupid.*

Bells rang out from the city above, letting all within earshot know of an event. Either a wedding or a funeral. Which meant that either Arie had been captured, or her father was dead. Either way, she needed help.

Gideon tapped his cane on the ground. "Tell me, why is it so important to you to save her?"

With my men listening, I struggled to form words. I could say so many things. She was the most confident girl I'd ever met. Fierce. Intelligent. It didn't hurt that she was gorgeous either. But none of that came out.

The men stared at me as we walked, eyebrows raised. A hint of a smile appeared on Gideon's lips.

"I don't know. It just is," I answered lamely. "But you need the lamp, otherwise you wouldn't have come all this way. You've gone to great lengths for it, don't you have any other tricks or Gifts you could use to help Arie?"

Though I'd always considered the Gifted to be selfish, I'd come to know Gideon well enough to believe better of him. To believe he had a heart. As I thought this, he nodded to me, just once. "I do," he murmured. I wondered whether he was answering my verbal thought or my silent one.

"Do you have a plan?" I asked him.

Gideon met my eyes. "This is your venture, Master Kadin. The plan is up to you."

People were staring at us. At Gideon, really. A Jinni in plain sight—whispers began to float along the air.

"I see them," Gideon replied before I could point out that he was drawing attention. He bent to pick up a stick, running his hand across it before handing the now engraved piece of wood to me. "Call me back when you're ready," he murmured, and disappeared before I could respond.

Chapter Forty-Three

Arie

THE WHITE SILK WEDDING dress flowed over my curves, hugging them until it hit my knees, where it flowed out in an abundance of fabric. The enormous tiara on my head belonged to my mother. I'd never worn it before today.

"You look just like her," Farideh breathed.

Havah wiped a tear from her eye. "You'll make a beautiful queen." As if this was what mattered most.

Like everyone else, they were convinced this was the wedding day of my dreams. Nothing I said could sway them. I knew, because I'd tried. If one more person told me it was just pre-wedding nerves, I didn't know what I'd do, so I clenched my teeth and stayed silent.

Without meaning to, I saw myself through Havah's eyes. Honey-toned skin, dark brown eyes flecked with amber, face framed with waves of black hair that touched my lower back, dripping with diamonds around my neck, hanging from my ears, and of course, a thick coating of them on my crown.

A vision, Havah thought as she sniffed, turning away to compose herself.

I supposed I was.

But I found no joy in it.

My wedding would take place at sunset in the midst of the Summer's Eve feasting and dancing. It seemed as if Amir had never bothered to cancel it. The whole castle buzzed with delight and anticipation.

Even though the young woman staring back at me in the mirror wasn't smiling, when I glimpsed myself through Havah's eyes once more, I was a vision of pure joy. How was that possible? This new trait of my Gift only made me feel more alone than ever.

Shaking the image from my mind, I avoided my reflection, remembering instead the vision of my father lying broken in his cell, which was burned into my memory. I needed to act quickly. It was tempting to use the tunnels and try to escape, but this time I needed to take a stand, otherwise Amir would never stop.

"Havah," I said, "would you be a dear and go fetch my mother's... perfume?" I grasped at straws, searching for something that hadn't already been provided to me. "I want something to remind me of her."

"Oh, how lovely!" Havah sighed yet again. "Of course, I'll be right back."

Alone, I hurried to dig through my drawers, searching for a weapon. Anything sharp really, but a dagger would be nice. I tried to remember where I kept that small blade from a childhood birthday. Had I left it in the stables after my last ride?

As I searched for it or a sharp object of any kind, I came up empty. "Come on, come on," I muttered as I raced to the closet, digging through the shelves in the back, making a mess. But if there'd been a weapon of any kind, it'd been stripped from the room.

I sank down on the bed. I'd never felt so alone.

At that moment, the door clicked open and Havah returned. "What's wrong?" she asked when she saw my posture.

"Oh, now you can tell something's wrong?" I snapped. It was unfair of me. She was under his influence, or she would've listened.

The bed dipped as she settled onto it beside me and wrapped her arms around my shoulder. "You can tell me," she said gently as she rubbed my arm.

I wanted to scream. Instead, I pulled out of her embrace and turned to look at her, taking her hands and squeezing. "Will you do something for me, Havah? Please? Without any explanation?"

Her forehead wrinkled at the pressure on her hands and my strange request, but I pressed harder. "Please. You've known me my whole life. Do you trust me?"

"Of course." Havah smiled as she tucked a loose strand of my hair behind my ear. "Tell me what's got you so upset?"

"I will, I promise." And if I lived through this, I vowed that I would. "But right now, I need you to do something for me, and I need you to keep it a secret. Can you do that?"

Slowly, Havah nodded, though her frown deepened.

"In the stables, I have a dagger," I began. When Havah reacted, trying to tug her hands out of mine, I squeezed tighter, leaning toward her so she couldn't help but meet my eye. "It was a gift, from my father," I added, stretching for an explanation that wouldn't raise any alarms. "I'm worried about him, Havah."

I hoped against hope that the mention of him might trigger some real memory of what was going on, but she raised her brows and asked, "Whatever for? He's just taking a short nap before the festivities begin." So, that's what he was telling them.

"It's hard to explain," I said finally. Harder still for her to understand with the fog of Amir's Gift clouding her mind. "But I need it. Would you get it for me?" I begged, tears coming to my eyes despite my best efforts. "Please, Havah? Would you help me?"

"Of course, I will, Arie-zada," she smiled, pressing my hands between hers before wiping my cheek where a tear had slipped out. "I don't know what's gotten into you, but if this will make you feel better, I'm happy to help."

We stood together and I hurried her toward the door. "Thank you," I whispered, voice cracking. "Promise me you won't tell anyone—do you promise?" I made her swear to me twice that she wouldn't tell a soul before allowing her to leave, but she paused at the door, hand fluttering to her heart as she teared up.

"What's wrong?" A flicker of hope mixed with worry rose in me. Was she finding her way out from under the compulsion? Or was she second guessing my request?

But she smiled through her tears. "I'm just so happy for you," she said, her voice rising high and squeaky. "You've found your prince!"

Whisking out of the room, she shut the door behind her before I could answer.

Alone, I wrung my hands, wondering if she'd keep her promise. Would she bring me my dagger or would she tell someone? Was the dagger even there to be found?

"I'm not looking for a prince!" I snapped at the closed door, kicking at my skirt as I paced. "I'm looking for a sword!"

Chapter Forty-Four

Kadin

MY MEN AND I slipped into the city of Hodafez unnoticed in the chaos and festivities. Fireworks sounded even though it was still daylight. Children ran about with sparklers and ribbons.

"Good sir," I stopped a man headed toward the castle dragging along a toddler while his wife carried the baby. "Where are you headed on this fine day?"

"Haven't you heard?" He hiked the child higher as he walked. "It's Summer's Eve—" My spirits lifted as he hoisted the child, but then he added, "and the royal wedding is tonight at sunset! The whole town is invited. We're going to get in line now."

I let the man go ahead, slowing as that sunk in.

Had Arie agreed to the wedding then? I'd tried not to think on it too closely, but somehow, I'd hoped she'd find another way.

I picked up my pace. "Looks like we're going to enter the castle the old-fashioned way."

"In broad daylight?" Bosh whispered loudly as he caught up to me. "How are we going to do that?"

"What about 'Ladies-in-Waiting'?" Ryo offered. "That might work during the day."

"I am *not* wearing a dress," Daichi argued. "'Ghost in the Stable' would be better."

"There's twice as many guards during the day," Ryo replied, smacking him on the shoulder. "Not to mention the *sun*. They'd never fall for that."

Twice as many guards. The wheels turned in my head as they argued and Naveed signed, all vying for a different scheme.

"I was thinking 'Pick Your Poison,'" I interrupted.

Ryo scratched the stubble on his chin and mumbled, "That could work."

Naveed nodded, and no one argued, which was enough for me. "Let's get to work."

Chapter Forty-Five

Arie

I WAS EXPECTED TO walk down the aisle on my own. I stood at the back of the Great Hall, built to hold a thousand and tall enough to stack the tables on themselves ten times before reaching the ceiling.

King Amir smirked at the opposite end of the long white runner on the dais, next to the holy man in his ceremonial robes. The Mere-girl, Rena, stood next to the holy man, wearing an enormous amount of jewelry, grinning like an idiot.

Other familiar faces sat in the audience. Lady Eiena from the northern kingdom of Ahdamon, King Zhubin of Keshdi, Tahran-Shah and Sirjan-Shah from my last courtship tour, and other royals from neighboring kingdoms, were all seated toward the front of the room, while the villagers of Hodafez were seated further back.

I hid my clenched fists in my skirts and struggled to keep my lips from pursing in disgust. I doubted I looked anything like a happy bride. Yet when the guests faced me, every single one of them glowed with happiness.

"Look how happy she is," King Amir said.

"Look how happy she is," Enoch intoned.

They beamed.

Only Rena seemed to sense that something was off, frowning from her place by the altar.

Digging in my heels, I refused to move. I stared down the aisle at Amir and wished my Gift could've been flames shooting from my eyes instead of this wretched mind-reading, which had grown increasingly out of control.

At this point, bits and pieces of every thought, along with all kinds of images, echoed in my mind, no matter if they were related to me or not. And no matter how important—or unimportant. The number of times I'd listened to someone wish for a washroom since the Summer's Eve celebration had begun was ridiculous.

Weddings were a solemn and silent occasion—yet I felt as if I was standing in the midst of a raucous crowd, everyone jostling and yelling over each other.

Amir waved for the guards to walk me down the aisle. I dragged my feet, but let them, fighting the urge to curl up in a helpless ball.

I imagined a jar to contain the thoughts like Gideon had taught me. But it felt as if thousands of them scurried around, vying for attention. Each time I put one in the jar, five more rose to take its place. There were too many to manage. The mental jar dissolved.

I concentrated my rage on Amir, which seemed to lower the volume in the room to a tolerable roar. Difficult to ignore, but manageable.

"Where is my father?" I called across the enormous room. Maybe not so controlled after all. My fury broke through the soft enchantment of the crowd, ruining the ambience, but though they murmured briefly, the response was contained. Muted.

"He'll be here shortly," King Amir replied. "Come to the altar now, Princess Arie."

Though there was no sign he was telling the truth, I nodded. A small part of me protested even as my feet kept moving.

"She's such a happy bride." His melodic, Gifted voice soothed those near the front. Faces smoothed over.

"She is such a happy bride," Enoch repeated, and this time, the wave of assurance passed over the room so deeply that I felt it in my bones.

Everyone's thoughts united as they repeated his words silently to themselves.

Even though Enoch's words weren't directed at me, I still had to fight them.

As they listened, the vast number of thoughts around the room dropped to a trickle. I'd never expected to want them back, but I wished for their presence now, for someone to still have enough awareness to resist.

The faces I passed by were blank. Empty. Void of self-control. Was resistance even possible?

No doubt Amir expected me to become docile as well. I didn't know what to do. If I struggled it would reveal my Gift. If I didn't...

"Why does she seem unhappy?" Rena asked, unfazed. I could've kissed her. Finally, someone was speaking up!

"It's customary to resist at a wedding." Amir smiled at her. "If she did not, I would be dishonored."

A tiny wrinkle stayed on her forehead as she watched me. Words wouldn't come.

Concentrating, I willed her to be aware of the lies.

"Isn't that right, Enoch?" Amir growled.

"Princess Arie's struggles aren't real," Enoch intoned. "She will stop resisting now."

And I did.

As they deposited me in front of Amir, I stopped thrashing, despite my best intentions. Seeing that I'd lost this first battle, I gave in to the Gift, allowing him to think it had removed my free will completely, willing my face into complacency.

I still had one last resort.

Chapter Forty-Six

Kadin

MY MEN AND I slipped behind the guard house. When one guard left to take a leak, Naveed glided out after him and disappeared. A pair of guards stepped out next, off to take a shift somewhere. I took the lead this time, and Bosh followed.

"Excuse me, sir," I spoke to the chattier guard, handing him a piece of rolled parchment. "It's your mother. There was an accident. You're needed at home as soon as possible."

"What is it? What happened?" Under the helmet, his eyes were wide and panicked as he took the parchment, but didn't unroll it.

"No time to explain, my friend," I urged him. "Just go. Run!"

He took off down a side street and I made to follow, hoping he wouldn't unroll the sheet and find it blank until a private alley. Behind me, I heard the other guard roar as Bosh did what he did best. "Stop, thief!"

A few minutes later, I returned to our hiding place behind the guard shack to find Bosh already there, tugging a helmet on. "I win."

I grinned as I pushed back the sword strapped to my waist to sit. "Yes, you do."

We waited for Naveed, Daichi, and Ryo to trickle back with their new armor as well. The two cousins returned last, bickering as usual.

"No time for that," I reprimanded them. "Let's go."

We stepped out in pairs, making our way through the small town toward the castle where it rose ahead of us. Bosh and I entered the crowd making its way toward the castle courtyard without a problem. A bottleneck at the gate slowed everyone down, but ahead of us, inside the castle gates, the vast courtyard swarmed with people, eating and drinking as they celebrated Summer's Eve.

Daichi and Ryo slipped into the crowd a few paces back, still muttering under their breath to each other, while Naveed took up the tail. Ryo dropped back to walk with him in a huff. They were slowing to a stop when I heard a guard call, "Where are you headed?"

I tensed, glancing behind me. Of all the people, he'd chosen to ask, he'd spoken to Naveed.

My friend pointed to the castle, but it wasn't enough. "I asked you a question, boy!" When the guard's hand clamped down on Naveed's arm, I slowed, gritting my teeth.

Naveed subtly signed, *Keep going.*

Behind me Ryo tried to explain, "The lad lost his voice when that last illness was going around. Don't pay him any mind."

"I'm going to need you to come with me," the guard's strident voice carried. He wasn't buying it.

I didn't need to look back to know when they ran. The courtyard erupted in chaos as the guard yelled and took chase, calling others to follow.

Bosh and I ducked through the archway, entering the courtyard. Daichi appeared a second later, out of breath.

"Member of the Guard, coming through," I called out, pushing forward, and the protests turned to glares.

We moved together through the mass of people. "Should one of us go back to help them?" Bosh asked.

"They'll be alright," I kept an eye out for other guards. "They're fast. And they'll shed the armor as soon as they're out of sight." I'd worry until we met up with them again, but the others didn't need to know that. "We should hurry."

Down to three now, we set a brisk pace. The guards would be wary of any soldiers they didn't recognize. "Let's split up. Find the ceremony. Shouldn't be too hard."

"Then what?" Bosh glanced back to make sure none of the guards had spotted us.

I shrugged. "Stop the wedding." I licked my lips, wishing I had a piece of grass or something to chew on. "Whatever it takes."

We took off, separating until there were a good dozen paces between each of us. The crowds made our job easier. No one looked at a guard twice; they were too busy celebrating. I took the lead, weaving past cheerful dancers and drunks, and didn't look back.

As soon as I stepped through the enormous castle doors, which were propped open, I found the foyer filled with people from the city. They milled about, chattering in hushed tones, waiting for the feast.

I cleared my throat and commanded the nearest man, "Direct me to the wedding ceremony."

He blinked, startled, pointing across the room to tall, wooden doors. "In the Great Hall..."

I shoved through the crowd, hoping my men wouldn't lose sight of me. On the other side, four guards stood at the Great Hall entrance. My uniform now had the opposite affect that I'd originally intended. They spied me coming long before I reached them. Stepping up to the two on the left side of the door, I placed my back to the wall, imitating their stiff stance, and didn't say a word.

Though I received a sidelong glance, their focus was on Bosh who followed close behind me. I tilted my head toward the opposite side of the door. The kid took the hint, stepping into position beside the other two guards.

Daichi arrived next, and this time the guard beside me spoke. "We don't need you here. Go guard the entrance."

Daichi turned to go, but I clapped a hand on his shoulder and shrugged. "We were told to come here."

"Well, I'm telling you to go," the guard snapped, stepping out of line. "The ceremony is already started. Now do as you're told or lose your post!"

Out of the corner of his eye, Daichi glanced at me and I nodded, yelling, "Now!"

He punched the guard in the gut. The clang of his fist hitting armor resounded. His face twisted and he groaned as the guard tackled him.

I spun to face the guard still by my side and threw my full weight into knocking him down. Wrestling on the floor, I pinned him, but he fought back, flipping me off and punching me across the face. I fell back into the crowd. They stared down at me gaping, unsure whose side to take when both fighters appeared to be the king's men.

The guard who'd thrown me climbed to his feet. Behind him, my men fought bravely with the other three guards. I scrambled to my feet as well. We were outnumbered. Bosh crumpled to the ground, knocked out cold. Daichi roared and rushed his attackers, taking on two at once.

I ducked when a fist came at my face, turning back to the guard before me, narrowly missing the next punch. I swung wildly. The lack of aim had me hitting his shoulder, but it was enough to knock him off balance. One swift kick to the back of his legs and he fell. I used the weight of my armor and dropped on top of him. The breath whooshed from his lungs. Placing my hands around his neck, I cut off his air. Though he struggled, he couldn't free himself. As I applied more pressure, he passed out.

I stood, only to find that Daichi was also on the ground and both remaining guards were headed right for me. My hand went to my pocket and I gripped Gideon's talisman. He'd said to call. He'd said he needed an invitation. Well, maybe it was time to invite him.

I rubbed the stick as I jumped to the side to avoid being tackled.

"Finally," Gideon said, as he materialized in front of me. He reached down to touch the shoulder of the guard at his feet. Both he and the man disappeared, then reappeared at the entrance. A second later, Gideon returned, alone, leaving the guard on the opposite side of the room yelling over the crowd between us. Gideon's mouth tilted in the slightest smile as he turned toward the remaining guards and said over his shoulder, "I thought you'd never take the hint."

Chapter Forty-Seven

Arie

I FELT THE SLIGHT weight of the tiny dagger tucked into my intricate braids—the only place I could think to hide it where it was still within reach. It was barely longer than my finger, but it was razor sharp.

I hoped it would be enough. I'd yet to decide on the timing—whether now, in front of everyone when he least expected it, or later tonight when we'd be alone, but it'd be more of a risk. Either way almost guaranteed my death. A monarch couldn't be killed lightly.

The guards held me at the altar like a butterfly pinned down, but over the din of everyone's strangely idyllic and happy thoughts, I realized Amir was speaking aloud. Channeling my rage, I glared at him, and again, it gave me focus.

"You will be a happy bride today," he murmured with a false smile. The power of his words flowed over the room like a soft gust of air. When Enoch repeated it, the strength of the words hit me like a wave. I smiled up at Amir. Why had I been upset? This was the happiest day of my life. Soft whispers from the minds across the room reached me, of how beautiful I looked, of how lovely the ceremony, the flowers, the sun shining in and blessing this glorious day. I reveled in each thought.

The guards let go and stepped to the side as the king took my hands, pulling me up the two small steps to stand beside him. His beard brushed against my cheek as he kissed it and his hot, moist breath touched my ear. In the midst of my excitement, my skin crawled. Some of the joy faded, leaving behind a strange sense of unease. Something wasn't right.

When the king pulled back, he faced our guests. The rest of Hodafez celebrated in the courtyard, while others waited in the castle entrance, hoping to be invited to the wedding feast. They must've been terribly excited because the noise was growing, even as we began to complete the marriage rituals. My sense of wrongness grew.

Stepping under the arch where someone had woven white roses through the thin wooden slats from top to bottom, we followed the path of the white runner, completing the symbolic matrimonial journey together and returning to the stand in front of the holy man.

She will die tonight, Amir's thought broke through the bizarre excitement. As I slowly came to myself, my instincts screamed to let go of his hands, but I forced a smile. I couldn't let the violet-eyed Jinni know his Gift of Persuasion had begun to wear off already.

Amir ignored tradition and gestured to me as he spoke to the room, "Isn't she a vision?" Everyone beamed and nodded like an ocean of idiots and I listened as he relished his hold over them. Under the influence of a full-blooded Jinni like Enoch, they were primed to obey his every word.

When he turned me to face the holy man, I let him, glancing over at Rena, who had the audacity to wink at me. My fury at my helplessness removed the last traces of the Persuasion, and I forced myself to do the hardest thing I'd ever done.

I pretended I wanted to be there.

Making my body relax and my eyes unfocus, I imitated everyone's cheerfully vacant expressions, as if his words had touched me too. "And *you* are a handsome groom," I crooned, swallowing back bile. "I'm so lucky to be marrying you."

His eyes widened as his attention returned to me. "Yes," he agreed and his smirk returned. "Yes, you are."

He waved an impatient hand at the guards who hovered close by, and they stepped down from the platform, so that it was only myself and Amir, with the holy man before us, a useless Mere on one side, and a chilling Jinni on the other.

Taking my hands, Amir pulled me closer to him and I obeyed as if entranced. The only way I kept the attraction on my face was to imagine Kadin instead. His warm golden eyes. The soft fuzz of a dark beard just beginning on his jaw. The tiny curls that formed around his ears where his hair had grown a bit too long.

The Jinni shifted behind the king, pulling me from my thoughts. His violet eyes held a touch of boredom.

I let my eyes unfocus even more, so that Amir was just a blur as I continued, squeezing those meaty hands. "I've always liked your eyes," I said, picturing the gold flecks in Kadin's eyes that I'd noticed from the beginning. "Your skin," I continued, thinking of the dark golden color of the ordinary boy without a drop of royal blood, unlike Amir—although the King preened at the compliment as I knew he would. I envisioned Kadin's dark, thick hair in place of Amir's thin, gray fuzz. "Your hair. And your lips," I added before I caught myself. That was too far. I was jolted back to the present as Amir pulled me uncomfortably close, flush against his body, his face inches from mine.

"My lips *are* incredible," he said, falling for my lies as quickly as I'd fallen from my balcony into the ocean. With all eyes on us and completely under his spell, he savored the moment of his assumed victory. "Kiss me and find out."

I ducked my head and tried to gather my wits about me. This was my opportunity. If I could stomach it.

Feeling numb, I lifted my face. *I can do this*. Preening peacock that he was, he simply closed his eyes and made me come to him.

I lifted a hand toward my hair. Hiding my revulsion, I pressed my lips against his and forced myself to hold there, against his cold, fleshy mouth, as I gripped the handle of the tiny blade. When he opened his mouth to kiss me back, I nearly lost the little bit of food I'd managed to eat that morning. I pulled the blade free from its sheath, careful not to slice myself.

The angle made it difficult, but I set it against his throat and stepped back immediately, pressing the blade against his skin so he could feel the prick. Amir tensed, as understanding and then anger crossed his face. "Unhand m—" he began, but I pressed harder and he cut off as blood trickled down his neck.

"Don't say a word," I hissed. "You will tell everyone here the truth—"

The enormous double doors to the Great Hall burst open with a crash and a voice I recognized immediately rang out. "Stop this wedding!"

Chapter Forty-Eight

Kadin

I SPIED ARIE'S BLADE pressed against the king's throat at the same moment as his guards. With her eyes on me, she didn't see them move in. They wrestled her away from his neck, wrenching the dagger from her hand. She cried out in pain.

My men followed close behind me and now that we'd opened the doors, the villagers poured into the room, mostly out of curiosity, assuming they'd been invited to the wedding as well, heading toward the tables filled with food along the back.

The volume went from nothing to bazaar-level noise in a heartbeat. Chaos broke out across the audience as well, as if everyone seated suddenly woke up. Some of them stood, and I lost sight of Arie briefly.

I swore as I sprinted out of reach of the guards. Bosh limped in the other direction, while Daichi disappeared in the crowd. I knocked one guard into a man behind me and ran while he was distracted. She'd had the King right where she'd wanted him, and I'd ruined it. I swore again.

"Gideon," I shouted, pulling off my helmet. "We need you here!"

Another guard took chase at my yell. Pulling a chair over to block him as I ran, I turned back as Gideon stepped into the room. I didn't know what I expected to see... Lightning bolts flying from the Jinni's fingertips. Or King Amir floating in the air at his command. Or even Gideon marching toward the king. I would've accepted any of those things as helpful.

Instead, our calm, dependable comrade had grown as still as the marble statues behind him.

While Bosh wove and danced to evade the guards, and Daichi dug in to fight, swinging wildly this way and that, knocking men across tables and chairs... Gideon didn't even seem to register the two guards taking hold of his arms. He just stared at Arie and King Amir.

"Gideon!" I yelled, but his gaze didn't flicker. What in all the lands was he staring at?

I risked his ire, snatching fruit off one of the tables, tossing it at him with all my might, glancing back. His fingers twitched, just slightly. Otherwise he didn't move. It was almost as if... he *couldn't* move.

I ducked behind a pillar, waiting for the guard still chasing me to come around the corner. I tripped him with an outstretched foot, grabbing his hair and smashing his head into the stone pillar. He fell, out cold.

I peered around the other side of the pillar, only a dozen or so feet from the front of the room now, scrutinizing the scene. What was Gideon staring at so intently?

King Amir shouted commands I couldn't hear over the din, but it caused villagers near him to quiet down, turning to face the room and spreading their arms wide, blocking others from reaching him. Arie screamed and kicked as the guards held her back.

And then I saw him.

Another Jinni.

His eyes were a strange violet color. And they were fastened on Gideon with the same intent, immovable focus as my friend, as if locked in an immense inner battle.

I hadn't realized until this moment that I thought of Gideon as a friend, but I did.

So, without thinking, I charged.

Chapter Forty-Nine

Arie

KING AMIR LOST HIS hold on the room seconds after Kadin and his men burst in. More specifically, the moment the violet-eyed Jinni faced the doors and froze.

Thoughts shifted from calm to chaos, relaxed to riotous, open to outraged. And as the villagers spilled into the room, my mind stretched and bucked against the vast number of thoughts filling it.

I fell to the ground, head pounding. Instead of imagining a glass jar and managing each individual thought, I envisioned a glass bowl settling around me, like a shield, sheltering me from them.

The relief was instant.

As the pressure eased, I opened my eyes. Amir struggled to maintain order and the violet-eyed Jinni ignored his demands for help.

"Guards," I shouted at my father's soldiers, testing the change in the air. "Seize King Amir!" They moved toward him.

"Be still," he snapped and their arms fell loosely to their sides like puppets. "Don't let her go." They grasped my arms again. "We have a wedding to finish."

"There's no way in this Jinni-forsaken land I'll *ever* marry you!" I screamed, losing control. "Tell your men to bring my father out of the dungeons *right now!*"

Voices rose with my cries. Some of the guests stood, as if ready to support me. "Everyone be calm!" Amir shrieked. Some sat back down, while others stayed standing; confusion trickled into their faces through frowns and open mouths, waiting for words that'd gotten lost. His hold was tenuous at best. He continued to order peace between yelling at the violet-eyed Jinni behind him, "Enoch! Stop staring at nothing and help me!"

Enoch ignored him.

In the back of the room, Kadin's form raced past and caught my eye. I yelled for help, but he couldn't hear me over the noise.

I blinked when he hurled fruit in Gideon's face. My mouth fell open when Gideon didn't respond. His eyes were locked with Enoch's in some mysterious, silent confrontation. I lost sight of Kadin in the chaos.

"Listen," I shouted over the noise, focusing on those further away, who seemed less influenced by the Persuasion. "This wedding is a sham. King Amir is trying to steal my father's kingdom."

"False!" He called on the heels of my words. "These are false accusations, pay her no mind."

I met the eyes of the villagers as they flowed into the room from the back, more curious than helpful. My gaze drifted to the nobles and royals who'd traveled to be here today. "If he succeeds, nothing will stop him from trying to steal your kingdoms as well! He's controlling your minds, you have to fight back—"

"Silence her!" King Amir shouted over my words to the guards. Even as I screamed, a filthy hand covered my mouth and I couldn't move.

Amir continued his cries for peace, and without my voice to stir them up, the crowd grew more and more docile. I thrashed harder, refusing to back down.

A blur of movement smashed into Enoch before I recognized his attacker: Kadin. Through brute force and surprise, he'd knocked the other Jinni to the floor, upsetting the strange duel between him and Gideon.

Between one blink and the next, Enoch was there beneath Kadin, grunting in surprise as he took a punch to the gut, and then he was gone, and Kadin's fist punched the marble floor instead, making him wince. He leapt to his feet, searching the room.

The strange Jinni had vanished.

The guards still held me, but at Enoch's disappearance, King Amir stopped ranting. The stupor over the room lifted. The hand over my mouth eased up.

Kadin turned to me. Before he took two steps, a guard knocked him over the head with the butt of his sword, and he crumpled to the ground.

I resumed my struggle, but they only gripped harder, and the hand over my mouth made it hard to breathe. Daichi yelled and thrashed against three guards who held him with effort, while Bosh struggled against one. What had happened to the rest of Kadin's men?

At the back of the room, Gideon still stood in the large doorway between two guards, as if too taken aback to remove them. A tiny fragment of hope rose in me. Had they come to help me? Or was he just here to retrieve his lamp?

Now that I'd placed the glass shield between myself and everyone's thoughts, I couldn't seem to lift it. The silence in my mind as I tried to mentally scream for his help was infuriating.

I stomped on one of the guard's toes, taking advantage of his surprise and ripping myself out of his grip long enough to yell, "Gideon, help!"

His gaze met mine across the distance. In one blink, he shifted across the room to stand in front of me, leaving his two guards blinking at the empty air between them.

The hands on my arms trembled at the sight of Gideon appearing out of thin air with his pale skin and sharp eyes.

He spoke to the guards in that deceptively soft tone, "Why don't you two take the day off."

Even without the use of Persuasion, they released my arms. I didn't bother to watch them leave.

"Thank you—" I began, gathering up the nerve to explain myself.

Amir didn't give me a chance. He shoved the guards and holy man aside to stand beside us. "Did Queen Jezebel send you to replace Enoch? Is that why he left so abruptly?"

I didn't miss the way Gideon's eyes flickered when Amir mentioned the name.

"No matter," Amir continued, waving arrogantly at Gideon. "Help me reclaim the room."

Gideon swiveled to face Amir with iron calm, ignoring his summons. "You think the Queen of Jinn sent me?"

The murmuring of the royals grew louder. I should be able to hear what they were thinking, but whatever I'd done seemed impossible to undo. I struggled to focus, pressing my fingers to my temple. In a room filled to the brim with people, the lack of thoughts made me feel strangely vulnerable.

"Stand up," Amir snapped at the holy man, as if he hadn't even heard Gideon. "We have a wedding to finish. Come." The holy man lurched forward at his command, opening his notes. My feet turned to obey as well, until Gideon put a hand on my arm. His blue gaze, pinned to Amir now, had turned cold.

"What's wrong with her?" Amir growled, as if Gideon was his servant. "Why does she not obey? I said *come.*" Though his Gift swept over me, I fought it. Outwardly nothing happened, but inwardly it felt like bracing myself against an enormous wave. Without the violet-eyed Jinni's help, Amir wasn't strong enough to overpower my will and I held my ground.

I envisioned mental fingers slipping under the edge of the glass bowl that shielded me, heaving it up and off. A flood of thoughts rained down with hurricane force, but I opened up to them, hoping desperately that Gideon would somehow see everything and help me as I gripped his arm like a lifeline. "He's keeping my father in the dungeons."

Ignoring the king and everything else at the panic in my eyes, Gideon nodded. "I'll find him." In an instant, he vanished, leaving everyone to blink at where he stood, unnerved by this strange Jinni magic.

King Amir strode toward me and his fingers closed around my arm, gripping hard enough to leave bruises as he spoke into the silence, "Tell everyone the truth—that you're happy to be married today."

"If that's the truth, I don't think we'd be here," Kadin's voice rang out only a few paces away, rescuing me even as my mouth opened against my will.

Everyone's attention snapped to where he stood on the side, rubbing the back of his head and wincing where they'd hit him. I blew out a breath. *He's okay.*

A thought from Kadin reached me, louder than the rest, as if he was speaking to me intentionally. *You wanna marry this guy? Or do you want us to bust you out of here? Just say the word.* I swung my gaze to meet his warm golden eyes, and he winked.

"You'll be quiet and sit down right now, young man." Amir's Gift made Kadin sit in the front row like a puppet. His golden eyes grew blank and unfocused; he couldn't fight it anymore than the rest of them. "I'll deal with you after," Amir said, then he turned to face me, stretching out his hands, palms up, expecting me to take them. This was the moment of truth.

Kadin had accepted my Gift. Kadin didn't think I deserved to die. Gideon didn't either. I felt a profound freedom even with a complete lack of control. I stared at Amir's hands. My own were suspended mid-air. I pulled them back and lifted my eyes to his as a slow smile formed. "No."

"Take my hands *now*, you little brat," Amir hissed at me under his breath.

Once again, I felt the full weight of his Gift flow over me, but I stood taller, letting my own Gift carry me above the waves of Persuasion. I lifted my chin to stare at him as I repeated myself even louder. "I will *not*."

"How are you doing that?" Amir hissed, eyes narrowing.

Everything in me wanted to give in. My lungs couldn't get enough air, but I stood stiff and held his gaze. *How is she resisting?*

I tried to ignore his thoughts as I faced the guests, addressing them instead: "King Amir's purpose with this wedding was to steal my father's throne. He planned to kill both of us before the night ended."

I felt their shock and horror as if it were my own. Glancing at Kadin, I expected him to verify my words with his own testimony—after all we'd all heard Prince Dev's words—but Amir's Gift still gripped him and his face was blank.

"How would you know that?" Amir's anger shifted into a calculating fury that gave me goosebumps. *No one else knows that plan. How would she know unless...* I saw him follow the train of possibilities to the logical conclusion as if he'd spoken it aloud. *She has some kind of Gift.* A wicked smile curved his mouth and made my heart beat faster as he said, "I've always thought there was something off about you."

I'd wanted to tell them myself, but before I found the right words, Amir began, "Your precious Princess Arie has been keeping a terrible secret from all of us. She is a *Gifted woman.*"

The way he said those last words sounded more like he was telling them I had the plague.

The reaction was deafening, even without my Gift.

"She *reads your mind,*" Amir continued. The terror spread, like shards of ice pelting my mind.

I stood tall, the way I had against Amir's Gift, lifting my chin and pressing my lips together. But my eyes betrayed me as I glanced at Kadin, still vacant and expressionless. Not that he could stop what was coming next. They could easily call for a Severance... for my execution.

Prior to this moment, the idea would've made my heart race... but I'd faced death once today already. Instead of fear from my secret being revealed, I felt pure relief, like an enormous weight being lifted off my shoulders.

"It's true," I called above the clamor of voices. "But I'm not the one abusing my Gift." I licked my lips, calling on my upbringing to find the right words to twist the public opinion in my favor. "Amir, with his Gift of Persuasion, has convinced each of you that you were attending a happy union today. You can see with your own eyes that this was never the case. My Gift is the *only* thing preventing him from taking my father's kingdom by force!"

"Your *Gift,*" Amir replied with a sneer, and once again I felt tendrils of Persuasion stretch out across the room, trying to touch each mind, despite how weak his influence must be when spread across such a vast number of people. "Your Gift is to rip open a person's innermost thoughts and use them to your advantage." Cries of outrage sounded. People were listening to him. "Someone with a power like that can't be trusted," he continued, pounding the nails in my coffin. "Especially not a Gifted woman. You should be put on trial immediately."

I swallowed, fighting the urge to run. "You're misusing your Gift right now," I shouted back, aware that I was losing. "Close your minds to him. Don't let him influence you."

"Be silent," the king said over me. "You will obey me now."

Pain built up behind my eyes, the result of my growing Gift clashing with Amir's. It felt like a losing battle, but I pushed further. "*He* should be put on trial. Reading minds is nothing compared to reshaping them completely without their consent!"

"So, you really can read minds?" Rena spoke up. I'd completely forgotten she was present. A silence radiated from her. This girl was undoing all my efforts with her innocent question.

I swallowed and it felt as if every single person within earshot held their breath, waiting for my answer. "Yes."

Spikes of emotion hit me as people digested my admission. Fear and surprise rose to new levels, as well as a fresh new wave of emotion that felt putrid and dirty. It took me a moment to recognize it: hate.

They muttered to each other, and I closed my eyes, wishing I could bring back the glass shield or find some way to hear one at a time instead of this swarm of thoughts like attacking hornets.

As I stood there taking deep breaths, I began to feel the differences between them. One silvery thread of hope stood out. When I focused on it, someone else's thought came through, clear and strong, stopping me in my tracks: *I'm not alone.*

Chapter Fifty

Arie

***NOT ALONE.* MY GAZE** shot toward the woman. Lady
Eiena. Tall, blonde, and formidable, she studied me solemnly.
Before I could acknowledge her somehow, another optimistic
thought surfaced across the room. *Another Gifted woman. If
they accept her, maybe they'll accept me too.*

As more and more of these Gifted women revealed
themselves, intentionally or not, I blinked at the overwhelming
strength and numbers. Before I could search them out, Amir
yelled over the murmurs, "She's a criminal! Stealing our
thoughts—she should be put to death!"

I backed away from his fierce screams, unable to stop the
trickle of fear as a wave of agreement crossed the room.

"If you kill her for her Gifts," a strong female voice rose above the confusion, "then you'll have to kill me too." It was Lady Eiena. She stepped out of her row and made her way toward us, stopping beside me to face the onlookers.

Was she truly declaring herself in front of all these people? Didn't she realize she couldn't take it back? I felt torn between thanking her and telling her to sit back down. They could easily take her up on her offer. But a slow smirk curved her lips as she added, "If you do choose that route, I guarantee you, it will not be easy."

My eyes widened. What was her Gift?

King Amir glared but didn't move as he wondered the same thing. The threat had silenced him.

The pause after her declaration stretched on for what felt like an eternity, before a small, dark-haired woman from the village stepped forward, trembling. "I have a Gift as well," she whispered. Her shaking increased, but she clenched her fists, determined. A Gifted commoner? The Jinni-blood was said to only run in royal veins, but this proved all those assumptions false. Similar thoughts floated around me.

Three of us. Enough to make people pause and King Amir reconsider his plans. But when the fourth woman stood, I could actually *feel* the shift in the room.

Her long white braid hung over her hunched back, but she tottered down the aisle toward us without help.

Recognition spread—the village healer.

Children had grown up learning from her. At least half this room had known her their entire lives. Someone like her— someone that everyone knew and loved—was far more difficult to hate. She stopped beside me.

I stepped forward, standing between the elderly woman and Lady Eiena, blocking Amir from their view. "We are not to be feared," I decreed, with confidence I didn't fully feel. "Not any more than Gifted men. The same rules that apply to the princes will apply to us." I spread my hands, gesturing across the Great Hall. Their thoughts had revealed at least three other Gifted women who'd yet to reveal themselves, maybe more. "Clearly, we've existed among you for years. I believe it's time to recognize that anyone can be Gifted."

Thoughts shifted, almost painfully, as they mulled over my words. "Guards, seize King Amir and keep his mouth shut. He will be held accountable for his actions today." They obeyed, hands clapping over his mouth as they dragged him down from the platform.

Using the momentum of the moment, I declared a bold proclamation in my father's absence, "From now on, the Kingdom of Hodafez will no longer require a Gifted woman to go on trial or sever her Gifts. They will be given all the same rights and privileges—along with all the boundaries and discipline—as the law allows Gifted men."

The same? Truly the same? No one knew how to respond. The whispers and shuffling made it hard to distinguish any one person's opinion unless I focused on them. My Gift threatened to overwhelm me, and I let the thoughts go out-of-focus, becoming one loud hum to find relief.

Lady Eiena spoke up, "My kingdom as well."

The floodgates opened as rulers across the room declared themselves supportive of Gifted women. Kadin's gaze grew more focused, taking it all in, but staying seated, still under the Persuasion. I tried to listen for his thoughts, but there were too many washing over me to single one out.

"Not in Keshdi," a man snapped as he stood, whipping his cloak out of his way. "I won't have it!" It was King Zhubin. His kingdom nestled just below ours, and I'd passed through it during my escape, not to mention spent multiple courtship tours under his roof, dining at his table. Despite all that, his hatred was palpable.

I started to back up, but caught myself and stood even taller, meeting his gaze without flinching. "You will abide by our laws as long as you are visiting Hodafez," I commanded.

"Anyone who abuses the rights of a Gifted woman in Hodafez will be brought before the royal courts for punishment."

To stand before the courts often meant imprisonment or worse. The threat was clear. Respect my wishes, or leave. His face twisted in a snarl. Pushing his way past those still seated, King Zhubin stormed out of the room.

Gideon returned then, holding my father's limp form in his arms.

With a gasp, I ran to him, kneeling as he set my father on the ground. Kadin stood, walking toward us as if wading through water, but I barely noticed. "Somebody help," I called, not caring that it wasn't dignified. "Please, somebody help him." The dark stains on the bandage wrapped around my father's head and his utter stillness terrified me. I dropped to my knees beside him. Those close by moved in closer, surrounding my father as they tried to get a better look. Kadin moved around them to stand by me in silent support.

The Gifted healer pushed through the crowd forming around us, and people let her through out of respect. "Let me," she said, leaning heavily on a shoulder as she lowered herself beside my father. "Someone get me warm water and fresh bandages." People obeyed.

As she unwrapped the dirty cloth from Baba's head, I whirled to face Gideon. "Can't you see how King Amir is abusing his Gift?" I cried. "Will you not bear witness to his crimes? He needs to be stopped!"

"Where is the king?" Gideon asked.

My gut clenched. When I spun to look at the dais, he was gone. Rena stood on one side, Lady Eiena and the holy man on the other.

But no Amir.

His guards stood dumbly, holding the air between them as if they thought they still held the king.

The coward had seen his chance during the chaos and disappeared.

Chapter Fifty-One

Arie

"CAN YOU SENSE HIM?" I clutched Gideon's sleeve in a panic. "Is he nearby?" If Amir escaped, there was no telling what he might do. What if he turned the people against me? What if he came back with a mob?

"I'm not a magical bloodhound," Gideon replied, but he held up a finger at the genuine horror on my face. "Hold on, one moment."

He flashed out of sight, and I choked back my anxiety under everyone's stares. Kadin pressed closer, though he never touched me, letting me know he was there.

We waited.

Out of respect, the guests stayed seated, whispering among themselves. I paced.

"I gather it's not actually tradition to struggle at a human wedding," Rena guessed after I passed her a third time.

I would've laughed if my eyes weren't trained on my father's still form. "No," I answered Rena softly. "No, it's not."

The elderly woman finished cleansing his wound and placed her hands on his forehead, closing her eyes. The cuts and scrapes along his forehead knit together, healing before our very eyes. The larger wound was slower to repair, but the sickly yellow and green hues along the edges faded into more healthy colors. The whole room watched the process intently.

"So, how do you know Gideon?" Rena asked lightly.

This time, I did laugh, though without humor. "How do I? How do *you* know Gideon?"

That stopped her questions.

The healer moved aside. Baba's wounds had turned to scars. Yet he still didn't move or open his eyes.

Gideon reappeared, alone, and all thought of the Mere girl flew from my mind. "Where is he?" I demanded. "What happened?"

"Amir is gone," he whispered, as if hoping to keep it private, but I had no such reservations.

"He can't be gone!" I yelled, "I need him to fix what he's done to Baba!"

A crease appeared between Gideon's sharp blue eyes as he frowned. He knelt beside my father, pressing a hand to his forehead.

I'd never seen the Jinni's expression quite this uncertain before. My heart pounded harder. "Something is wrong inside his mind," Gideon said finally. His soft voice carried in the stillness of the room. "I've seen it before. The human body grows ill if a Gift is pressed onto it too strongly or for an extended period of time."

Amir had been here for almost two full weeks. And I had no doubt he'd pressed. Guilt suffocated me.

Gideon stood slowly as he added, "I don't have the skills to heal this kind of injury."

I wanted to crumple. The only thing holding me up was the knowledge that Baba wasn't dead yet. I'd never imagined King Amir would go this far when I ran away. This was all my fault.

"What do I do? There has to be someone who can heal him!" My voice broke. Kadin stepped forward, breaking all rules of etiquette to wrap an arm around me. I let him, but resisted the urge to bury my face in his chest. I needed to be strong. "Tell me what to do, and I'll do it. You," I pointed to the Gifted healer, "can you fix him?"

She met my eyes and shook her head. "I've no experience with this sort of malady, Your Highness."

Tears filled my eyes. I refused to let them fall while we had an audience. I was still struggling to find words when Gideon stepped closer and murmured, "There may still be a way to help him. There are healers trained in lacerations of the mind."

One of my tears escaped.

"I will find a healer for your father, for your sake," Gideon said, adding for only me to hear, *And also for your mother's. I knew your face was familiar when we met, but I didn't recognize Hanna until you told me your Gift.*

My lips parted. *You knew my mother? How? When?*

Gideon took my hands between his own, clasping them once, and then again twice more, in the way of the Jinn making a promise. *That's a story for another time.* "I'll come back as soon as I can."

He vanished.

So many unanswered questions flew through my mind. But besides Gideon, the only other person who could answer them lay unconscious on the ground. His chest moved with each breath in and out, but he was otherwise still as death.

"Bring my father to his rooms," I commanded the servants. "Make sure he's comfortable."

Our kingdom was vulnerable. My people looked to me now. I pulled away from Kadin and stepped past the holy man, who moved to the side. With everything that had taken place, especially the revelation of Gifted women, I needed to show strength. No doubt Amir had spies in place for the slightest opportunity to return.

I knew what I had to do.

Reaching for the heavy gold crown on the dais, meant to replace the one on my head during the wedding ceremony, making me a queen by marriage, I lifted it gently for all to see.

"Please be seated," I said, though many already were. As the few remaining lowered themselves into their chairs, I waited.

Kadin raised a brow, but he sat as well. Rena didn't take the hint until I waved for her to join him. That left only myself and the holy man at the front of the room.

I let the silence stretch until even the shuffling in the crowd ceased.

Carefully, I handed the crown to the holy man, maintaining ceremony as best as I could, considering I was breaking it.

Understanding my decision, he moved up the stairs to stand at the top of the dais.

Before I followed, I lifted my mother's silver crown off my head. The diamonds sparkled in the sunlight. It only served to remind me of Gideon's history with my mother.

Setting it on the cushion where the other crown had rested, I faced my guests. "My father is *temporarily* indisposed." I emphasized the fleeting aspect. "In these difficult circumstances... I will rule in his place."

I forced an edge to my tone so it wouldn't crack. "With everyone gathered here for a ceremony, you will all bear witness to my coronation."

They didn't miss my choice of words. Bearing witness was usually reserved for the Jinn and meant to be taken with utmost gravity.

I knelt on the steps before the holy man.

Signaling for him to begin, I listened to the thoughts and outright whispers across the room that it wasn't right, that a woman couldn't rule—especially not a Gifted one.

I ignored them.

My wedding was now my coronation.

With everything that'd happened over the last hour, everyone was too shaken to protest. They sat shell-shocked as the ceremony unfolded.

When the holy man spoke the final rites, he raised the crown above my head, jewels glittering in the last bits of light as the sun set.

He lowered the crown onto my temples, and I felt its weight, cold and solid, heavier than I'd ever imagined.

No longer the princess of Hodafez.

I was the reigning Queen.

Chapter Fifty-Two

Arie

I HEARD HIS THOUGHTS before he spoke. "You're free now," Kadin said softly. We stood on my balcony overlooking the ocean. He'd used the tunnels over the last few days, though I suspected he would've found a way in even if I hadn't shown him. I stared down as waves crashed into the cliffs below, creating white surf. The sound usually calmed me.

Not today.

"Free?" I scoffed, glaring at the waves. "I've never been less free." My father was still in a comatose state—only in Rena's presence, under her enchantments, did he occasionally wake. Over three days had passed this way. If he didn't get better soon, I worried he'd never recover.

When I'd imagined becoming queen, it'd never felt like a burden. And there was no one to share it—most of the Shahs were avoiding the castle. It had become a silent tomb with servants tiptoeing through it.

"You mean Amir?" Kadin hopped onto the marble ledge to sit facing me, trying to catch my gaze. He misunderstood, but he was right about that too. The king of Sagh was still a threat. "Why does he want Hodafez so badly anyway?"

"He needs it to reach the other kingdoms." I finally met his gaze, but I couldn't hold it. The ocean didn't stir up feelings the way he did. "And yes, I'm worried he'll try again, but it's more than that… It's also the people…" My new rule was so fragile. The other Gifted women depended on me, yet if even one of them made a mistake, it would demolish the delicate peace I'd created. And I couldn't comfort them—the entire kingdom feared me more than anyone else.

Kadin waited.

"And… I'm worried about my father."

That was an understatement. Gideon had promised to save him. The Jinni had come back only once, for mere minutes. No news. He'd asked for the lamp, and vanished once more. I feared his own mission came first. And that there might not be a solution to be found.

"There's another healer on the way," Kadin murmured. "Bosh sent word he found someone. And the others haven't given up searching.

I nodded, turning to pull myself up onto the ledge as well, swiping the tears away while my back was turned and keeping my voice steady. "How are they doing?"

"Good. You've given us more than enough," he waved a hand and I stared at it where it landed on the balcony next to mine. I'd pardoned Naveed and Daichi, who'd landed in the dungeons, and given each of the men a handsome reward for their aid. "They just want to help. *I* just want to help," he added.

I already knew that. It was impossible not to hear his thoughts when he let his walls down. Even now, he pictured wrapping his arms around me. It was more a warm sensation than a full thought, but I could sense it all the same. I put a palm on the stone between us, and he covered it with his own, leaning toward me.

Instead of moving away, I held my breath, hoping the kiss would be as good as he was imagining. The seagulls called to each other, the waves crashed around us, and I let myself forget everything else, just for a moment. I closed my eyes as his lips brushed softly against mine, light, tentative. I leaned toward him and kissed him back.

He pulled away first, rubbing the back of his head, as if it still ached from the guard's blow during the fight. *Tell her how you feel,* he urged himself. I blinked, and the spell was broken. This couldn't happen.

As much as I wanted to give in to the feelings, I pushed off the balcony until my feet touched the ground, putting distance between us. He was a weakness. If Amir found out, he'd exploit it. If the people found out, they would add his lack of nobility to their list of reasons I shouldn't rule. And most importantly, I couldn't fathom allowing myself a moment of happiness when my father was in this state. When it was all my fault.

"He'll be okay, Arie," Kadin whispered, as if it were him who could hear thoughts, not me. He'd jumped down as well to follow me inside, but stopped a few feet away on the threshold, unsure of himself. It was a side of him I'd never seen before. I supposed now that I was queen, he wasn't sure how to act.

His words pulled me out of my thoughts, as if dragging me to the surface of the water where I could breathe, penetrating the fog in my mind. I clung to the hope. But out loud, I only said, "You don't know that."

The sunset glowed over the rippling waves and created a halo around Kadin's form. His warm eyes shone golden-brown in the fading sunlight as he stared back at me. He didn't make promises he couldn't keep, didn't lie, just stood there, opening his mind.

It was comforting. And at the same time, too soothing. It wasn't right.

"You should go." I crossed my arms, bracing myself against the cool evening wind. "Thank you for this latest information. I'll make sure you and your men are well compensated."

"Thank you," he said slowly, studying me with those golden eyes as if solving a puzzle. "If you need anything—"

"I don't," I interrupted, spinning to pass through the marble archway that led into my bedchambers, speaking over my shoulder. "I'd rather you didn't come here again, actually, unless you have further information."

Kadin had followed, but he stopped in the middle of my room, blinking. Hurt.

I felt that brief moment of pain as if it were my own, before he slammed his walls into place, hiding his thoughts from me. He'd accepted me as I was, accepted my Gift, only for me to reject him.

I pulled on the mask of a queen, cold and alone. I had to fix this by myself. I'd been weak before, when I'd run away; I couldn't allow that again. And Kadin was my biggest weakness.

Settling onto my seat in front of my dressing table, I watched him in the mirror as he searched for words, even though I could no longer hear his thoughts. In typical Kadin fashion, he avoided the argument. "That's fine. It doesn't matter."

I dropped my gaze to the jewelry, sorting through it so I wouldn't have to see his hurt.

A quiet formed around him so deep that I couldn't sense him at all anymore. Unsettled, I whirled to face him, but he was already gone.

My heart broke. It struck me as funny how it wasn't in two pieces, the way I'd always pictured, but more like how glass would shatter if dropped from a high point, into thousands of tiny slivers so fragmented they could never be put back together again.

Utterly destroyed.

Though he couldn't hear me anymore, I wiped a tear that slipped down my cheek and whispered, "I think that's the first time you've ever lied to me."

THE END.

...

If you loved this book, support the author by leaving a review—it helps more than you know!

**TURN THE PAGE FOR A SNEAK PEEK AT
BOOK TWO IN THE SERIES, THE JINNI KEY!**

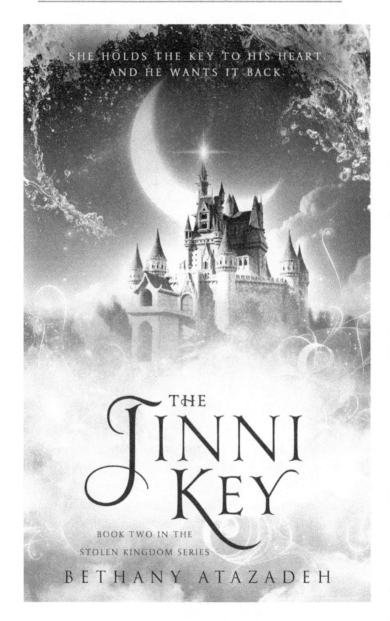

SHE HOLDS THE KEY TO HIS HEART,
AND HE WANTS IT BACK.

THE
JINNI
KEY

BOOK TWO IN THE
STOLEN KINGDOM SERIES

BETHANY ATAZADEH

THE JINNI KEY

JUST A SHORT YEAR ago, on my birthday, I met him for the first time. My family sent me off covered in pale ceremonial shells, fixed to me from my neck all the way to the tip of my tail. My mother adjusted the colorful crown of vibrant ocean flowers before I waved her away. Nearby Mere-folk stared, unashamed, as I swam past. My long, red hair flowed behind me. *Regally, I hope.* The heavy attire weighed me down. With effort, I swam on, waiting until I reached a deep canyon that curved out of sight before I shucked the ensemble to swim faster. This was the day I *finally* saw the surface.

As a young Meremaid, only sixteen, I'd looked forward to this rite of passage my entire life. *Watch out for sharks or stray squid,* my father's voice echoed now as I swam alone through dark caverns, slowly leaving the depths behind. I clutched the remaining shell necklace around my neck. Occasionally I stopped to rest, but other than the occasional whale, the hours of swimming passed without incident.

Breaking the surface, a light breeze hit my skin and air filled my lungs. I feasted my eyes on my first sunset and gasped. *Yuliya was lying. The color is nothing like her pet fish. I've never seen anything like it.*

I only had an hour or two before I'd have to return to our underwater kingdom. So, I'd make the most of it. A small rock jutted out of the water a short distance from land; I dragged myself up onto it.

Outside of the water, I felt heavy. The rock dug into me far more than it would at home. *Nadia said the human world would lose its charm quickly.* I pushed the thought away, settling onto the rock, savoring the sunset. My sisters wouldn't ruin this for me.

The burning orb hurt my eyes; I took a break from staring at it to admire the rest of the sky. Brilliant blues with streaks of orange, gold, and pink.

I almost missed him. A dark shape fell through the clouds and splashed into the ocean in the distance.

For a moment, I almost turned back to the sunset, but my curiosity got the better of me. Diving into the water, my powerful tail carried me to the spot in moments. The ripples on the surface above me showed the impact, but nothing else. Below, drifting toward the ocean floor, I spotted him.

Was it a human or a Jinni?

Either way, I knew the rules: stay away.

I touched the shells around my neck. No one was around. *Maybe I'll swim a little closer. Just to see.*

The fallen creature was a male with pale skin, almost translucent, and deep black hair like I'd never seen back home.

A Jinni.

According to the elder-Mere, they were far worse than humans. But this one wasn't doing anything particularly evil, that I could tell.

Fascinated, I swam closer to admire him. His eyes were closed and he continued to sink. Bubbles escaped his mouth. I chewed on my lip, growing worried when I noticed his lack of gills. *Is he drowning?*

I didn't know what to do. A Jinni in the sea was on my mother's list of the vilest things that could ever happen. Interacting with him was, if possible, even worse. But I couldn't let him die.

I swam closer and reached out to poke him. Nothing. Feeling skittish, like he might open his eyes at any moment and surprise me, I swept up behind him and pulled him by the arms. He was heavy compared to the Mere. Larger and taller than me, and muscular. I kept my tail away from those strange legs as I began to swim back toward the surface. Who knew what he might do?

Our heads burst above the water and I inhaled a deep breath for him, showing him what to do. His head lolled to the side.

Glancing around, I found my sunset-gazing rock. I tugged him through the waves and dragged him onto it. Flopping him onto his back, I lay my tail alongside him, leaning in. The longer he didn't move, the less I worried about my mother and the more I worried about him.

I pulled myself even closer until I could lean down and listen to his chest for a heartbeat. My mother said they were heartless—did she mean literally? I nearly gave up, but then I heard it, faint, but beating. As I lay on his chest, staring at the shadow of a dark beard on his chin, and that sharp jawline, I was puzzled. *Why isn't he waking up?*

It dawned on me that his chest wasn't moving at all. His heart might last a bit longer, but he needed to breathe!

Sitting up, I pushed him onto his side and beat on his back. It was like hitting a whale. No results, no reaction. I let him drop onto his back again and eyed his lips.

It was just a fairytale. Told at bedtime to little-Mere. Kissing didn't really bring humans back to life. And he wasn't a human anyway, so even if it did work, that solution didn't apply... *Did it?*

I licked my lips. Reaching out, I touched one finger to his mouth, softly, tracing the shape. Putting my hand on his chest to stabilize myself, I leaned forward, bringing my full weight over him in a hurry. I tilted my face toward his, prepared to do the unthinkable, when he coughed. Water spewed from his mouth and hit my face. I jerked back as he vomited up what seemed like half the ocean.

When he finally fell back, his eyes were closed and his breathing came in ragged gasps. I pulled my tail away, prepared to leap into the water the moment he saw me, but he didn't even open his eyes. *I should stay to make sure he's okay. And to see what color they are.* The way he lay there unmoving made me think he might still need a kiss.

"What happened to you?" I whispered, mostly to myself.

"Banished," he spoke between ragged breaths, startling me again.

Mother always said my curiosity would land me in the belly of a shark. Instead of listening to her and leaving him to his exiled fate, I slid a few inches closer, carefully lowering my upper body onto the rock next to him. Propping my head in my hand, I said in an even softer whisper, "Why?"

When his eyes flashed open, I froze. Just inches away from my face, they were light blue, the color of the icebergs in the north.

They closed as suddenly as they'd opened. "You're so beautiful," he said, and my heart fluttered. No one called me beautiful. Not when they'd seen my sisters. "I must be dreaming."

Half of me wished he could see me in the ocean, where my hair would swirl around me instead of hanging limp and wet on my shoulders, and the water would make my tail shimmer. The other part reminded me that Mother would kill me if she found out what I was doing. A dream would be better for both of us.

"You *are* dreaming." I smiled down at him. He blinked in confusion, squeezing his eyes shut again, rubbing a hand across his face.

I wanted to lift my tail and let the beautiful red scales shine and sparkle in the sunlight to convince him further. But my mother's voice in my head stopped me. The Mere and the Jinn didn't get along very well; it wouldn't do to upset him in his condition. Thinking this, I tucked the Jinni Key I always wore underneath my thick shell necklace to hide it before he opened his eyes again. Better not to overwhelm him.

"What's your name?" I asked to distract him. Those blue eyes flew open, landing on my face. I brushed my hair back, feeling self-conscious. Nobody looked at me like that back home.

He sighed, staring openly in his supposed dream state. His eyes traced the shape of my face, my lips. I blushed, thinking about how I'd done the same thing a few minutes ago. But he didn't know that. *Did he?*

"Gideon," he told me. His eyes were growing more alert and his breathing came easier now.

I should go. Can the Jinn use their Gifts outside of their land? That made me nervous all over again. He hadn't done anything yet... but would I see it coming if he did? *Would I even know what to look for?*

"What's your name?" He rolled over to face me. The sudden movement made me flinch and slide away instinctively. "It's okay," he said, reaching a hand toward me. "I won't hurt you."

But I panicked.

Leaping off the rock, I dove into the water away from the hand that had almost touched me. *A Jinni hand.*

He leaned over the rock and peered down into the deep, searching for me. I let myself sink lower, into the protective darkness. Though his face was distorted, he looked sad. I sighed and watched the bubbles float up to him, jealous of them. But my mother's voice in my head held me back.

I stayed close, as the water grew darker. The sunset was ending. I'd missed it. The whole reason I'd come here in the first place. But for some reason, I didn't care anymore.

Gideon gave up looking for me and crashed into the water, swimming like a little-Mere toward the shore. It was only a short distance away, but at the rate he was going, it would take him a while.

I'd never answered his question. "Rena," I whispered, wishing he could hear. "My name is Rena."

ORDER THE JINNI KEY NOW!

SIGN UP FOR MY AUTHOR NEWSLETTER

Be the first to learn about Bethany Atazadeh's new releases and receive exclusive content for both readers and writers!

WWW.BETHANYATAZADEH.COM

ACKNOWLEDGMENTS

It took 22 people + one pup to create this story. Writing a book is not a solo journey!

But before I tell you all about these incredible folks, it's important to say that none of this would be possible without Jesus. I wouldn't be here without the hope that I have in my savior.

Secondly, I have to thank my husband, Mohsen (who asked to be named specifically this time, you're welcome, babe). He has supported my dream when he didn't have to and that means a lot. Also, like I mentioned above, my corgi puppy, Penny, even though of course, she can't read and doesn't care. I never feel like I'm writing alone because she's always snuggled up next to me (or bugging me to play laser).

My family has cheered me on since I began writing, and I know they will continue whether it keeps going well or not, because they have to… just kidding, it's because they're also the best, love you guys. Special shout out to my mom, Kris Cox, who has read all my books and is always willing to help edit and proofread for me, love you mom!

My critique partner and one of my closest friends, Brittany Wang, has been instrumental in shaping the plot and characters in these pages. Talking to a friend and fellow author who has read my story (multiple times!) and understands good writing, characters, story structure, and so much more, has been revolutionary to my writing process. Thank you, Brittany!

My editor, Claerie Kavanaugh, taught me about RUE (Resist the Urge to Explain) which is one of my biggest weaknesses. She tightened up the writing and made it overall more enjoyable to read, which I appreciate.

My beta readers were enthusiastic cheerleaders who kept me going by pointing out the good qualities in the story, as well as offering much needed outside perspective on what *wasn't* working in the draft stages. Huge shout out to: Amelia Nichele, Bri R. Leclerc, Brooke Passmore, E.A.Hamm, Emma Woodham, Falan Rowe, H.J.Stack, Kaylee White, Lia Anderson, Maddy Bourman, Maverick Moses, Mickey Miles, Peggy Spencer, Renee Dugan, Tianna Peterson, and Valerie Wheeler. And an extra big shout out to my proofreaders, Bri R. Leclerc, Brittany Wang, and Kaylee White, who saved me from some embarrassing boo-boos.

In this second edition, I also want to thank my new cover designers for The Stolen Kingdom. First, huge props to the new front cover, which was designed by Guilherme Ambrósio and the model photography which was done by Oswaldo Ibáñez—this cover perfectly embodies Arie and how I always imagined she would look! The full hard cover wrap and finished design is by my friend Mandi Lynn at Stone Ridge Books, and I'm so thankful that I got to work with her on not just this cover, but also the other four covers in the series!

I also want to thank my Patrons—I didn't tell them I was doing this, but their support lifts a lot of the burden of the unknown within the writing business, and getting to know each of them has been such a joy. I really appreciate each one of you and want to say thank you!

And to you, my reader—you are amazing. When I picture you reading this book, well, it's hard to imagine, send me a picture. Just kidding, but I hope you enjoyed this story! If you did, spread the word, review the heck out of it, and please let me know—it means so much to me!

GLOSSARY

Aaran-Shah (AIR-rin-Shah) – Shah in Hodafez

*Ahdamon (*AH-da-MON) – Lady Eiena's kingdom in the north

Amir (Ah-MEER) – King Amir of Sagh, a wealthy neighboring kingdom of Hodafez

Arie (ARE-ee) – princess of Hodafez (means Lion in Hebrew)

Arman (Are-MAHN) – owner of the Red Rose

Azadi-Shah (Ah-ZAHD-dee-Shah) – Shah in Aziz

Aziz (Ah-ZEES) – the kingdom where Arie and Kadin meet (loosely translated it means sweetheart)

Baba (BAH-buh) – means father

Bafrin (BAF-frin) – kingdom to the East where Daichi and Ryo are from

Baradaan (Bar-rah-DON) – kingdom where Kadin and Naveed grew up

Berange-Shah (Beh-RANGE-Shah) – Shah in Hodafez (berange is also the persian word for rice)

Bosh (BAH-sh) – orphan adopted into Kadin's crew (persian word for yes)

Captain Tehrani – Captain of the Guard in Aziz

Chimigi (CHEE-mee-gee) – language and home country of the woman who speaks with Prince Dev (loosely translated it means what do you mean?)

Daichi (DIE-chee) – member of Kadin's crew

Dev (Deh-v) – prince of Baradaan

Dusa (DOO-sah) – the name for Arie during the heist; Dusa means sweetheart

Eiana (EYE-nah) – the Lady Eiena

Elam (EE-lahm) – creepy man in Aziz

Enoch (Eee-knock) – the violet-eyed Jinni who helps King Amir

Farideh (Fair-REE-duh) – Arie's lady-in-waiting

Gaspar (Gas-SPAR) – king of Aziz

Ghormey-Sabzi – a traditional persian dish (roughly translated it means green stew)

Gideon (Gid-e-un) – Jinni they meet in Aziz

Haman (HEY-mun) – shopkeeper in Aziz

Hanna (HAH-nah) – Arie's mother (means grace or favor in Hebrew)

Havah (HAH-vuh) – Arie's lady-in-waiting (persian word for sky)

Hodafez (Ho-DAH-fes) – Arie's kingdom (loosely translated persian word for goodbye)

Illium (ILL-ee-um) – member of Kadin's crew

Jezebel (JEZ-zuh-bell) – queen of the Jinn

Jinn/Jinni (Gin/GIN-nee) – Jinn is the name of the country and the race of Jinn as a whole (i.e. *the Jinn, the land of Jinn*); Jinni is the singular, used to refer to an individual Jinni and also as a possessive (i.e. *a Jinni, a Jinni's Gift*)

Kadin (KAY-din) – leader of the crew of thieves

Madani (Muh-DAWN-ee) – one of the families in Hodafez

Mahdi (MAH-dee) – king of Hodafez (persian word for guided one)

Marzban-Shah (MARS-bin-Shah) – Shah in Hodafez

Mere (Meer) – meremaids and mereman, also known as mere-folk

Naveed (Nah-VEED) – member of Kadin's crew

Piruz (Peer-ROOZ) – town Arie is originally aiming for

Red Rose – the inn and tavern in Baradaan

Rena (REE-nah) also known as the *Grand Tsaretska Marena Yuryevna Mniszech* (Zar-ret-ska Mar-reen-na Yer-yev-na Nez-zich) – youngest daughter of the Sea King and Queen

Reza (REH-zah) – Kadin's youngest brother

Rusalka (Roo-SULK-ah) – the underwater kingdom of the Mere

Ryo (RYE-oh) – member of Kadin's crew

Sagh (SAW-gh) – King Amir's kingdom (persian word for dog)

Severance – when a Jinni's Gift is severed from its owner

Shah – interchangeable title for a governer of provinces within a kingdom or for a monarch (persian word for king)

Shazada (Shah-ZA-dah) – title that means princess (Arie's informal nickname is Arie-zada)

Shirvan-Shah (SURE-vin-Shah) – Shah in Hodafez

Sirjan-Shah – Shah from Arie's courtship tour

Tahran-Shah – Shah from Arie's courtship tour

Tohmans – name for a large amount of coin

Yazdan-Shah – Shah in Hodafez

Yik-Shah – Shah in Hodafez

Zhubin (ZOO-bin) – king of Keshdi

Three Unbreakable Laws of Jinn:
1) Never use a Gift to deceive
2) Never use a Gift to steal
3) Never use a Gift to harm another

Bethany Atazadeh is a Minnesota-based author of YA novels, children's books, and non-fiction. She graduated from Northwestern College in 2008 with a Bachelor of Arts degree in English with a writing emphasis. After graduation, she pursued songwriting, recording, and performing with her band, and writing was no longer a priority. But in 2016, she was inspired by the NaNoWriMo challenge to write a novel in 30 days, and since then she hasn't stopped. With her degree, she coaches other writers on both YouTube and Patreon, helping them write and publish their books. She is obsessed with stories, chocolate, and her corgi puppy, Penny.

CONNECT WITH BETHANY ON:
Website: www.bethanyatazadeh.com
Instagram: @authorbethanyatazadeh
Facebook: @authorbethanyatazadeh
Twitter: @bethanyatazadeh
YouTube: www.youtube.com/bethanyatazadeh
Patreon: www.patreon.com/bethanyatazadeh